D0242003

Kinley MacGregor

A Pirate Of Her Own

AVON BOOKS

An Imprint of HarperCollinsPublishers

AVON BOOKS
An Imprint of HarperCollins*Publishers*
10 East 53rd Street
New York, New York 10022-5299

First Avon Books paperback printing: June 2005
First HarperTorch paperback printing: March 2003
First HarperCollins paperback printing: April 1999

Avon Trademark Reg. U.S. Pat. Off. and in Other Countries, Marca Registrada, Hecho en U.S.A.
HarperCollins® is a registered trademark of HarperCollins Publishers Inc.

Printed in the U.S.A.

10 9

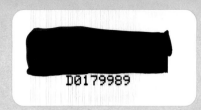

This book is dedicated to two of the most wonderful people I know. May God protect and bless you both always:

For Laura Cifelli, whose humor, support, and encouragement made this one of the best experiences of my life. I owe you so much more than I can ever express.

For my husband, who has brought untold joy to my life, and who gave me strength when I needed it most (not to mention all the babysitting you did while I worked on this)!

Thank you both for being there when I needed you.

And in loving memory of my grandmother. I wish she could have lived long enough to see it published. I hope you know, Grandma, that I spelled "milch cow" correctly—I really was listening to your stories.

A Pirate
Of Her Own

Savannah Dispatch

THE LEGEND OF THE SEA WOLF

S. S. JAMES

Savannah, Georgia, 1793

I have been told, by sources most reliable, of an incredible hero. Of a man so cunning, so courageous, that none can touch his skill. He is as dark as the night, his ship as black as a raven's wing. Like a phantom wind, he comes upon unsuspecting British ships and reclaims that which those wretched British have taken from us.

He is all things American. Proud and true, like Nathan Hale, who gave his life so that the rest of us could live free. Holding true to his mission, begun during our War for Independence, he returns our impressed men back home to their loving families.

But who is this man, our hero?

Some say he was once a pirate prince who decided to make good his life. Some say he was a destitute orphan left to brave the harsh realities of life alone. Others have told me that he was once a British sailor who knows firsthand the cruelties of the British navy.

One thing I know for certain, this man is like no other. He answered America's call to arms. He is our legend, the savior of our seas.

But guard your heart well, ladies. For I am also told that he is dashing and handsome. A man well used to feminine company. Like Lancelot of old, he has left behind numerous Ladies of Shallot who mourn for his loss.

For his is a mission of passion far greater than the lure of a woman's arms. The Sea Wolf can never be tamed. He will never be leashed. He is as unpredictable as the sea and every bit as dangerous.

So look twice at those sails in the distance. Do they belong to some passing merchant or a navy ship? Or are they the white sails of *Triton's Revenge*?

Look again, and pray God, you foes of America, that those sails come no closer, lest you find out.

Prologue

Cannon fire roared as waves of thick gray smoke billowed across the deck of *Triton's Revenge*. Even after almost an hour of battle, Morgan Drake was still amazed that the English frigate had actually tried to defend itself from him.

It'd been a long time since anyone dared such an affront. Most captains knew his flag on sight, and after firing a round or two of initial rebuttal, they docilely submitted to his plunder.

But not the *Molly Doon*. For some reason her captain had taken on a fool's crusade. What could the ship possibly carry that would make her captain so willing to risk the lives of all his crew?

He would know soon enough.

Another blast sounded. Morgan barely had time to duck before a cannonball whizzed past, only to land harmlessly off the starboard prow. He sucked his breath in sharply between his teeth. A few more feet and he would have been searching the waves for his head.

"A captain's share to the crew who disables the main mast!" Morgan shouted to his gunners. He was bored with this game, and it was time to end it.

Eight of the cannons on the main deck of his ship were pushed forward while four more were reloaded. He could feel the deck beneath his feet jar as the cannons were pulled back and forth by their crews. The cotton fuses hissed just before the cannons fired, almost in unison.

After pulling back the cannons, his gun crews dumped water over the long iron barrels to cool them off before they repeated the loading process.

Morgan smiled at their efficiency, at the symphony of their movements.

How he loved this! Every bleeding part of it.

His ears ringing from the fight, Morgan watched his men fire another volley at their target. A few seconds later wood began splitting as rigging fell from the *Molly Doon*. The main mast made a tidal splash in the ocean and his crew raised a cacophonous bellow of victory.

The pungent smell of sulphur circled around him and stung his eyes. For hours he and his crew had been pursuing the English frigate *Molly Doon*, and at long last the chase had ended. With one final shot, the *Revenge* had crippled her prey.

"Bring her about, Mr. Pitkern," Morgan shouted to his quartermaster. "The *Molly Doon* is listing to port."

"Aye, aye, Cap'n," Barney Pitkern responded, whirling the wheel. The *Revenge* cut a smooth course through the waves until it drew broadside with the *Molly Doon*.

"Stand ready to defend," Morgan called to the twelve sharpshooters who were positioned in the rigging as a precaution against whatever other surprises might be lurking aboard the *Molly Doon*. "Fire upon my orders."

Their answer to his words came as each man trained his sights on the enemy vessel.

To safeguard his identity, Morgan placed his mask over his face.

On the main deck of his ship, sixteen members of his crew drew swords and pistols as they made ready to board the smoking frigate. Grappling hooks whistled through the air as four men whirled and tossed them to catch the thick oaken boards of the *Molly Doon*'s side and haul the lumbering ship nearer.

He found it surprising that none of the English sailors had bothered to arm themselves, especially given the fact that they had fought him so ferociously just moments before.

Instead, the English stared at him as if they were seeing a terrifying phantom. Even their captain, dressed in the dark blue coat, white breeches, and powdered wig of the Royal Navy, did nothing more than open and close his mouth like a gaping fish.

As they drew close enough for him to see the individual faces, Morgan could pick out the English sailors from the Americans who had been impressed into service. The American sailors' eyes burned with great relief while their British counterparts shook visibly with fear of his retribution.

Barney gave a raspy laugh. "Looka there, Cap'n. They've finally got the white flag."

"Aye, and from the look of the English captain, it's not from his drawers," Kit added.

Morgan laughed at his boatswain. For a youth barely old enough to shave, Kit had seen more than his share of blood, and battle.

And soiled English breeches.

"Bring 'em aboard, boys," Barney shouted to the small group of their men who were pulling out boarding planks. "Reclaim America's riches from them thieving Brits."

In only a few minutes his crew separated the Americans from their slavers and sent the newly freed men across the small makeshift gangplank to the safe deck of the *Revenge*.

His crew was well accustomed to such skirmishes, and Morgan knew it wouldn't take his men long to ferret out whatever stolen American goods might be hidden aboard the fallen ship. Once they'd reclaimed all that property, they would head home for a well-deserved liberty.

Barney shouted orders to two of the men to help lift a crate of American spice over the last plank. Morgan smiled at the old man's efficiency. At sixty-two, Barney looked like a withered up piece of driftwood, but his small stature and bald pate hid the fact that he was one of the finest quarter-masters to ever sail the seas.

"Cap'n!" one of the men called as he helped set the crate on the deck. "This be too heavy for spice."

Curious, Morgan removed his long dagger from his belt and pried loose a board. He searched through shredded pieces of paper until his hand brushed against something smooth and hard. Seizing it, he pulled out a piece of raw gold.

Morgan laughed. No wonder the British had risked their lives. Even though he would have to give the new American government a share of the bounty, there would be plenty of gold left to make all of his crew happy men.

"What be the fate of the *Molly Doon*, Cap'n?" Barney asked as soon as the last crate was brought over.

Morgan glanced about the terrified faces of the Brits and pondered the answer. None of his crew had been seriously hurt, and with the exception of a few pieces of split rigging and nicks in the railing, his ship stood sound.

And, they had taken a king's ransom in gold.

Today he was feeling merciful.

"Raze all the jib and mizzen sails," he told Barney. "That should keep them occupied for a while and eliminate any thought they might have of renewing our fight."

"Nay!" the English captain begged in a raspy whine. "That shall leave us prey for pirates."

Anger creased Morgan's brow and he curled his lip at the man. "Well then, you should be grateful. My experience with pirates is that they treat their captives much better than the English navy treats its impressed sailors."

Kit laughed at his words. "Aye now, Captain, don't you think that he'd make a fine cabin boy for some pirate prince?"

Barney slapped the youth on the back. "Better a swabber. What with those pudgy fists and fat bottom, he could cover the decks in a matter of minutes."

Morgan shook his head at their banter. "Raise the sails and chart a course for home," he called to Barney. "I think our guests are more than ready to weigh anchor on solid ground."

His words brought a cheer from the newly freed

Americans as his crew rushed to carry out his orders.

No sooner had they drifted past the *Molly Doon* than one of the American sailors came forward.

Gratitude burned brightly in the man's brown eyes as he pulled his ragged English scarf from his head and stopped in front of Morgan. "I don't know how to thank you, Captain. We've all prayed many a night that one day *Triton's Revenge* would cross our paths and make us free."

Morgan remembered a time when he, too, had whispered such desperate prayers. Only, his prayers had gone unanswered until he'd been forced to take matters into his own hands. He'd learned early in life that he could depend on no one but himself. "I'm glad that I had the chance to free you."

"Aye," another sailor said, moving up alongside the first. "You're just like the story said. Proud and true."

Morgan went cold at the words. "What story?" he asked.

"Why, this one here that I picked up from a colonial ship last month," the man said while he fished inside his pocket. After a moment he produced a crumpled scrap piece of parchment and handed it to Morgan.

As Morgan scanned the writing, anger throbbed

through every fiber of his body. God's blood, someone had found out who he was!

"Mr. Pitkern!" he shouted, gaining Barney's attention. "Shift course and head us for Savannah."

"Savannah, Cap'n?"

"Aye, I've got a fish to fry."

Chapter 1

"Well? What do you think?"

Douglas Adams smiled at the hopeful enthusiasm on Serenity James's face. She looked much as she had the very first time he'd met her almost twenty years ago. Only, then she'd been covered in dirt, her dress and stockings torn, while she clutched a shiny apple to her tiny five-year-old chest. An apple she'd climbed high into a tree to claim.

Though her face no longer bore the childhood cherub quality he'd first grown to love, it still held that sparkling romanticism that had prompted her to climb the tree and proclaim herself Helen of Troy clutching the Golden Apple of Venus.

"I think it's your best story yet," he said at last, deciding he had kept her long enough in suspense.

His reward was an even brighter smile, one that lit her face and made her eyes glow like indigo fire.

Though far from a stunning beauty, Serenity held her own special quality that set her apart from the other women her age. Even a married man of Douglas's advanced years couldn't quite deny her unique charms or appeal.

Serenity leaned over his desk and looked upside down at the sheets of paper he held. "You don't think the ending is overly dramatic, do you?" She looked up to meet his gaze. "I tried not to make it too dramatic. But you know how I can get sometimes when I—"

"Nay, I don't think so," he said with a smile, cutting her off.

That was one thing about Serenity—any time she became nervous or excited she tended to babble off whatever was on her mind. If one didn't take charge, then one could become blindsided by her chatter. "I think the idea of a far-reaching conspiracy was quite clever."

Her delight over his praise died and she pulled her spectacles from the bridge of her nose. In her familiar nervous habit, she toyed with the left earpiece of the spectacles and drew her brows together into a deep frown. "Do you think Father will like it?"

An ache seized Douglas's heart. How she longed to please her irreconcilable father, but after working for the man these last twenty years, Douglas had come to the realization that nothing would ever please Benjamin James. "I can't see why he'd *refuse* to publish it."

She smiled halfheartedly. All too well, she knew why her father might refuse the story, why he continued to refuse his daughter.

"How I wish I'd been born a man," she said with the same longing Douglas had heard countless times. "Then I could report real news like you, Father, and Jonathan. I could go down to the docks and interview witnesses, go into taverns and ..." She shook her head, sighed, and pushed herself away from his desk. "I know you're tired of hearing me say that."

She left his side to walk toward her mahogany desk, the top of which was piled high with the manuscripts she dutifully edited for them. The hem of her plain, practical black dress rustled slightly with her steps as she paced their tiny work area.

She stopped and looked wistfully out the large bay windows, down the busy street that was filled with sailors, fishmongers, filthy children, and businessmen rushing to and from the docks.

How she yearned for things they both knew she could never do. If it were within his power, Douglas thought, he would gladly give her the autonomy she craved.

Unfortunately, all he could offer her was a sympathetic ear, and some encouragement.

"Don't give up hope, Miss Serenity," he offered, hoping to cheer her. "One day adventure will come bounding through that very door and you'll—"

"Run for cover," she said with a sigh.

Turning to face him, Serenity replaced her spectacles and squared her shoulders into the no-nonsense stance that she wore like a protective mantle.

"We both know what a milch cow I am," she said. "I shall never be a bold woman who flouts societal rules like my idol, Lady Mary. I'm afraid I'm far too practical for that."

Crossing the room, Serenity took the pages from his hands and flipped through them. "But at least I can pretend."

The door to their small printing shop opened, ushering in a crisp autumn breeze that rustled pages of the journals lining the tops of tables set around the room.

Douglas straightened in his chair as his employer, Benjamin James, came into the office, wearing the stern frown that had etched permanent lines in his weathered features. "Good afternoon, sir," Douglas said quietly.

Benjamin responded with a cool *harrumph.*

"How did it go, Father?" Serenity asked.

"They wouldn't tell me anything," he snapped. "I'll send Jonathan down there later today. Mayhap your brother can get them to open up. Great Caesar knows, he seems to do better than me most of the time, wastrel mix-nut that he is." His cold blue eyes focused on the pages in her hands, and he lifted one white bushy brow that made his scowl appear even more ominous.

Douglas sank lower in his chair, wishing he could vanish into the very floor, while Serenity met her father's stare unflinchingly. Douglas had never understood Serenity's immunity to her father's black moods. If only he could learn her secret.

"What's that?" Benjamin snapped. "Another one of your infernal stories?"

"Yes, I just finished it this—"

"I don't know why you bother," he grumbled, taking the pages from her and crinkling them.

Douglas clenched his teeth at the visible cringe in Serenity's shoulders. How could her father treat her hard work so callously?

No, he corrected himself. It wasn't so much all the work she put into her stories, it was her soul. Those were her dreams she wrote down. Dreams they both knew would never come true.

But he could never tell her that. She heard it enough from her splenetic father. Douglas would never be so cruel as to remind her that childhood dreams should be left behind along with dolls and frilly, smocked dresses.

Reality was just too harsh sometimes to face without them.

Shaking his head, Benjamin waved the pages

under her nose. "Blasted waste of time for a girl your age. On the shelf, that's what you are. You ought to have callers. I should have a grandson or two by now. But no, what do I get? One daughter who runs off in the middle of the night, another daughter who thinks she's some sort of solicitor, and a son who can't be trusted to tie his own stock."

He ran his gaze over her, his eyes flaming with anger. "And if they aren't enough to drive me mad, then what little sanity I have left is jeopardized by a daughter who thinks she's Lady Mary Wortley Montagu."

He rolled his eyes heavenward and implored her mother's spirit with a litany Serenity had long ago memorized. "Why did you leave me with *them*, Abigail? She, like the rest of her wayward siblings, needs your gentling influence. Not mine." He shook his head again and dropped his gaze back to his daughter. "Never would listen to me."

His tirade finished, he made his way into the back of the shop to his desk, where he tossed her pages down upon the other pieces that littered his work space.

Serenity crossed her arms over her chest and offered Douglas an encouraging smile. Still, he noted the flush of embarrassment staining her cheeks.

"He'll publish it, Miss Serenity," Douglas offered again. And in an effort to restore their usual comradery, he added the same phrase that had become their own private jest. "And one day your adventure shall come."

Her smile turned genuine, whimsical. She gave a light laugh that made him smile in return. "Just so long as it comes with wavy ebony hair, flashing eyes of danger, and dressed like a pirate."

Douglas laughed, glad to see her father hadn't dampened her spirit. "Aye, your pirate shall come on a rainy day like this, with the wind whipping his hair and his hat askew."

Two days later, Serenity watched once more as the world walked by outside the windows of her father's printing office.

"Twenty-four years old today," she breathed to the dozing calico cat sitting in her lap as she reshuffled the pages she was proofreading. "And I'm no closer to being the writer I wanted to be than when I turned five."

"Writer, bah!" her father's impatient voice thundered across the office, making her jump.

Though they were alone in the office, she had been sure he was far enough away not to hear her musings. Too bad he had drifted closer while she'd been reading. She should have looked up before she spoke her thoughts aloud.

"You should be minding my grandchildren," he

continued to rail as he came to rest just before her desk. "That's what would make you happy. Not sitting here doing men's work!"

He lifted her right hand up to where she could see the ink stains that covered her fingertips and nails. "Look at that mess! Why, I should never have published any of your stories or even let you come near this office." He dropped her hand and scowled. "All I've done is encourage you to be willful and stubborn!"

Serenity refused to cower before her father. Or let him get the last word about this personal matter that they both knew rubbed her raw. "If marriage be such a blessed state, how comes it there are so few happy marriages?"

Her father glared indignation at her and slammed his hand down on the mahogany desk. The loud thump echoed in the room, and several papers fluttered from the force of the gesture. Her cat, Pris, jerked her head up, looked at Benjamin James, then lay back in Serenity's lap.

"Don't you be quoting any of that social reform rhetoric to me, girl. Lady Mary—"

"'Tis Mary Astell, Father."

"I don't care if it's the Virgin Mary, I'll have no more of this disobedience from you. By God, I'll find you a husband by the end of this week if it kills me."

Serenity bit her lip to stifle the words that leapt into her mouth. He'd never find a husband for her. They both knew that. Even with the modest fortune her father had, he would be hard pressed to find a man who'd be willing to wed what the town biddies had dubbed that "poor James girl."

The familiar voices of the town matrons filled her head. *That girl should have been given the stick years ago, before it was too late for her father to find her a suitable husband. What man would suffer through one of* her *lectures?*

That poor James girl. Too old, too drab, and far too opinionated.

The type of man her father thought respectable would never agree to marriage with one such as she. No, those men sought younger brides. Girls with underdeveloped minds who were just waiting for a man to fill them with whatever nonsense *he* deemed suitable.

She was cut from a different mold.

Serenity sighed in sudden regret. Not at being different. Nay, she would never regret that, but what ached inside her was her inability to agree with her father's wants and desires where she was concerned.

When had they become so different?

There had been a time once when she and her father had been close, inseparable. A time when he had agreed with her about such matters as women taking on an important role in the emerging American utopia. Of women being well educated.

Her mother's death had changed all that.

Still, he did support her writing in his own way. In spite of his complaints and harsh remarks, he did publish her stories, and those he refused often found their way into the *Dispatch* anyway. And though it irked him when she published a story behind his back, he had yet to banish her from the office for it.

Maybe it was foolish of her, but she liked to think that in some way he was proud of her and that was why he allowed her to continue working for him.

"Here," he snapped, laying more papers on the desk before her. His brow drawn into a stern frown, he crossed the room to the coat tree to retrieve his hat and overcoat. "I need those edited by the end of the week."

"Yes, Father," she said quietly as she watched him shrug on his overcoat.

He gave her one last imperious scowl before reaching for the brass doorknob.

Rubbing her eyes beneath her spectacles, Serenity nudged her cat from her lap and sat forward.

"And get rid of that blasted stray!" he snapped an instant before he slammed the door shut behind him and braved the pouring rain.

Pris lifted her nose in the air and gave an indignant sniff as if she'd understood his order.

"It's all right, girl," Serenity said. "You know I'll never get rid of you." With a haughty flick of her tail, Pris headed off toward the back of the shop.

Suddenly the sharp scent of ink stung Serenity's nostrils, distracting her from her father's words.

Serenity froze. Surely she hadn't smudged ink against her cheek or eye again. Not today of all days! Not with a party that very evening.

It had taken a month for the last smudge to wear off her skin. Mr. Jones, the baker, had thought it a black eye and had given her father dirty looks for weeks.

She laughed at the thought. Though gruff, her father would never hurt her. At least not physically, though there were times when his caustic remarks did sting as much as a blow.

If only she could find some way to prove herself to him. To prove to everyone that Serenity James was just as capable a writer as her brother.

"Oh, Pris," she said to her cat. "What I wouldn't give to have a great lead. To find the one story that would also rivet the entire country!"

She sighed in sudden defeat as she watched her cat sit in the corner and clean her right paw. "Who am I kidding?"

Wiping a towel soaked with turpentine against her cheek, Serenity swept a glance to the work surrounding her. "Dreary. My whole life is nothing but dreary drudgery. I can edit *men's* articles, but no one trusts me to write them."

She would probably live and die right here in this office, shuffling paper, reading exciting stories about exciting people, while the only excitement she could look forward to was a few fireworks on the docks during celebrations and holidays.

And if she were *really lucky*, she thought sarcastically, Charlie Simms might join her.

She shivered at the very thought of the gangly coopersmith who could never take a hint that she had no interest in him. He was nice enough, but he had the type of wandering hands that kept her hopping.

And breath that would shame a frightened polecat.

Sighing, she set her towel down on the desk and gazed longingly out the bay window covered with droplets of rain, toward the docks filled with people who had lived incredible lives. People who had seen incredible sights.

Oh, if she only had a tiny bit of the courage her idol Lady Mary Wortley Montagu possessed. To marry for love and travel the world, learning languages, visiting harems!

What she wouldn't give to be swept away from her endless monotonous cycle of home and work.

To find a dashing dark pirate who would come and spirit her away to far adventures the likes of which she could barely conceive.

Serenity laughed at her immorality. Her father would have an apoplexy if he even suspected she held such a notion.

"If only it could really happen..."

Shaking her head at her foolishness, she laughed. "Well, if ifs and buts were candy and nuts, then we'd all have a Merry Christmas."

The little bell above the door chimed. Her cheeks warming at being caught in the midst of her indecent thoughts, Serenity straightened up in her chair.

"Did you forget some..." Her voice trailed off as she looked up and saw the black-garbed mountain entering her office.

The man had his head bent to shield his face from the storm. With water dripping, he swept into the office and in one graceful movement, removed his hat from his head and threw back a corner of his black cape.

By heaven!

He was certainly not her father!

Nay, this man was her dream pirate come to life. A man of unspeakable handsomeness. A man of broad, corded muscles that rippled beneath the damp cream waistcoat and white shirt.

His stock had come untied and dangled loosely

about his wet shirt front, exposing a sleek neck. A sensuous neck that appealed to a part of her she'd never before met. A part of her that wanted to run her fingers over his exposed flesh to see what it felt like.

By heaven! her mind repeated.

Hair as black as pitch was pulled back into a queue. And he possessed a face that was neither pretty nor fair, but one that was decidedly masculine.

Granite. That was the only word for his sharp, aristocratic features. Aye, they looked as if they'd been carved especially for him, and right now those features were rigidly stern, his dark eyes terrifying in their heated intensity.

Obviously unaware of his disheveled condition, he had the look of a man who had ridden hard and with a purpose.

Shaking the water from his hat, he stepped forward.

Serenity finally gathered enough wit to close her gaping mouth and swallow hard. "May I help you?" she asked, her voice trembling at the incredibly fierce sight he posed.

"Aye," he said, his stare intensifying. "I'm looking for a Mr. S. S. James."

The butterflies in her stomach multiplied. Whatever could *he* want with *her*?

Well, she certainly knew what she would want

him to want with her. Even with her eyes wide open, she could imagine him leaning close to her, feel his breath prickling her neck as he whispered poetry in her ear ...

Get a hold of yourself!

Blinking to banish the image, she forced herself to remain as calm as was possible when one confronted a come-to-life dream. "That would be me. Serenity James. How may I help you?"

Surprise flickered in the magnificent hazel depths of his eyes a moment before they hardened. Serenity had the impression that it wasn't often something took this man by surprise. And that thought gave her an unexpected feeling of delight.

He dropped a portion of the *Savannah Dispatch* down on her desk. "Then tell me of this story you wrote."

She glanced down at the scrap piece of paper and realized it was the past month's edition where she had published the Sea Wolf article without her father's approval.

Heaven above, would this piece ever cease haunting her? Her father had only stopped railing over it yesterday! Even the reserved Douglas had had a few choice things to say about it. Now this man wanted to start where they'd left off.

What was it about that one article that made every man want to strangle her?

Greatly miffed, she returned his stare evenly. "What do you wish to know of it?"

"I want to know everything you know about the Sea Wolf and his ship *Triton's Revenge*."

In spite of her anger, her lips curled into a smile as she recalled the romantic buccaneer who preyed solely on British ships.

"Oh, isn't it the most incredible story you've ever heard?"

He arched a brow.

Though her common sense told her to stop, as usual when she talked about one of her stories, she couldn't keep her tongue still. Especially not about this particular story of a true American hero whom she worshiped.

"The minute I heard of him and his bravery, I just couldn't keep myself from becoming entranced. The Sea Wolf is the most courageous hero to ever roam the billowing waves. Kind, but fierce, he protects those who can't protect themselves. And his crew! Don't you just love the motley bunch who sail with him?"

His look turned murderous.

A sudden wave of fear crept along her spine, and she had the distinct feeling that he didn't care for her writing one little iota.

"Why is this so important to you?" she asked.

"I think you know well enough why."

Confused, she shook her head. Why would he assume such? "No, I can't say that I do."

"What do you take me for, a fool?"

"Certainly not," she answered. Indeed, she took him for a most marvelous specimen of male physiology. He reminded her much of the hero she had dreamed of for the Sea Wolf. Aye, the Sea Wolf would have that same fiercely stubborn jaw and those dangerous eyes that flashed like burnt cinnamon.

"You talk about sources in your article. Who told you about the Sea Wolf?" he demanded.

She shrugged. "I overheard my brother talking to my father about him."

"Your brother and father? How did they learn of the Sea Wolf?"

She bristled. "What is this? The Inquisition?"

When he spoke, he enunciated every word slowly and carefully, his voice dark with warning. *"I want his name."*

What would it hurt to humor him? If it would appease him, far be it from her to keep silent. After all, silence was not something she was good at.

"My brother heard the story from a sailor down on the docks who said that he'd seen the Sea Wolf's ship from a distance. He said he was sure it was the same Sea Wolf who had been a blockade runner during the War of Independence."

"I want that man's name."

"I don't know his name."

His eyes darkened in such a way that she could tell he didn't believe her.

How dare he come into her father's shop and interrogate her like a prisoner of war! She wasn't about to let *anyone* intimidate her.

Just who did this man think he was?

The Sea Wolf?

"Why are you so interested in him?"

Morgan Drake took a deep breath to calm his raging temper. With as much patience as he could muster, and that wasn't much, he placed his hat on her desk and braced his hands on either side of the paper pile that rested in the center.

Leaning forward, he gave her the glower that had driven grown men to their knees in terror. It was his fail-safe glare that always broke the spirit of whomever he was trying to intimidate.

Instead of cringing, she stiffened her spine!

Damn. He needed answers, not a ruffled hen. And damn the imbecile who had allowed a woman to write for his paper.

She leaned back in her chair as if his temper didn't concern her in the least. As if she were well accustomed to dealing with irate men.

"I don't see why a fictitious piece has you so angry," she said at last. "It's just a little story I made up."

"Made up," he repeated in disbelief. "You couldn't have made it all up. Too much of it smacks of truth."

"Truth?" she asked, her eyes wide. "Why, sir, the piece is *fictitious*. Completely and utterly."

Why was she lying about her knowledge?

This was certainly no random fictitious piece just thrown together by a girl's whimsy. She had included everything, from his being an orphan impressed in the British navy to his days as a privateer.

And then to talk about his exploits of freeing the American sailors who were still being victimized by the British navy...

Nay, there were far too many details of his life that she knew. This woman's story did all but list his name and address. He couldn't afford for her to reveal his identity. The British government would like nothing more than to lay hands on him. But right now all they had was an alias.

And he would do *whatever* he had to do to guard his secret.

Suddenly a light flashed behind her empyrean eyes and humor danced in their depths.

She stood and gave him a bright smile that lit up her entire face. *"Oh, my goodness, I know who you are."* Laughing, she winked at him. "Douglas sent you, didn't he? I should have known from the instant I saw you!"

Completely baffled, he straightened.

Was this some trick to throw him off guard?

Aye, distraction was a clever ruse. One he had used countless times against his opponents. Blindside your foe with inconsequential matters until he loses his focus. Then he's yours. It was a ploy that worked almost as well as his glare.

But he wasn't one to fall for such trickery. No one made a fool of Morgan Drake. Nor did anyone *ever* get the better of him.

"Who is Douglas?"

Moving to stand by his side, she laughed again. "As if you didn't know," she said, laying a gentle hand on his arm and giving a light squeeze.

Was she daft? Morgan opened his mouth to speak.

"I can't believe I didn't know it when I first saw you coming in," she said before he had a chance to say a word.

Her smile widening even more, she walked a slow circle around him, talking all the while. "You're perfect. Absolutely perfect. Just as I described you. Why, it's even raining outside. If I didn't know better, I'd think Douglas had even ordered *that*."

She lifted his hat off her desk, turned it around in her hands, then tapped the brim. "Why, you even had your hat perched precariously on your head, just as Douglas said you would." She placed his hat on her head as a demonstration.

Morgan went cold.

So, she did know him. Somehow this little chit had learned his identity.

Once more he tried to speak.

"Why did you agree to this?" the girl asked, removing his hat.

"You couldn't have made it all up," she said, dropping her voice two octaves as she attempted to mimic his earlier words. "Of course I didn't make it all up. I did do some investigating. Even if I am a woman, I'm also a good reporter when I *do* get a real story to report. I can't believe Douglas would have you interrogate me so. It's probably his way of showing me why my father won't let me go down to the docks. Imagine my trying to gain information from a man like you!" She rolled her eyes dramatically. "Why, my father would have my head. You can tell Douglas I got his point, but he could have made it in a much gentler fashion."

Her smile enchanting, she brushed a piece of lint from his hat. "Oh, he's a clever one to be sure! It'll take some doing to top this. But I'm definitely up to the challenge."

As she continued her babbling, a strange odor caught him by surprise. It seemed to be encircling him.

Turpentine?

Confusion dampened his temper while he glanced about for the source. It had to be turpentine, yet he couldn't imagine where it came from.

Then he realized its source.

It was *her*.

No, his logic argued. It couldn't be. He leaned forward a tad and took a discreet sniff as she passed once more before him.

It was definitely turpentine and she was wearing it like French perfume!

Cocking a brow, he took a second look at the strange woman who continued to talk about this man Douglas and some sort of ongoing dare they had between them.

Serenity James was an odd one, to be sure. Never before had he known a woman who would willingly walk about drenched in such a pungent-smelling concoction. Yet this one seemed completely oblivious to it.

Her chestnut brown hair was pulled back into a sleek, severe knot at the nape of her neck, not the alluring soft ringlets preferred by most women. And rather than wear a soft color that might complement her pale features, she wore a modest gown of solid black with only a ruffled white neckerchief to break the somber tone.

If not for the ruby and diamond brooch that

clasped the neckerchief just between her breasts, he might have thought her in mourning.

"Poor Douglas, no wonder he'd protested being sent to St. Simon's Island today to interview that poor man whose house was burned down by his angry wife. I'm sure he wanted to be here to see my face when you walked in! Oh, but I'm ever so glad he wasn't here. No doubt, he would have laughed at me from now until kingdom come."

As his gaze wandered over the length of her, the most amazing thing happened. He began to fancy her dressed in a blue ball gown, her hair dressed down and soft.

Aye, behind those spectacles she had eyes the color of the brightest sea. Sensuous lips that begged for kisses, and pale, creamy skin that . . .

Morgan blinked.

Was *he* mad?

Naw, just bloomin' horny, Cap'n.

He tensed as Barney's voice drifted through his mind. The thought of that old randy barnacle was enough to snap his attention back to the matter at hand.

"Miss James, I have no—"

"Please," she said, cutting him off and linking her arm in his before leading him toward the door. "I deeply appreciate what you're trying to do. But today really isn't a good day for an adventure. I have piles of articles to review and my sister should be by any minute now to fetch me home where I have a party to supervise. Why don't you thank Doug—"

She stopped dead in her tracks and stared wide-eyed at the large glass window at the front of the shop.

Following her line of vision, Morgan found himself face-to-face with two members of his crew. Barney and Kit were staring in at them.

Would today's aggravations never cease?

They were supposed to wait for him down at the docks, not follow him about like two lapdogs with nothing better to do than yap at his heels.

The two of them stood with their legs braced far apart as if standing on deck in the middle of a typhoon, and they leaned against the glass, their hands cupped to shield their sight from the outside glare. All he needed now was for Barney to grin and wave at him like some half-wit.

He growled low in his throat. May the rains soak their rotten hides!

Well, he'd deal with them later. First he had a mystery to solve—how this woman had learned who he was and whom she had told so far.

And most important, how far would he have to go to make sure that their secret went no further.

He started to return to his interrogation when

all of a sudden a brown and gold coach pulled up in front of the shop.

Barney and Kit glanced around as a footman dressed in green livery jumped off the top of the coach. He opened the coach's door.

A huge black umbrella was shoved out into the rain and opened, then tilted upwards to reveal an elderly woman whose dress would rival Serenity's for plain ugliness. She scowled at Barney and Kit before holding the umbrella over the coach's open door. A young, attractive blond woman emerged from the coach an instant before the footman closed it.

With a frown on her pale, angelic face, the young woman cast furtive glances at Kit and Barney as she and her chaperone made their way into the shop.

"Goodness, Sister," the blond woman breathed, her attention still focused on the two sea dogs behind her who had returned to peeking inside. "What strange admirers have you gathered now?"

"Good day, Honor, Mrs. O'Grady," Serenity said in greeting. "He's a friend of Douglas's who just came by for a birthday surprise. But as I've already explained to this gentleman, I haven't the time."

"Ach now, lass, what were you thinking by letting him in here? You should know better than to be letting a man such as this one into the shop while you're here alone," Mrs. O'Grady warned in a thick Irish accent. Era O'Grady was the self-crowned matron of propriety. Her gossiping tongue had sealed the fate of many a young woman, and Serenity wasn't happy at having been caught by her.

Still, Mrs. O'Grady was loyal to Honor, whom she planned on grooming to take her place of town gossip should anything ever happen to her. With a few heartfelt apologies, Serenity should be able to allay any of Mrs. O'Grady's concerns.

Besides, Serenity was a plain woman who would never catch the fancy of a man such as this. Everyone in town knew that.

Even Mrs. O'Grady herself had said such.

Mrs. O'Grady raked her gaze over the stranger, and if Serenity didn't know better, she'd swear the old woman's eyes gleamed with appreciation.

"I've seen men like him talk a woman out of her virtue countless times," Mrs. O'Grady warned. "Be too late for you when it's done. Your father will have your head over this. Just see if he doesn't."

"You're quite right, Mrs. O'Grady," Serenity agreed. "Men are the blight of the world and hazardous to all women."

Morgan lifted his brow at her words. Even

though she spoke with a hint of sarcasm in her voice, he didn't like being called the blight of the world.

"I was just escorting him to the door when you arrived." Serenity shoved his hat into his hands and eyed the matron, who was scowling at the two of them. "It was a pleasure to meet you, sir, and I'm grateful for your sense of humor, but I must be going."

With an expediency that astounded him, he found himself back outside in the drizzling rain, standing next to his two men. A moment later he watched while Serenity and her sister were whisked away by the speeding brown coach.

"Well, Cap'n?" Barney asked as rain dripped off of his brown-colored tricorn hat and into his face. "Did you find out about that there paper story?"

Dumbfounded, Morgan could only stare after the departing coach. Never in his life had he been dismissed so easily. He found it downright... humbling.

Infuriating!

How dare she dismiss him as if he were nothing but a nuisance! Women had fainted at his mere presence. Fought one another for just a smile from his lips.

By God, kings had *begged* for an audience with him. A sultan had even offered him his daughter's hand. And this little chit had rushed him out into the pouring rain without so much as a by-your-leave.

Remembering her words about his hat and its precarious perch, he jerked it down low on his head. "All right, Miss Serenity James," he said as her coach disappeared from his sight. "When next we meet it'll take more than your sister and a scowling Irish biddy to protect you."

Chapter 2

"Beg pardon, Cap'n?" Barney asked with a serious frown. "What scowling Irish biddy do you mean?"

Angry at Serenity, her chaperone, himself, and the reminder that his men had disobeyed a direct order, Morgan glowered at Barney. "What in Triton's hell are the two of you doing here?"

Kit turned a bright shade of red and Barney drew himself up to the full five feet six inches of his height.

"Why, we've come to help you, Cap'n," Barney said with a wide smile that showed off the gap between his two front teeth. "Thought you might need a good pirate sword to silence the tongue of that thieving dog what went and wrote about you in his story."

Growling low in his throat, Morgan knew all too well that nothing short of bloodshed would intimidate Barney. "How many times do I have to tell you that we're not pirates?"

"Right," Barney said with a conspiratorial wink. *"I know we're not pirates."*

Morgan wanted to throw up his hands in defeat. With Barney practically bragging they were pirates, it was only a matter of time before someone believed the old sea dog and hung the lot of them.

If you had any brains about you at all, you'd throw the old barnacle and his bird off the ship at next sail.

But no matter how angry Barney made him, Morgan could never do that. Nay, he owed the old man much more than could ever be repaid.

If not for Barney, he would never have survived his years of imprisonment in the British navy. And though Barney's grip on reality was sometimes shaky, the old man had a generous heart.

"So Cap'n, do we drop that there blooming writer into Davy's Locker?" Barney asked.

"Nay," Morgan said quietly, even though he did rather enjoy the idea of Miss James walking the plank. Perhaps a mouthful of seawater would quiet the wench. "It turns out that the *he* in this case is a *she*. And I shall deal with her in my own way."

Thunder clapped above their heads and the slow drizzle turned to a hard rain. Morgan scowled up at the sky, then at the pair before him. "Dammit, Kit, take Barney back to the ship and see to it that he's dried out before he catches his death."

"Bah," Barney snorted. "What's a little water to a pirate?"

"A bout of pneumonia if he's not careful," Morgan warned.

Lifting his tricorn, Barney curled his lip and ran his hand through what little gray hair remained. "You treat me like I'm nothing but an old woman."

"Well, maybe if you didn't follow me about like a mother hen I might not—"

"All right, Cap'n," Barney interrupted, setting his hat back into place. "You just go on about your business and me and Kit will see to it that the *Revenge* is ready to sail when you are."

Now, why did he have a hard time believing that?

Because it would be the first time in your life that you ever won an argument with Lord Thick and Knotty Pate. Resigning himself to the inevitable, as well as to the fact that he might not get a chance to finish a single sentence for the rest of the day, Morgan left them there while he retrieved his horse from the nearby hitching post.

He pulled himself up into his saddle and directed a meaningful gaze to Kit. "Take him home."

"Aye, aye, Captain Drake."

With one last look at the incorrigible pair, he set

his heels into the horse's flanks and took off after Miss James's coach.

Hours later, dressed in her best gown, and standing in the middle of her father's ballroom, Serenity forced herself to smile.

The open room was surrounded by Grecian columns wrapped with pink satin and ivy. A thousand beeswax candles flicked from the eight crystal and gold chandeliers and torchères positioned strategically around the room. The orchestra balcony overhung the right corner, and dancers twirled about while the other guests stood in clusters talking about politics, recipes, and the latest scandals.

Since the party began, Serenity had been pulled aside countless times by matrons wanting to know if she'd heard from her runaway sister, Chastity, and by kinder souls who wished her a happy birthday.

But it was terribly difficult to focus on her birthday party guests while her mind kept drifting back to her encounter with her mysterious man.

It wasn't every day that one of her characters manifested himself in her office. Especially a character so handsome.

If only she had learned his name.

If only she could quit thinking about him!

There were over two hundred guests in attendance, not the least of whom were the parson's family and hopping-hands Charlie Simms, who kept trying to drag her out into the gardens.

People drifted around her as they went about their regular lives, while she had experienced something miraculous today. Something she knew she would never forget.

Enough, Serenity! Pay attention to the dancers. Look at the matrons chaperoning their young charges.

Concentrate on poor Parson Jacobs!

The parson had already had to repeat himself three times while he talked to her. Even now she wasn't really sure what he was talking about. Something to do with Jonah. Or was it Job?

Oh bother!

Nodding at the parson and murmuring what she hoped was an appropriate response to fill the few lulls in his conversation, she let her gaze roam about the room in search of Douglas. Maybe he could answer all her questions about her mysterious visitor.

A flash to her right caught her attention. Turning her head, she looked up just in time to see her sister rush toward her with rosy cheeks and sparkling eyes.

"Please excuse us, Parson Jacobs," Honor said breathlessly an instant before she seized Serenity's arm and dragged her rather rudely toward the open French doors.

Serenity frowned. "Whatever is the matter—"

"He's here!"

"Mr. McCarthy?"

"Nay, not my beau, silly. Yours!"

Completely confounded, Serenity stared at Honor as if she'd gone daft. What was she talking about?

Hopping-hands Charlie?

Nay, her sister wouldn't be so cruel. "My suitor?"

Honor grabbed her about the waist and swung her to face the crowd.

Serenity swept her gaze across the marble and gold ballroom where dancers twirled about in time with the minuet. Candlelight flashed against jewels and brightly colored gowns and even a few outdated wigs. She saw a number of men she knew fairly well, but none of them would have elicited such a response from her sister.

A sudden hum of voices permeated the room. Voices that grew louder and louder until the musicians stopped playing.

Dancers faltered in their steps, and all of a sudden the dance floor cleared.

"Holy Christmas," Serenity breathed. It was *him*. And everyone in the place was obviously as entranced by his presence as she.

And if she thought her mysterious man handsome before, she was wrong.

He wasn't handsome, he was...

Whatever there was that went beyond handsome—that was what he was!

Her breath caught in her throat and an electric charge ran the length of her body, riveting her.

No longer disheveled and rain soaked, but still dressed in black, he had the bearing of a prince and the aloofness of a king.

Until one noticed his eyes. Eyes that betrayed his studied nonchalance. Like some exotic predatorial beast, he scanned the crowd, taking in every detail. Sizing up every man as a possible opponent and every female as a possible conquest.

As his gaze touched on the women, feminine heads came together behind fans that fluttered and swayed. It was obvious he was on a quest, and in that second of realization, Serenity knew he sought *her*.

Her heart pounded in expectation. In excitement.

"Oh, my word," Heather Smith gasped from where she stood about four inches from Serenity's right. Heather, whose virtue was more than questionable, had been talking to Felicity Jacobs, the parson's daughter, for most of the evening. And it was to Felicity her comments were now directed. "Tell me, Felicity, have you ever seen the like?"

"Nay," Felicity answered back. "But I tell you

this, that man is certainly a devil out to ruin some poor woman this night."

"Well, if he be the devil, you can chain me to *his* throne anytime."

"Heather Smith," Felicity snapped. "You'll lose your soul for such words!"

Then their conversation vanished into the crowd, lost in the sudden buzz of female voices and the clearing of masculine throats.

The sound became deafening.

Serenity couldn't take her eyes off the source of everyone's speculation.

Paying no attention to the people around him, her pirate strode across the room with a masculine swagger. He was dark and deadly and mesmerizing.

"He *is* the Sea Wolf," Honor whispered in her ear. "He's just as you described in your story. Where on earth did Douglas find someone so perfect?"

"Out of my dreams," Serenity breathed.

Morgan Drake scanned the women, but none of them bore any resemblance to Serenity James. Belatedly he realized that he had become the topic on everyone's tongue.

The last thing he needed was for this many people to take notice of him.

His crew was ready to sail and he was anxious to

leave the busy harbor before someone recognized his ship. But until he could be certain that Miss Serenity James would exercise discretion regarding his identity, he couldn't risk another mission.

It had taken him hours to find out where she lived.

If only he could find her . . .

His gaze darted over two young women standing just outside the center pair of French doors. He well remembered the petite blonde with her luscious curves from the paper's office.

There was also something about her companion that seemed oddly familiar.

It struck him like a pugilist's fist.

Nay, it couldn't be.

Stepping closer, he finally recognized Serenity James.

How she had changed! Gone was her hideous black rag, and in its place she wore a stylish gown of pink. Though she lacked the voluptuous curves of her sister, there was a glow to her face that made her stand out.

Her chestnut-colored hair had been swept up into the type of style that made a man yearn to free it, and he had no doubt that the soft ringlets would be like satin in his palm.

And her eyes . . .

Without her spectacles to overshadow them, they were mesmerizing. Fire and intelligence sparkled deep within their depths. And something about them sent heat straight to his groin.

Morgan tensed. Whatever was the matter with him?

She was not his type. Indeed, her stunningly beautiful sister should have tempted him more.

But there was something about Serenity that made a mockery of her name.

Morgan closed the distance between them. She greeted him with a suspicious smile, arching an inquisitive brow that made her look like some impish elf out to make mischief. "Why, sir, I don't seem to recall your name on our guest list. Perhaps if you give it to me . . ."

"And what name would you call me?"

"Sea Wolf."

His gut tightened in response. Aye, she knew him. And now she'd involved her sister. So be it. "We *must* talk."

"Go on, Serenity," her sister whispered.

Her gaze uncertain, Serenity glanced back at Honor. "I have no chaperone," she said under her breath.

"You do now!"

Morgan watched the two women as Serenity frowned at Honor, but judging by the determined slant of her sister's eyes, he doubted if the whole of Washington's army could deflect Honor from getting them alone.

Why? It was strange to him that he had such an unlikely ally.

What did Honor hope to gain?

"I believe the library is empty," Honor said, taking Serenity's arm. "If you'll follow us, Mister ...?"

He said nothing.

Serenity exchanged quizzical looks with Honor, and he wondered what game they played.

Could it be trap?

It could. And well he knew it.

His senses sharp and alert, he detected no imminent threat. He followed them through the crowd of people that no longer seemed quite so curious about him, other than to speculate what it was he wanted with Serenity.

Now that he knew for certain Serenity James had learned his identity, he needed a plan of action.

But how in the world could he keep silent a woman who loved to babble as much as this one?

Hang her out to bake in the bleedin' sun, Cap'n. Let the gulls feast on her gizzard.

Well, that would certainly be Barney's answer. As well as his own.

Honor ushered them into the library across from the ballroom, then closed the elegantly carved mahogany door behind them. As Serenity walked past him, Morgan realized she had bathed and found a decent rose-scented perfume.

Her pink dress rustling slightly with her steps, Serenity moved to stand in the center of the room. A slight shake to her hands, as well as the fact that she wasn't chattering, alerted him that she was already nervous about this meeting.

Good, she feared him. Now, if he could play up that fear, perhaps it would be enough to quell her pen.

Her sister crossed the room to stand beside her. Both women waited while he purposefully remained silent. Let them anticipate his words, then they would pay him more attention when he did speak.

"Miss James," he began after a long pause.

"Yes," they both answered in unison.

Honor blushed a becoming shade of pink. "I'm so sorry," she said, taking her sister's hands. "You meant Serenity, of course. Go ahead, forget that I am here."

Clearing his throat, Morgan wished again that they were alone. It was enough that one Miss James threatened his secret identity. Two of them being able to identify him was two too many.

"Back to our earlier discussion, I want to know the name of the man who gave you the Sea Wolf's identity, and everyone's name you have given that information to since."

"His identity?" they answered together. They turned their heads to look at one another.

A sudden doubt prickled the back of Morgan's neck. Either both women were consummate liars or the confusion that creased both their brows was sincere.

"Why, sir, I have no idea of his identity," Serenity said, releasing her sister's hand and taking a step toward him. "I wrote the story as a piece to rally support for his efforts. If I knew his name, then I would have gladly sought him out and I would have written his views about his activities. I would be honored to report such grand news."

"She'd be the envy of all!" her sister piped in.

For the umpteenth time since he first met Serenity, Morgan was baffled and unsure. Could it all be just a coincidence?

Surely not.

What were the odds?

Suddenly the door to the library swung open. An older man entered the room, and then catching sight of Morgan, he paused.

"Forgive me if I'm intruding..."

"Oh, Douglas, no," Serenity said as she left her sister to greet the gentleman. "I am so glad you're here. I've been wanting a chance to speak with you all evening."

Morgan watched as she took Douglas by the hand and led him to stand before him. She gave both of them a dazzling smile, then turned back to Douglas. "I can't tell you how much I appreciate

your sending this man to the office this afternoon.
Why, it was the best surprise I've ever received. He
almost had me going again just a second ago, but I
realize now he's still—"

"My sending what?" Douglas interrupted.
"Who?"

Serenity's mouth dropped open and she looked
back and forth between them. Morgan suppressed
a groan, realizing finally that Serenity had no idea
who he was.

"You don't know this man?" she asked.

Douglas lifted his brows. "Should I?"

"You didn't send him into the office as a birthday prank?"

Douglas shook his head slowly. "No."

Serenity covered her mouth with her hand and
took a step back. "Oh, heavens to Betsy," she murmured, her face pale and mortified.

Morgan lifted one corner of his mouth into a
smile. God's blood, it *was* all just a bizarre coincidence.

Then Douglas smiled. "Is this another of your
games, Miss Serenity? You really should warn me.
I'm getting far too old to keep up with you and
your shenanigans." He extended his hand to Morgan. "Douglas Adams."

Morgan wanted to laugh aloud. So, this was the
man she'd been talking about earlier.

And she had assumed . . .

And then *he* had assumed . . .

Oh, this was rich. Truly rich. His anxiety had finally come home to roost.

Wouldn't Barney have a good laugh about this?

On second thought, he better keep it to himself. The less Barney knew, the more peace he'd have.

Morgan took Douglas's proffered hand. "Pleased to meet you, Mr. Adams."

Douglas turned back to Serenity. "I just wanted to let you know that Annie isn't feeling well. I thought that I should take her home, but before we left I had to wish you a wonderful birthday."

Finally her gaze settled on Morgan and for a moment she became so pale he thought she might actually faint. "You must think me the greatest of fools."

The irony of the incident amused him. Besides, it was his initial assumption that had begun this whole ridiculous misunderstanding. "Not at all. I think we have both been made the brunt of fate's folly."

Her laughter rippled. It was an enchanting sound, deep and throaty, not the silly little giggles practiced by most women of his acquaintance.

"What is going on?" her sister asked from behind them. "I don't think I understand."

Serenity turned to her sister. "'Twould seem that honest business brought this good man to my office, but he bore such a striking resemblance to my hero that I merely assumed Douglas had hired him as a prank."

Douglas joined her laughter. "I wish I had thought of that."

Now it was Morgan's turn to feel foolish. All this time he had been ready to threaten and intimidate, even abduct her if necessary, and it had all been just a strange quirk of fate.

"Forgive me for intruding on your party," Morgan said, giving her a curt bow. "'Twould seem we have both jumped to conclusions."

"Well, Serenity certainly does that enough," her sister said indelicately.

Pulling his gloves on, Morgan smiled again. "Allow me to wish you a happy birthday, Miss James, and I shall take up no more of your time."

Serenity watched as her mysterious visitor walked out of the library.

He was gone.

A strange feeling enveloped her. One that warned her she had somehow just defied fate.

"I, too, must be going," Douglas said, then followed after Morgan.

For several thundering heartbeats, Serenity stared out the open door. Her pirate was truly gone, and now she knew they would never again meet.

Nor would she ever know his name.

Oh, what did it matter? It wasn't as if there could have ever been anything between them anyway. Handsome men like him never paid heed to women like her. Nay, such handsome men were always attracted to beautiful women like Honor and Heather Smith.

"What a strange thing to happen," Honor said, her voice breaking into Serenity's thoughts. "Who would have thought a man like that would want to investigate your sources for your story. What could have caused him to pursue you all the way to the house?"

"What?" Serenity asked, her mind whirling at the significance of the question.

"I said, who would have thought that such—"

"Yes, who would have."

Honor took a step back. "Serenity, you've got that look on your face."

"What look?" she asked, arms akimbo.

"That you're-thinking-something-you-shouldn't look."

Relaxing, Serenity smiled and tapped her forefinger against her chin while her thoughts tumbled around. "Tell me, Honor. Why *would* a man like that pursue me so?"

"He was curious about the story."

"Yes, but *why* would he be curious?"

"Maybe he wants to meet the Sea Wolf?"

"Or maybe he *is* the Sea Wolf."

Chapter 3

"He's what?" Honor asked, her eyes wide.

"Don't you see?" Serenity asked Honor excitedly as the full implication hit her. "'Tis the only thing that makes sense. He was so angry this afternoon, so accusatory. He has to be the Sea Wolf and he thought I knew him! That *I* would betray his identity."

Honor scoffed. "Serenity, you're jumping to conclusions again."

"Nay," she said, her mind positive. "Not this time. I know I'm right."

"That's what you said about the butcher being in league with a French spy to steal the secrets of our new government."

"'Tis not the same."

"What about thinking the Widow Pennington was the one who was pilfering the collection plate, or that the chandler, Mr. Phipps, was working with the British government to—"

"Very well, Honor," she said, irritated at her sister. "You've made your point quite nicely."

Honor put her arm around Serenity's shoulders and gave a comforting squeeze. "I'm not trying to be harsh, sister. But God blessed you with an incredible imagination and I'm grateful for the wonderful stories you create. It's just that you need to remember that life is never as incredible as your dreams. Fantastical things just don't happen to everyday people like us."

Too bad Serenity didn't believe that. Incredible things could happen to people who were just minding their own business. After all, Moses had just been tending his flock when the Lord spoke to him. David had been a humble shepherd until he faced Goliath.

Extraordinary things could happen. Extraordinary things *did* happen!

And her pirate could be the Sea Wolf.

Nay, she corrected herself. Her pirate *was* the Sea Wolf. She would prove it!

Hours went by slowly as Serenity waited for the house to quiet. She'd never noticed before how long it took her father and brother to find their beds.

Nervously she paced the floor of her darkened bedroom, her black kidskin riding boots whispering across the pine boards.

An hour ago she'd sneaked into her brother's room to borrow some clothes while he sat below discussing his latest story with her father.

Jonathan's large black breeches felt strange, and not very secure; she'd made a belt from one of her sashes, and Serenity prayed it wouldn't break and send her pants falling into a pool around her feet.

She must blend in with the dock workers tonight. No one must ever suspect she was a woman alone, or there would be much more than Mrs. O'Grady's gossip to fear!

She knelt by the fireplace and smeared soot across her face, neck, and hands, hoping to conceal herself in the darkness.

As she continued to wait, she debated the sanity of her mission.

How was she to ever find her mysterious hero? She didn't even know the name of his ship.

Yet she was confident that she knew enough details to distinguish his ship from the others. Pulling out from her pocket the small book where she made notes for her stories, she reviewed what Jonathan had told her about the Sea Wolf's ship. It was a hundred-gun frigate, painted black and trimmed in gold with a serpent masthead.

How hard could *that* be to find? Out of the six ships that had come in today, only two had been black—one trimmed in red, the other in gold. And that one had also been a frigate.

She smiled.

Imagine, an interview with the Sea Wolf! She would be the talk of the Colonies.

For once she would be like her idol, Lady Mary. She would brave unknown dangers to uncover this story.

No matter what, she wouldn't return home tonight until she had interviewed the Sea Wolf.

"Hold me tight, sweet courage." She tucked her book back into her pocket.

Then she saw her opportunity—the flickering of a candle's light beneath her door as her father made his way down the hall to his room. The door handle rattled, then she heard his door open and close.

This was it.

She carefully left her room and headed for the stairs. Just as she reached the front door, she heard the raspy shuffle of boots moving toward her. Her heart hammering, she dodged into the drawing room.

"Goodnight, Kingsley," her brother called to their butler as he trudged up the stairs.

"Goodnight, Master Jonathan."

Serenity trembled in the shadows as another wave of apprehension washed over her. Maybe she should stay here and let Jonathan have this story.

After all, anything could happen.

True, she was dressed like a man and it was a dark night, but what if someone should realize she was a woman? A woman alone on the docks at night was a disaster just waiting to happen.

Come now, her mind snapped. *What is this cowardice? Would Lady Mary shirk at such a challenge?*

Well, nay. Lady Mary would carry on regardless of the danger. Indeed, she would revel in it.

Besides, the Sea Wolf was a man of honor. It showed in the way he carried himself, in the fact that he risked his very life to save others. He wouldn't dishonor her. He was the noble Sea Wolf. The protector of innocents.

This was her chance to be the person she wanted to be.

With that thought foremost in her mind, she slipped out the front door, into the cool night and into her future.

It was just after midnight. Jacob Dudley sat waiting beneath the bower of a weeping willow, his eyes trained on the James household, and most importantly, on the single light in the upstairs window. He was waiting for it to go out.

You're a fool on a fool's mission, he groused at himself as he shifted a large package in his lap. He'd come to Savannah just that afternoon to pick up his wife's dress, and he'd been delighted to find Morgan in port. Of course, Morgan's dinner story about his near miss with Serenity James had been less than amusing.

But they had laughed anyway and shared drinks until Morgan had taken his leave. Jake had been just about to follow when he'd overheard a man in the tavern questioning the patrons about the same story that had brought Morgan to town.

Wayward Hayes.

It was a name he knew as well as his own. A name any good profit-minded sailor kept his ears open for word of. Hayes made his living by tracking down pirates and privateers and handing them over to the governments who paid the most for them.

Now that man sought the Sea Wolf.

Just like Morgan, Hayes had decided the author of the newspaper article knew the Sea Wolf by sight; only, Hayes had yet to learn S. S. James was a woman.

That gave Jake enough time to make sure Morgan escaped before Hayes learned his identity.

But first he must make certain Serenity was secure. Hayes wouldn't ever believe she'd written her story without firsthand knowledge of Morgan. Nor was he the type of man to go easy on her just because she was a woman.

Nay, with the price the British had on Morgan's head, Hayes would interrogate her every bit as thoroughly and painfully as he would a man. And

Jake wasn't the kind of man to leave a woman to suffer. Not when he could help it.

The light went out.

Scooping up the package, Jake rose to his feet. Just a few minutes more and he would make sure Serenity and Morgan were safe from Hayes's clutches.

He sneaked across the yard.

It had cost him quite a bit to learn about the James family. There were three women living in the house—the brown-haired Serenity, her blond sister, and an elderly housekeeper.

Jake smiled. True, it'd been a while since he'd infiltrated a home for such mischief, but he'd done it enough in the past to believe he'd have no problems finding the chit and getting her out. He could move as stealthily as a ghost, and in his bachelor days, he'd roamed in and out of many a woman's room without her husband or family being the wiser.

He drew even with the sweeping front porch.

The front door creaked open.

Jake froze. And before he could move, a small form ran from the house. Like lightning, someone scampered across the porch, down the steps, and straight into his chest.

A startled cry escaped before the person who hit him stumbled back, tripped over a root, and fell to the ground with a solid thump.

Bemused, Jake dropped his package and knelt down to check on who had accosted him.

"Well, fate be damned," he laughed as he caught sight of the pale form in a buttery shaft of moonlight. She was dressed as a man, but only a fool could miss her curves, and Jacob Dudley was anything but a fool.

Jake looked up at the bright, star-filled sky. "Thank you, Lord," he said. "You've helped me out once again."

And surely He had, for she'd knocked herself unconscious in her fall. A quick check assured him that she still breathed and hadn't broken the skin of her skull, though from the knot that was forming he could tell she'd have a wretched headache when she awoke.

Now all he had to do was get to Morgan and see to it he sailed before Hayes identified his ship. Easy enough.

His spirit light, Jake hefted Serenity up over one shoulder, grabbed Lorelei's package, and headed for his concealed horse.

Serenity came awake to a fierce pounding in her temples. Moaning softly, she tried to put her hand to her head only to learn her hands weren't free. Someone had tied her to a chair! A hard, wooden chair that seemed to be in a small cabin on a ship ...

Her blood racing, she remembered running out of the house and into a tree.

Nay, she thought, her body going cold. It had been a man. A huge man.

"Listen to me, old man, we've not got enough time for you to argue."

"But Jake, the captain'll have me head if he finds her on board. And you know how he is when he gets riled."

Her vision blurry, she blinked her eyes. The man called Jake came into focus. He was extremely tall, at least six foot five. He wore the humble clothes of a farmer, and his long blond hair had been pulled back into a queue.

However, it was the coldness of his eyes that held her transfixed. They were steely, devoid of emotions, and they were set into a face that would rival her pirate's for sheer handsomeness.

"Barney, I swear I'll hang you myself if you don't give the order to sail."

"Sail?" Serenity gasped, wincing as more pain sliced through her head. "Sail where?"

The old man stepped around Jake and eyed her curiously. "See now, she's awake. You can be taking her with you."

"Barney," Jake growled, his voice laced with warning.

"All right then, I'll tell the captain about her and—"

Jake grabbed Barney by the arm and turned him around until they faced each other. "Listen, unless you want Wayward Hayes to hang Morgan, you'll get this ship out of here while you're still safe. *I'll* deal with the woman, and with Morgan."

"Fine then, it's your arse he'll be skinning." Barney gave her one last look, then headed out of the tiny cabin.

"Excuse me," Serenity said, her voice cracking with alarm. "But I really don't think you'll be sailing with me on board."

Jake quirked a smile. "And what do you intend to do about it?"

"Scream?"

His laugh was low and evil. If it were true that the eyes were the window of the soul, then this man didn't possess one at all. His intense gaze betrayed no emotion whatsoever as he reached beneath his navy cape and pulled out a long, wicked knife. "Try it and I'll have your tongue." He fingered the shining blade.

"You wouldn't dare," she squeaked, her voice constricted by terror.

"I've done worse things in my life."

And by the light in his eyes, she could see he spoke honestly. Dear Lord, how could this man have so little regard for human decency?

For the very tongue she loved so well!

"Why have you taken me?" she asked.

He returned his knife to the folds of his cape and sighed. "Believe it or not, it's for your own good."

"My own good? Pray tell, how do you figure that?"

"Under the circumstances, I fear I don't have time to explain it. I have to make sure Barney carries out my orders and that a stubborn man sees reason. So, if you'll excuse me..." He started for the door.

"Wait!"

He paused and turned back to face her with one arched brow.

"I won't tell anyone you kidnapped me," she begged. "Just, please, let me go."

"Unfortunately, that's not possible." He cocked his head to one side and eyed her like a hawk watching a hare. "Now, do I need to gag you before I leave?"

Serenity shook her head. She was quite attached to her tongue and she was determined to keep as much of her freedom as she could. One way or another, she was going to get off this ship, even if she had to jump off and swim back home; sharks and sea monsters be damned.

Two hours later, Serenity sat in the small crevice that Jake had called Barney's bunk room. Bunk water-closet was more like. She owned hatboxes that were bigger.

She'd been doing her best to free herself, but it was too late.

She had felt the ship leave its moorings and now it rolled across the waves at full speed.

Whatever was she going to do?

You should have screamed anyway, she said to herself in frustration.

Well, had I done that, Jake would have cut my tongue out.

Yes, well, better he cut out your tongue than your father get ahold of you after this.

Closing her eyes, she could just imagine the look on her father's face.

What had she done? This was not the adventure she had wanted. She had never once dreamed of being trapped in the belly of a ship headed for who knew where.

Oh heaven, this was definitely not a good day for an adventure.

Suddenly she heard steps outside. She held her breath in fear.

The door swung open.

"Barney, I need..." The familiar voice trailed off as her dream pirate looked up from the fob watch he'd been checking. His gaze touched on her, and if she thought he had looked angry that afternoon in her shop, she had certainly underestimated him.

"Barney!" he bellowed with a force that shamed the raging sea.

"Good evening, Captain," she said in the calmest of voices. She was proud of her poise, given the ridiculousness and horror of her situation.

"What the devil are you doing here?" he asked between clenched teeth.

She twisted her hands that were held in place by the ropes so that he could see them. "I am sitting in a most uncomfortable chair."

"I can see that," he said moving forward into the room. He knelt down in front of her chair. "How did you get there?"

Her eyes widened as he pulled out a huge dagger. An image of it plunging into her breast flashed before her eyes as Jake's words echoed in her ears.

Serenity took a deep breath.

Footsteps thundered down the hallway. "I can explain, Captain," Barney said as he appeared outside the door.

"You better," the Sea Wolf said in the most intimidating voice she'd ever heard as he slashed the ropes holding her arms and legs to the chair.

More rushing footsteps.

Jake came to stand by Barney's side, and the two of them stared into the cabin at the captain. "I was going to tell you about her," Jake said.

"When? After she died of starvation?" The Sea

Wolf's jaw ticked as he rose slowly to his feet and turned to face Jake and Barney. "Dammit, Jake, what kind of mess have you dragged me into now? I would have thought you'd learned your lesson about kidnapping women."

In spite of the anger in the Sea Wolf's voice, Jake cracked a roguish grin. "Don't take that tone with me, Drake. You know what I do to people who make me angry. Besides, would you have had me leave her behind for Hayes to question?"

The Sea Wolf returned his dagger to its sheath. "There were other alternatives."

"Such as?"

"You could have warned her of the danger, and her father could have seen to her protection."

Jake snorted. "Do you really think her father could have kept her safe from Hayes?"

The Sea Wolf tensed, and Serenity could see him debate Jake's words.

Jake met her gaze and his smile died. "We just have to decide what to do with her in the meantime. I figure we only need to hide her out a couple of weeks before Hayes will pick up someone else's trail and leave Savannah."

"Weeks?" she asked in disbelief.

The Sea Wolf placed a comforting hand on her shoulder, which kept her from rising. "Her reputation's ruined if we do that."

"That's not as bad as what Hayes will do to her," Jake said nonchalantly.

"Who is Hayes?" Serenity demanded, and then she listened in horror as the Sea Wolf explained. Not that she had a problem with Hayes hunting down the dreadful pirates. They deserved to be hung for their crimes. But any man who would hand over a hero like the Sea Wolf, well, she certainly had a problem with that.

"You *can* take me home," she said. "I could go stay with some of my family in Marthasville."

"Aye," the Sea Wolf agreed. "We could do that. I doubt if he'd—"

"*I* found her with very little effort," Jake interrupted. "And you don't want to know how much information about her family I was able to purchase. Hayes could easily track her to the home of a relative. And to get a prize like you, you better believe he would."

The Sea Wolf raked his hands through his hair. "Jake, keeping her doesn't make any sense. She doesn't even know who I am."

"That's not entirely true," Serenity couldn't resist adding. She didn't know why, but she liked taking the upper hand with the good captain. Maybe it was the arrogance of his stance, that devil-may-care attitude that seemed to bleed from every pore of his skin.

The Sea Wolf cocked a surprised brow. "What's that?"

She rubbed her chafed wrists. "I didn't know who you were until you came to the party. Your ire gave you away, sir, and as I told you then, if I knew the identity of the Sea Wolf, I would get his views on his activities."

Ignoring Barney and Jake, who still watched them from the doorway, she retrieved her glasses from her coat pocket, along with her book and pencil. She put her glasses on, opened her book to the correct page, positioned her pencil for notes, then locked gazes with the captain. "So tell me, what got you interested in freeing American sailors?"

"Ah, bloody hell!" he cursed.

Jake folded his arms across his chest. "Now what do you think?"

"I think the girl's ruined and you and I are going to hell for it."

Jake laughed. "Given our past sins, I doubt if she'll be the stone that tips the scales of our damnation."

The Sea Wolf sighed. "Well, I guess there's nothing we can do but make the best of it. It looks as if the girl's to be our guest. Barney, see to it Kit makes my room ready for her." He pinned his stare on Jake. "I really wish you'd told me what you had planned before you took it upon yourself to abduct her."

Jake shrugged. "As if you would have come up with a better idea." He clapped Barney on the back. "Come on, old man. Let's go see to that room."

Once they were alone, the captain turned to face her with arms akimbo. "Well, Miss James, I don't suppose I'll be able to keep my name from you much longer. Allow me to present myself, Captain Morgan Drake at your command."

Morgan Drake. The name suited him.

"I wish I could say that I was pleased to meet you, Captain Drake," she said with a curt sigh. "But under the circumstances I hope you will forgive me for being less than cordial."

"I fully understand, Miss James. I suppose the last thing you intended tonight was a voyage."

Serenity released her breath slowly at his words. She had finally done it. Instead of a quick and quiet adventure where she had planned to interview the Sea Wolf and gather a spectacular story before returning to the safety of her neat and organized little world, she now faced the most unsure future imaginable.

Even for her.

And she wondered if Lady Mary had ever felt as alone, as terrified, as she did now.

Morgan pulled out a small, engraved silver flask from his coat pocket and handed it to her. "You look as if you could use a stiff drink."

"No, thank you," she said, attempting to return it to his hands. "I don't imbibe."

He placed one lean finger on the bottom of the flask and lifted it to her lips. "Nor do you run off in the middle of the night with a shipload of men—unchaperoned."

Her hand trembled to the point she could hear the liquor slosh inside the flask. He was right. Her life would never again be the same. There was no going back.

With a deep breath, she lifted the flask in a mock salute. "To adventure, then," she said, taking a quick swig. The rum scalded her throat and burned a path to her stomach.

Gasping for air, she tried to force her lungs to work.

Through the tears in her eyes, she saw him smile. Heavens, he was dashingly handsome. Especially when he wasn't scowling.

"You're a bold one, Miss James," he said, taking the flask from her.

She watched in awe as he took it to his lips, his mouth touching the very spot from whence she had sipped.

"And you're a brave one, Captain Drake."

He laughed and duplicated her toast.

"To adventure the likes of which I think neither of us has ever seen."

"And to fate," she whispered. "To the very fate that has abandoned us to turmoil."

Chapter 4

To the very fate that has abandoned us to turmoil.

Why did that echo in Morgan's head? Because in his short acquaintance with this particular woman, she had done nothing but turn his orderly world inside out.

What could possibly be more torturous than spending the next few weeks trapped on board a ship with a woman who tempted him so mercilessly?

And she managed to do it effortlessly!

Even now, covered in grime and looking like a half-drowned pup, this woman had something about her that made a certain part of his anatomy sit up and beg for her.

Great hooks and crooks, why did this have to happen now, when the last thing he needed was something, or most especially someone, to get in his way?

He must stay focused with his thoughts.

He must...

Morgan looked at her and he sighed. With her eyes lowered, she rubbed her arms against the chill. She looked so vulnerable and timid.

Worst of all, she looked a mess.

But when not covered in soot, she was a pretty little thing, with a keen mind and fiery spirit that attracted him to her every bit as much as if she were a raving beauty.

Morgan clenched his teeth. He must have done something horribly wrong in his past! He must have committed some awful, wretched sin that fate was now punishing him for.

Yes, well, you better make sure you don't do something wrong in the future, his mind scolded as he tried not to notice just how perfect Serenity's cupid's-bow lips were.

She was a decent woman, not some wharf-side doxy. Though he may have ruined her reputation, the least he could do was see to it that she was returned to her father every bit as intact as she had been when she left his home.

"I find it odd, Miss James, that you don't demand I return you," he said, noting the resignation in her posture.

"If I thought it would make you release me, Captain, I would. But you and Jake have made it quite clear that I have no voice in the matter."

"And are you always this compliant?" he

couldn't resist asking as he remembered the way she'd boldly walked and talked circles around him that afternoon.

"Seldom."

He laughed at her honesty. Still, he must make her understand the very real danger she posed. Not just to him, but to all of them. "Well then, Miss James, let me remind you that you're on a ship *full* of men. Rough men who will be at sea for quite a few weeks. Men who aren't used to having a decent woman near them."

She sighed. "I believe it's what my mother used to call a recipe for disaster."

"Without a doubt."

She nodded in understanding, her eyes bold and brave. The only clue he had of her nervousness was when she began to chew the corner of her bottom lip.

"Which brings me to my next point, Miss James. Though I trust my crew with my life, I don't trust them with yours. There are several of my men who were Caribbean pirates before I took them on, and though I've had no problems with them before now, I have no idea how they will react to your presence."

"An ounce of prevention—"

"Please spare me the old wives' sayings."

Serenity clamped her lips together as if in effort

to stifle more sayings. Though he wasn't sure, he suspected that she liked rankling him.

Mayhap it was the mischievous gleam in her eyes belied by her nervousness. Whatever it was, he had an impression that she wasn't always so forward with men. Somehow he was different, and if the truth were known, he liked the thought that she might see him as different. That she wasn't this forward with all men.

Rising to her feet, she covered a yawn with one hand, and it was then he noted the dark circles under her eyes. Aye, it was after three o'clock in the morning, and no doubt she was used to being long asleep by this hour.

Just as she opened her mouth to speak, the ship lurched beneath her feet and sent her flying toward him.

Morgan barely had time to prevent her from colliding with the wall. The weight of her body threw him against the rough boards, but he didn't even notice. Nay, how could he notice any pain when a pleasure so sweet swept through him.

Her soft, supple body ran full-length against his, and even though she wore rough clothes, he could feel her body's heat. Smell the sweet scent of rose wafting from her hair.

Her lips were parted slightly from her gasp of alarm, and wide, cobalt blue eyes stared up at him.

A searing heat tore through his groin as his body reached out for her, and he swore that he could taste the sweetness of her honey breath.

What he wouldn't give for a taste of her.

"Will I be safe with you, Captain?" she asked quietly, her voice like a shout in the tiny room.

"Most assuredly, Miss James," he answered back. *About as safe as a lamb in a wolf's den.*

Serenity swallowed and her body tensed. "I believe I have my balance again," she whispered.

Yes, but I seem to have lost mine. Morgan reluctantly let go of her. And in that instant, he decided it was a good thing for Serenity that he wasn't the sort of man who took advantage of young women. Because if he was, she'd be his this very night.

Grime and all.

"Follow me," he said, his voice sounding odd even to him. Yes, it would be best to put as much distance between them as possible.

As quickly as possible.

Serenity followed him up the short ladder back to the main deck. The sky was as black as pitch, and only the ebony waves broke the monotony. A stiff breeze whipped the sails and made the wooden boards creak. It was a deafening symphony.

Salt stung her nose and she wondered how long it would be before she saw her family again.

What would her father say?

And did she really want to hear it?

Her heart heavy, she wished herself home, safely asleep in her own bed. Indeed, she was sure her father's wrath would make the raging sea around her seem mild.

Would he ever forgive her? Or would he turn his back to her as he had done to Chastity? Abandon her to the same vicious gossips that had finally driven her sister away?

Don't think on it. There is nothing you can do but go forward. Fate has deemed this time and place for you. And to everything there is a season.

Yes, but what season was it? A time to weep, or a time to laugh?

Taking a deep breath for courage, she swore that no matter what fate had planned for her, she would meet it bravely. Honestly. And if those old Savannah biddies treated her the way they had treated Chatty, then she would give them their full due. This particular James girl had more than enough brass to take on any gossip.

Morgan led her down below the deck, through a tight corridor until they reached a small door. He shouldered it open, then stood aside for her to enter.

Serenity wasn't sure what to expect. She'd seen thousands of ships from the outside, but this was the first time she had actually been aboard one.

Stepping through the door, she was somewhat

disappointed. Once again her imagination had run away with her. She had envisioned his cabin as an opulent room with rich satins hanging from the walls, maybe like a sheik's tent. Of numerous chests spilling over with booty taken from English warships.

What she saw was a nice orderly room, low of ceiling and decidedly masculine.

The large bunk on her right was made right into the wall of the ship and covered with a beautiful blue and yellow charm quilt. Behind the bunk was a small cabinet that held a wash pitcher and basin.

To her left was a medium-sized trunk, and directly in front of her was a large oak table. But what commanded her attention was the wall of glass windows that looked out on a sea so dark and mysterious that it kept her transfixed.

"How beautiful," she breathed.

"I often have that same reaction to it," Morgan confessed from behind her.

"Do you ever grow accustomed to it?"

"Never."

She looked back over her shoulder to see him staring out at the sea as well. With the lantern light shadowing his face and his hair tousled about his tanned cheeks, he reminded her much of the wolf for which he was named.

Serenity found it overwhelmingly attractive.

And deeply disturbing.

Time seemed suspended.

He stared at her with a raw hunger burning bright in his eyes. His entire body tense, he stood as frozen as she.

Kiss me.

Serenity felt her face grow warm at her thought. Oh, but he was so very handsome. Just the type of man she'd dreamed of on so many lonely nights. The type of man she'd giggled about with her sisters and friends as they exchanged stories on what features and characteristics they wanted for their beaux.

But it was a foolish thought.

He was a man of the sea. A man who would no doubt live and die on board a ship, and she was just the plain spinster daughter of a printer.

It wasn't for her to have such thoughts.

Clearing his throat, he moved to his trunk and pulled out a towel and shirt. "I'm afraid we're lacking in feminine garb. You'll have to make do with this until we can find more suitable clothing."

Serenity took the clothes from him, stung by his obvious rejection. She had been so sure he was going to kiss her. He'd had the same look Charlie Simms got right before he made free with his hands.

"I'm sure I look a fright," she whispered, moving toward the table. Morgan came up behind her so close that she could smell the salt of his skin, feel the heat of his body.

Until he put a small mirror up to her face. "I must say I've seen you look better," he said.

Serenity gasped. Goodness, she looked worse than she'd feared.

"I should caution you against any further inclination to roll around in the dirt, Miss James," he said, with a teasing note in his voice. "Fresh water is scarce on a ship and we have very little for washing."

That said, he took a pitcher from the cabinet in the wall and poured a small amount of water into the washbasin. Before she could move, he dipped a small cloth into the water and brought it up to her face.

She couldn't move. She held her breath as he slid the cool cloth over her face and neck. His long, lean fingers brushed her skin, raising chills all the length of her. And even stranger than the chills was the sudden warmth that began to drum through her entire body.

"Captain?"

"Yes, Miss James?"

"I..." Serenity couldn't finish her sentence. All she could do was stare up at him, aching for something she couldn't name.

And then he did it.

His lips claimed hers with a firmness that took

her breath. Arms as strong as steel wrapped around her and brought her up close against a body so hard and solid that she couldn't imagine any man feeling better.

Her legs weak, she surrendered her weight to him.

Now, this was a kiss, she thought, as he parted her lips and explored her mouth with the expertness of Don Juan. This was the wonder, the thrill that romantic authors wrote of, and in that instant, she knew that she would never want another man to hold her so intimately.

Serenity felt him tense an instant before he stepped away. Her mind numb, she could do nothing but stare at him in confusion.

What had prompted him to kiss her so passionately?

And why did he look so upset now?

Did he regret it?

He ran his thumb over his lips and stared at her with an unreadable expression on his face. "You are a very dangerous woman, Serenity."

"Me?"

"Aye. And the worst part is, you don't even know why."

Completely baffled, she stared at him as he strode to the door.

"There are extra blankets in the chest, should you need them," he said, pulling open the door.

He paused in the entrance and turned to face her. "And Serenity?"

Still dazed, she looked up and met his dark stare.

"Make sure you lock the door."

Chapter 5

Serenity stared at the closed door. Lock the door indeed! Yet even through her mortification, she was thrilled that a heroic man like Morgan could be attracted to her.

Her heart light, she placed his shirt on the oak table and quickly locked the door as ordered. Not that she was afraid of him, nay, far from it.

Her Sea Wolf had proven himself a most honorable man.

"My Sea Wolf," she repeated, wondering if any woman could ever lay claim to such a man.

Butterflies fluttered in her stomach. She felt giddy, even a little silly. Oh, but it was an incredible feeling. One completely new to her.

Her thoughts still on her magnificent Captain Drake, she finished scrubbing the soot from her cheeks. Even now with the cold water splashing against her skin, she could feel the heat of Morgan's touch, smell the raw and wild scent of the untamed sea. It was a heady concoction.

Was this what her sister Chatty had felt on those nights when she would sneak out of the house to meet Stephen alone? No wonder Chatty had run away with him. At the moment, Serenity held little doubt that if Morgan asked her to, she would follow him to the ends of the earth.

She heard his voice from outside the door as he called orders to one of his men, and another warm rush ran through her. What a man!

Strong, proud ...

A little on the arrogant side and somewhat domineering, but then, who was without flaws?

Sighing, she pulled her brother's shirt off and replaced it with Morgan's. The white lawn swept against her skin, raising chills along her arms. It had his scent. Raw and wild, and she fought the urge to bury her nose in the soft material.

A knock at the door startled her.

"Miss James?" a timid voice called. "The captain wanted me to bring you some ..." The voice trailed off and for several seconds no sound followed.

She lifted her brow in question.

"Some lady things," the voice finished, rushing as if the words embarrassed him.

Opening the door, she met the young man who had peeked into her shop earlier that day. He stood on the other side, looking sheepish and unsure while he clutched at an armload of material.

"They call me, Kit, ma'am," he said, his light

blue eyes meeting hers for an instant before he glanced back to the floor. "Barney and the captain told me to look after any needs you might have."

"Thank you," she said with a smile.

He handed her his armload of clothes. "These are from Captain Dudley. They were supposed to be for his wife, but after Captain Drake had a few words with him, he said that you might have more use of them for the time being."

Who was Captain Dudley?

"Dudley?" she asked.

"Aye, Jake Dudley. He was the one who brought you on board."

"Oh yes, I remember him quite well."

Kit hung his head and nodded. "I thought you might."

He started to move away, but Serenity stopped him with a light touch on his arm. "Who is Jake Dudley, Kit?" she asked, remembering the way he'd spoken to Morgan. She didn't know for certain, but she suspected that Morgan Drake didn't allow many men such liberty with their words. "Is he a member of the crew or just a friend of Captain Drake's?"

She watched the color fade from his cheeks as if the question terrified him. "It's not for me to say, Miss James."

With that handful of mysterious words, Kit took his leave. Chewing her lip, Serenity shut the door and crossed the room. A mystery. How she loved a mystery to solve. And just who should she bother for the details?

Surely not Morgan, he was too clever and cautious by half. And Jake himself scared her to pieces.

Hmm...

It would take some doing, but she was certain she could find a member of the crew who liked to talk as much as she did. Someone who with a few well-placed questions would spill like an overfilled barrel. First thing in the morning, she would find that person.

Shaking out the bundle Kit had left behind, she was surprised to find a modest rose and white striped gown, as well as a couple of things that made her blush every bit as much as Kit. No wonder the boy had been embarrassed. Imagine bringing a corset and pantaloons to a woman! Good gracious!

She started to put the light silk chemise on, then stopped herself. The truth be known, she didn't want to take off Morgan's shirt. For some reason she *really* liked wearing it. It was as if he were holding her, protecting her.

What would it hurt to keep it on for the night?

After refolding her bundle of clothes, she placed them in the chest and settled into Morgan's bunk. Chills spread through her, and she twisted her hands in the warm quilt. Just think, this was where her infamous pirate captain rested his head every night after he'd spent a day chasing the evil Brits.

This was where he came to relax and think through his...

"Oh, no," she breathed. She suddenly realized that he must view her as a horrible intrusion into his life. This cabin was like her father's study. Morgan surely thought it to be his refuge—his one private domain.

And he had given it over to her.

Where was he going to sleep from now on?

She couldn't accept his room for the duration of the trip. Other arrangements would have to be made.

Pulling the quilt up closer to her, she caught another whiff of him and sighed. Her heart fluttered.

Give up this bunk, she said to herself, *and you won't feel this close to him anymore.*

But, I will keep my self-respect, she countered.

Aye, but since when does self-respect feel as good as this bunk?

Serenity laughed at herself. *You are an immoral, wanton woman, Serenity James, and for the sake of your sanity, as well as your virtue, you will give Captain Drake back his bed!*

All right, self, you win. Tomorrow he gets his bed back.

But tonight was hers to savor.

* * *

"Looking a little green gilled, Drake."

Shaking his head, Morgan rubbed his tired eyes. "Don't you ever make any noise when you walk, Jake?"

"Well, the way this ship's creaking tonight, I think I would need a cowbell for you to hear my approach."

Morgan gave a short laugh as Jake took a seat across from him. The galley was dark, the coals of the fire burning very low. Only the light of a single tallow candle safely ensconced in a glass lantern provided light for the two men. Morgan wasn't sure how long he'd been down here. It seemed in some ways like an eternity.

"It's not like you to drink with a storm brewing," Jake said as he reached for the bottle of rum next to Morgan's elbow.

"Who says I'm drinking?"

Cocking an amused brow, Jake held the half-full bottle up before the flame. "I guess the bottle drank itself."

Morgan said nothing, instead he stared at a black spot on a board just over Jake's head.

"You know, Drake, I seem to recall this impertinent young pup who once told me that problems shared are problems solved."

Morgan had never been one to appreciate hearing his words flung back at him. Especially not by the infamous pirate king, Jack Rhys. "And I seem to recall a surly pirate telling me to mind my own business or I'd find myself gutted."

Jake laughed and poured himself a liberal amount of rum. "Careful with that word, lest Barney hear it. If anyone finds out who I am, I'll be in a worse fix than you. Which leads me to my next question. What do you plan to do about Hayes?"

"What I should have done years ago."

"Kill him?" Jake asked in all seriousness.

Morgan smirked at the pirate's answer for everything. "*Confront* him."

Jake expelled a snarling breath before curling his lip in disgust. "Since when do you take the sissy way out?"

"Excuse me?" Morgan asked, infuriated by the insult.

Jake laughed good-naturedly, dispelling Morgan's anger. "Face it, Drake, that good English breeding of yours is showing itself. Talking ain't a man's way of doing things. You know that. You got a problem, you cut its heart out and then it's not a problem anymore."

"Last time I checked, following that philosophy is what has you one step away from the gallows. Forgive me if I don't take your advice."

Jake shrugged off Morgan's words. "You, my friend, have come a long way from the piss 'n' vinegar youth who used to try my patience. But then, you were always too honest for your own good.

"By the way," Jake said before taking a swig of rum. "I'm sorry for getting you mixed up with that wench."

Morgan snorted. "What possessed you to take her hostage?"

Jake shrugged again. "You ought to be grateful. My first impulse was—"

"To cut her throat."

"Exactly."

Morgan rolled his eyes. Tolerance had never been a strong point for Jake, and it seemed not even these last years away from the sea had managed to mellow him any. "Just answer me one question. How did Lorelei ever survive long enough for you to marry her?"

Jake guffawed loudly. "What can I say, she puts up a good fight." He downed the last of his rum. He laced his hands behind his head and sat back with a satisfied smirk. "And she handles a sword better than most men."

Morgan laughed, remembering Lorelei's intrepid spirit as she stood toe-to-toe with the surly pirate.

But who would expect less from the granddaughter of the infamous pirates, Anne Bonny and Calico Jack?

"You must be mellowing with age," Morgan said at last.

Snorting, Jake poured himself another mug of rum. "I think it's too many years of being around you." He eyed Morgan keenly. "So, what do you plan to do with *her*?"

"I don't know," he answered with a sigh. "In all honesty, Jake, I have so many problems right now, I don't know where one ends and the next begins."

Jake gave a knowing nod. "You're thinking of Penelope?"

Morgan sighed. "Aye," he said. He could never hide his thoughts from Jake. "I keep thinking that I'm no better than Winston."

Jake's gaze hardened. "What, are you daft? How do you figure that?"

"We've ruined Serenity every bit as much as Winston ruined my sister."

Jake frowned. "Last I checked, we weren't planning on selling Serenity to a wh—"

"*Don't you say it!*" Morgan snarled.

Jake held his hands up in truce. "I'm sorry, Drake. I know how much you loved her."

And Jake did. If any man alive knew how much Morgan Drake's sister had meant to him, it was Jake. Jake had helped Morgan track her down and it'd been Jake who'd paid to free her from the bordello she'd been sold to.

"You know," Morgan said, scratching his chin in thought. "I was actually thinking we might be able to turn this around with Hayes."

"What do you mean?"

"Well, this time of year, he usually heads toward the Caribbean to try and roust some of our good brethren from their winter homes. If we were to head that way, we might be able to cross paths with him."

Jake took a deep swig of rum. "You know there's nothing more I'd like than to see that bastard dead. But you go after him and the Brits will raise their price."

"Aye, but maybe the next person will think twice before coming after me."

Jake snorted. "Leave him be, Morgan. You got more important things to attend."

"Such as?"

"For starters, you can buy Lorelei a new dress from one of those expensive London designers. She'll have my head when she finds out I let your woman have that flimsy pink thing she's been asking for."

"Serenity is not my woman. You're the one who trapped her here."

"Yeah, well, if I had a woman on board *my* ship, I wouldn't be down here making love to a bottle of rum. I'd be up there showing her the better part of my sex."

Morgan placed his finger above his brow and traced a line that ran the same length and shape as the scar above Jake's brow. A scar Lorelei had delivered during one of their numerous and notorious fights. "I think I'll spare myself the grief."

Jake laughed. "I assure you, Drake, I *thoroughly* enjoyed earning that scar. And it was certainly worth every stitch."

With that, Jake took his leave, and Morgan noticed the bottle of rum took its leave as well. *Same old Black Jack*, he thought with a smile.

Some things never changed.

Morgan sat quietly, thinking over Jake's words. And the fact that Serenity was only a few yards away, no doubt tucked safely in his bed.

In *his* bed.

Would the insults never cease?

Serenity came awake to the sound of rain tapping lightly against the windows. Opening her eyes, she watched the drops run down the thick panes of clear glass.

The ship!

"Oh no," she gasped, realizing in that instant that the night before hadn't been a nightmare.

Well, okay, maybe *nightmare* wasn't the right word. The point was: *It all had really happened*.

She was ruined.

By now her father would have been up for hours

and was no doubt scouring Savannah looking for her. He had no idea where she was, or when she would return.

"Oh no," she repeated.

The permanence of her predicament hit her like a shot. This was really it. There was never any going back to the life she had lived before.

Serenity prayed for courage and strength to face her future—to face the stinging gossipmongers who would follow her for the rest of her life. Even now, she could hear the vicious comments made about Chatty.

That's the James girl there. She's the one they caught kissing that young boy down at the lake. Little harlot. That's what happens when a woman starts talking social reforms for women. Benjamin should have taken a strap to his wife and never let her fill her daughters' heads with such tripe. I pity that poor man, left behind to cope with the mess his wife left him.

How many times had she heard a variation of that story? And how many more times in her life would she hear the new one?

That be the poor James girl there. She done run off with pirates in the middle of the night. . . .

She had brought it on herself, and it would haunt her forever.

Serenity pushed herself out of bed and quickly dressed. There was no need in moping around and bemoaning her fate. She had chosen this course and it was time to follow it wherever it led.

And right now her rumbling stomach wanted it to lead to a kitchen somewhere. She unlocked the door and tripped over a lump.

Only, it wasn't a lump.

The Sea Wolf had slept at her door.

Morgan came awake with a curse and a mouthful of pink silk. A sudden sharp pain stabbed his side as limbs and silk engulfed him.

"What the devil?" he asked. His hand brushed up against something warm and velvety. Something that felt incredibly good against his palm.

"Captain Drake, remove your hand from my thigh this instant!"

It was a wonderful wake-up surprise to find the woman he was dreaming of sprawled in his arms. Serenity's outraged voice brought a rakish grin to his face. Before he could curb the impulse, Morgan ran his hand over the cool silk stocking, along the sensuous curve of her leg, feeling the supple muscles and delicate softness. But what he really wanted to do was cup the inside of her leg, especially the soft, warm juncture of her thighs.

What he wouldn't give to trail his lips over the soft flesh. To peel back those stockings and . . .

"Captain Drake!" she shouted, shoving the hem

of the dress down over his hand and forcing him to withdraw it. Her cheeks were flaming red. "Release me."

"I believe you are the one holding me down, Miss James."

Not that he minded. With Serenity lying atop him, he was tangled in her skirts and enjoying the press of her breasts against his chest as she struggled to right herself, all the while choking on indignation.

His grin widened. Oh, her outrage was delightful. He knew his smile infuriated her, which amused him all the more.

With one sharp elbow in his side, she pushed herself to her feet. "You are the devil!" she snapped, turning about in a huff.

Morgan's laugh rumbled deep in his throat as he rose to his own feet and watched her head for the main deck. "You're wrong, Serenity James," he whispered. "Were I the devil, you wouldn't have gotten away so easily."

Serenity didn't slow her pace until she saw Barney shouting orders up to a crewman in the crow's nest.

"Excuse me, Mister..." she paused as she realized she didn't know his last name, and calling him "Barney" seemed just a little too forward.

"Pitkern," he supplied for her. "They call me Mr. Pitkern, lass. Now what can I do for you?"

It was then that she noticed the crewmen had all stopped their labors and were now staring straight at her. The two men behind Barney had stopped scrubbing the railings and water dripped from their sponges. Even their bawdy singing had ceased.

The ship was as silent as the dead of night, and only the snapping of the rigging and cries of birds broke the sudden stillness.

The hair on the back of her neck raised. This was not good. Not good at all!

Morgan paused at the top of the deck and noted the reactions of his men as they became aware of her presence. It didn't bode particularly well. A woman on board a ship was exactly what Serenity had said, a recipe for disaster.

With purposeful strides, he crossed the deck to where she stood.

"Men," he called, shifting their attention away from her pale form. "We have a guest for our trip. Miss James is a lady of decent temperament and is to be accorded respect. Any man who fails to show her anything less will have me to deal with."

"Aye, Captain."

He turned to face her. "I should have dressed

you like a powder monkey," Morgan said in a low tone, his voice strained.

"I beg your pardon?" she asked.

"He means like one of the boys in charge of fetching powder for the cannons during a fight, Miss James," Barney explained for her.

Serenity thanked the man before she looked back at Morgan. "Need I remind you, Captain. I *was* dressed like a powder monkey."

"And you still managed to get into trouble."

By the look on her face, he could tell she longed to argue, but she knew he was right, and that alone must have been what kept her silent.

Morgan rubbed his rib cage. "Now tell me what was so important that you almost punctured my lung with your foot to come out here?"

She crossed her arms over her chest. "What were you doing on the floor outside my room?"

"That happens to be *my* room."

"Not until I'm returned home."

Morgan took a deep breath. Why was he arguing with her? And why over something so stupid? It wasn't like him to even care about such matters.

"Where were you going?" he asked again, not wanting to investigate his feelings any further.

"I was going for food, if you must know. I happen to be hungry. Now tell me why you were outside my door."

"A man has to sleep sometime, Miss James, and on a ship a man makes his bunk wherever he can find space."

"Aren't there guest quarters, or ..."

"This is a warship, Miss James, not a passenger ship."

"But what about the other sailors? Don't they have beds?"

"They make pallets or string up hammocks wherever they can. And I'm not beast enough to oust poor Barney from his room. He needs it to keep his bird happy."

She looked around at the men who surrounded her, performing numerous duties.

Morgan could see the confusion on her face. "It's not the glamorous life you wrote about in your story," Morgan said, softening his tone. "Life at sea is hard. And often deadly."

"Then why do you do it?"

"Because we love it."

She arched a brow. "A glutton for punishment, aren't you?"

Morgan laughed low in his throat as he swept his gaze over her trim figure and remembered just how good her thigh had felt in his hand. Aye, he was definitely a glutton for punishment.

Too bad she didn't know just how true her words were.

"I've been accused of worse." He moved back from her. "Now if you'll follow me, I'll take you to the galley."

Without another word, she followed him back below deck.

The galley was a large room with a huge cast iron stove. A bald, surly man stood making bread at a wooden table while he barked orders to a young boy of about fourteen who hustled around the room.

"I said to fetch more flour, boy! I'll be needing it before the winter season is upon us."

"Yes, sir," the boy breathed, rushing over to a barrel and pulling out a cup of flour.

Morgan cleared his throat and the middle-aged man looked up from his task with a sour frown. It instantly changed when he recognized Morgan. "Need some bread to break the fast, Captain?"

Morgan turned to her. "What would you care for, Miss James?"

The cook's ominous frown now turned her way. Deciding an omelet and bacon would probably strain the man's already weak patience, she shrugged. "Bread and cheese will be fine," she said.

"Court," the cook snapped to the boy. "Get the captain's woman what she wants."

Stunned by his words, Serenity stuttered. "Um ... I'm not *his* woman."

"Well, you needn't sound so offended," Morgan said beneath his breath.

Bemused, Serenity caught the twinge of anger in his eyes. "So I *am* your woman?" she asked.

"That's not what I said."

"It's what you implied."

"No, it's not."

"It's not?" she asked in wide-eyed innocence.

Scratching his neck in discomfort, he ground his teeth. "You cross-examine like a bloody solicitor."

Pleased with herself, Serenity smiled. Why she enjoyed his discomfiture she didn't know, but one thing was certain, she loved every minute of harassing him.

Court came forward with her food and a cup of milk. "The milk's fresh, me lady," he said with a heavy Cockney accent.

Serenity smiled her gratitude. "Thank you, but I'm not a lady."

"Aye, mum, but you certainly ain't a tart."

Serenity was somewhat stunned by his words. How many tarts had the young boy known?

"We need to talk," Morgan said, pulling at her elbow.

Without another word, she returned with him to his cabin. Primly she took her food to his table and sat down to eat.

Morgan barely caught her tin cup of milk before a lurch in the ship sent it flying. "This is one of the things we need to talk about," he said, setting it back by her plate. "We have rules on a ship that everyone must follow."

"And they are?"

"The first is that you avoid being around Cookie. If you need something from the galley, you find Kit, Barney, or myself and we'll get it for you."

"But that's a waste—"

"Serenity," he snapped, interrupting her. "Cookie is a surly old seaman and we know how to handle him. You don't."

Her eyes darkened in anger. "And you would abandon that child to his care? What kind of mon—"

"Court happens to be Cookie's son and to date he has never harmed the child. Well, that's probably not true. I'm sure Court's hearing has been somewhat dulled by Cookie's shouts, but he's never physically harmed the boy."

"Oh," she said before taking a bite of her food.

Morgan leaned one narrow hip against the edge of her table and Serenity did her best not to think about how nicely his pants fit him.

She forced her eyes to her milk.

But it was hard to keep her gaze from trailing back to his . . .

"The next thing," he said, distracting her, "is that a ship is unpredictable, especially since we have a storm moving in. As you've noticed, the decks are constantly rolling, and every now and again a sharp wave or break in the ocean will cause the floor to lurch out from under your feet."

She gabbed her mug as it teetered once more. "I think I follow that."

"For that reason," he said, indicating the mug with a tilt of his head. "I want you to stay away from the railings lest you stumble overboard. We lost our netting a few weeks ago and until we replace it, it's not safe to stand near the edge of the ship."

"Wise rule, that."

Morgan ignored her sarcasm. "When you need light below deck, then use one of the lanterns that are available. But whatever you do, don't set one down. They are suspended by ropes to keep them from hitting the deck and setting fire to it."

"An extremely valuable safety tip."

His glare intensified.

"What?" she asked in all innocence.

"These are serious matters."

"And I'm taking them as such." She lifted her hand and counted off his rules. "One, don't irritate the ill-tempered cook—as if my presence is innately irritating," she said with a shrug and it was all Morgan could do not to laugh. "But that's fine, I'm willing to abide by your order anyway. Two, don't get myself thrown overboard because you might not stop and come back for me."

"I didn't say that."

"And three," she said, ignoring him. "If I need light, don't start a fire. I think I have it. Is there anything else?"

"Yes. Never—" he leaned close to her and pinned her with a fierce scowl. "*Never* wander around below deck without me or Barney with you."

"What about Kit?"

"I repeat, *never* wander—"

"Without you or Barney. I understand. I'm not allowed to walk topside, nor can I walk below deck. What could possibly be left for me to do? Oh, I know. Die from boredom!"

Bemused, Morgan took a step back, not really prepared to have this discussion with her. But he had to make her understand just exactly what kind of danger she could find herself in. "Miss James," he said, reverting to a formal tone— anything to hide his discomfort. "I don't know how much your parents have told you about men and . . ." He paused, searching for words.

"Their base cravings?" she supplied.

He nodded. "That term will suffice."

"They gave me adequate advice and warnings," she assured him, then she paused for a minute as if thinking something over. "You know, Captain," Serenity said, sitting back and pursing her lips. "It seems to me that we have a problem with these rules."

"And what is that?"

"That they are made on the presumption that I'm stupid."

He lifted a brow. "Now, how did you get that—"

"I'm a grown woman, Captain," she said, rising to her feet to confront him. "I can even walk and whistle at the same time without fainting. I do, after all, work alone in my father's paper shop, which happens to be walking distance from the wharf. Believe me, Captain, I am fully capable of watching after my own affairs."

Morgan smiled at her bravado. "I believe you said earlier, Miss James, that an ounce of prevention—"

"Is worth an army of pistols," she said. "I agree. It is, after all, why the Good Lord gave us brains. I fully intend to keep myself out of harm's way."

Grateful for her sense, Morgan nodded. "I know you can't stay down here all the time, so if you want to go topside, you can. Just make sure you're not alone for the journey."

"Aye, aye, Captain Drake," she said with a mock salute.

She finished up the last bite of her breakfast, then faced him. "Now, Captain, if I may make a small request?"

"The water-closet is—"

She cleared her throat, cutting his words off. Color rose high in her cheeks. "I already found *that*."

"Then what did you want?"

"Show me where I may make mischief and mayhem."

Chapter 6

"I beg your pardon?" Morgan asked, temporarily stunned by her request.

Serenity gave him a huge smile. "Forgive me, Captain. 'Twas a small jest. I wanted to see the look on your face. And it's priceless. Truly, truly priceless."

He groaned. How could she gain so much satisfaction out of making him insane?

"If you're through with your games, then I have serious business to be about."

"What a novel idea," she said, pulling her small book and pencil from her pocket. "If you'll just—"

"What do you think you're doing?"

She paused and looked up at him. "I'm going to work. You have a ship to run and I have a story to research."

Morgan stared at her in disbelief. How she could even think about writing after all that had happened was beyond his ken. "Isn't writing a story what got you into this trouble?"

Her face lit up as if she were proud. "Absolutely, and if suffer I must, then far be it from me to suffer in silence. I plan to make a great novel out of this ordeal."

"Ordeal?" he asked, offended by her choice of words. If she wanted an ordeal, he could certainly give her one!

But then he reminded himself that she was sheltered and naive, and to her this *was* an ordeal.

"Adventure, then," Serenity amended. "Actually, it's hard to say whether it'll be an ordeal or adventure until all this is behind me. Not that it matters right now." Putting her glasses on, she gripped her book and pencil like a soldier would his musket. "Now take me topside, Captain."

"I'd rather take your bottom side and spank . . ." he said under his breath.

Serenity tensed, and gave him a look that said she wasn't quite sure she'd heard what he said. "What was that?"

He sighed. "I feel blindsided by your chatter, Miss James."

He watched the comical expression on her face as she tried to match the syllables he supplied her with the ones she'd originally heard.

By her frown, he could tell she knew they didn't match.

Irritated and yet somewhat amused, Morgan headed out of the room and did his best not to grumble or curse as she followed behind him.

After several steps, Serenity asked. "You're thinking, 'Why me?' aren't you?"

He paused at her question and turned around to look at her over his shoulder. "How did you know?"

"You have that same look my father gets right before he says it out loud and implores my mother's soul for help."

"Does that a lot around you, does he?"

"Well, only every now ... hey!" she snapped as she caught his meaning, not to mention his teasing smile. "That was rude. You don't know me well enough to be so insolent."

"No, but I'm learning fast."

She gave him a damning look that told him she probably had a sudden impulse to shove him up the ladder. And under her breath she whispered, "I'll get you!"

I wish you would, Morgan thought to himself as he turned around to help her up the short ladder that led to the deck. There was nothing he could think of that would be more pleasurable than being *had* by Miss Serenity James.

"Now, remember rule number two," he said in warning, "If you fall overboard, I won't go back for you."

"I thought you said you would."

"I said, I never said it. Now I am."

"Well then, Captain, let's go see what trouble I can go stir up before I manage to fall overboard."

Now, that was something to fear. There was no telling what trouble a woman alone could stir up on board a ship of renegade pirates.

Morgan reached out and lightly grabbed her arm. "Remember our talk, Serenity. There are a lot of rough men aboard my ship and I've already breached one of the pirate's ten greatest commandments."

"Which is?"

"Never bring a woman on board a ship. It's rather like storing gunpowder in the galley, next to the stove."

Serenity cocked her head, and too late he realized what he'd let slip. Holding his breath, he hoped she hadn't caught his words.

"It's true then," she asked, "that pirates have a code of honor they observe?"

"Yes, they do," he answered, thinking the danger had passed.

"And how is it you know about this code?"

So much for that—damn the wench for her intelligence. He should have known he couldn't slip anything past her. Aye, she was a sly one. And Morgan wasn't about to divulge his past to her. "I sail for a living."

"But you're not a pirate..." She paused and watched him closely as if trying to see through him. "Or are you?"

Morgan decided on the truth. "Depends on whom you ask."

And with that flippant response, Morgan crossed the deck to speak with Jake.

"Fine," Serenity whispered. "You go your way, but I promise I shall get to the bottom of all your secrets, Captain Drake. Just you wait and see."

Chewing the tip of her pencil, Serenity glanced around the deck at the men who were now working quietly. A few of them glanced her way, then quickly looked back at their tasks. None of them seemed approachable.

Who looks like the most interesting member of the crew? she asked herself, looking around.

Serenity glanced up at the sails flapping in the wind. It was a gray morning, uninviting. But at least the light drizzle had stopped for the time being. By the look of the clouds, she could tell the rains would be back.

She walked around the center of the deck. Heavy winds blew at her skirts and hair, making it difficult to walk.

There was a young man of about twenty climbing up a mast with rope curled about his torso. He might have a story, but she wasn't about to go up the sail to find it.

Maybe later.

Three men were to her left, folding the canvas sails, while another man scrubbed at the decks. To her right was a large, well-muscled black man who sat to the side with a huge rope and some long, thick, needle-shaped tool she couldn't name.

There was something about the man that warned of danger, but even so he looked to be the crewmember with the most interesting stories.

Which meant he was the perfect man for her to talk to.

Crossing the deck, she stopped directly in front of his stool. "Hello," she said, offering him her warmest smile.

He glanced up with a feral snarl. "I've killed over a hundred men," he growled out in a low and vicious voice. "Half of them I kill for simply saying hello."

Her heart instantly sped up.

Run away, Serenity!

Nay, she told herself. A good writer doesn't turn tail and run. A good writer gathers the story in spite of danger.

Besides, there was something about this man

that belied his fierce voice, a kindness in his dark eyes that bespoke a more gentle nature.

At least she thought she perceived that.

On second thought, she *hoped* she perceived that.

Deciding to test her theory, she asked, "Is that the greeting you always use when someone approaches you?"

He turned his dark stare toward her, appraising her. After several seconds of silence, he grinned. "You are a *majana*. Maybe we should call you *ushakii*, too!"

It took her a minute to translate his melodious accent. *"Majana?"*

"Aye, it means fine child, in my language."

"Oh," she said, making a quick note on her pad. "What language is that?"

"Kiswahili."

Serenity sank to her knees on the deck next to him. "Could you spell that?"

He did and she quickly took notes, then offered him her hand. "My name is Serenity James."

His huge, callused hand swallowed hers as he shook it. "They call me Ushakii, which means courage."

"Nice to meet you, Mr. Ushakii."

"Please, *majana*, call me simply Ushakii." Now there was no mistaking the kindness in his eyes.

Grateful his malice had melted away, she

watched as he returned to splitting the rope with a huge iron needle. "What are you doing?" she asked.

"I am splicing the rope, then rewrapping it to make it stronger."

"Is this what you do mostly on board the ship?"

His smile widened. "No, I have many duties. This is just the one that currently needs to be done. We will need more ropes for the storm that is to come." He stopped his work and watched her make more notes. "What is it *you* do, *majana*?"

"I'm taking notes to write a story about Captain Drake and his crew."

His look spoke loudly in the ancient male domination language—*What, you female, write?*

"It's for my father's paper," she explained, and then wished she could bite her tongue off. There was nothing wrong with writing for her father. Jonathan did it.

Yet she'd always felt the need to supply that information like some sort of ready-made excuse as to how *she*, a woman, could get a story published. It should be enough that she was a good writer and *that* was why she was printed.

But it wasn't.

Refusing to let it daunt her, she shrugged away the sudden lump in her throat and pursued her story like any man would. "Have you really killed over a hundred men?"

His deep laugh rumbled like thunder out of his chest. "Between us, *majana*, no. But it is what I tell the others. The mark of a man is not so much what he is, but what others think him to be."

She pondered his words for a moment. That was the motto that her father lived and died by—protect your reputation at all cost.

Though she might hate the hypocrisy, she knew it was true. People's opinions did matter, regardless of truth. In private, a person could be the most evil of people, cruel, vicious, but so long as the public never knew, then that person would be touted as a saint.

"Then I shall put you down as having killed over two hundred men." She made a quick note. "Why is it you wish people to think you're a cold-blooded murderer?"

He shrugged. "What can I say? It makes them leave me and mine alone."

Serenity frowned at his words. "But isn't it lonely to always be left alone?"

He looked up at her, his eyes as wise as a sage. "A man can be in a crowd always and still be alone, *majana*. I like my own company. You like your own company, too, I can tell. I think you know what you want."

"Sometimes."

He gave her a knowing stare. "What brought you to our company?"

"Stupidity mostly."

He cocked a brow.

Serenity was reluctant to share her dreams with this man. But something in his patient expression encouraged her to trust him not to laugh at her. "May I be honest with you, Ushakii?"

"Only fair. I was honest with you."

"I want to be a great writer," she said, her voice heavy with her desire. "I want people everywhere to know my name and long after I die, I want people to read what I have left behind."

"But you are a woman. It is not for you to want such things."

He had mocked after all. "Yes, I am a woman. But I want so much more."

His smile widened. "Like Lou, you are."

"Lou?"

He nodded up the rigging to the young man Serenity had seen earlier. "Lou came to sea for adventure, too. He didn't want to be a farmer like his father and brother. He wanted adventure and danger. But he is young. I think one day he will realize the sea hasn't as much to offer as a place on the earth that you can own yourself. Raising sails is not nearly as satisfying as watching a harvest grow."

What an odd view for a sailor, she thought. "If you feel that way, then why do you sail?"

"I have no reason to leave the sea. This ship is my home, these men my brothers. Unlike Lou, I have no other family."

Serenity picked up her pencil and began taking more notes. "How is it you came to sail on *Triton's Revenge*?"

Anger flickered through his eyes, stunning her with its intensity. She hated that she had dredged up such an unpleasant memory for him.

"I was being beaten in Cairo by a slaver," he said, his voice filled with hatred. "The captain stopped him and bought me."

"You're his slave then?"

He shook his head. "Nay, the captain set me free. He said no man should be forced to serve another, said I could do whatever I wanted."

"Why didn't you go home?"

He sighed and looked out over the sea as if he were looking back into the past. "My village was destroyed by an enemy tribe. I had no home to return to."

"I'm sorry, Ushakii." She placed a hand on his arm.

He covered her hand with his and lightly stroked the backs of her fingers in a gentle caress. "Don't feel for me, *majana*. Things are good here.

Fate has given me this life and I vowed long ago not to dwell on things I could not change, but to focus on making my life the best it can be. I am happy to sail with the captain and see many things."

She smiled. "I know exactly what you mean."

Morgan looked over Jake's shoulder and stopped midsentence when he saw Serenity talking to Ushakii.

Jake turned and followed the line of his stare.

"Well, I'll be," Jake said with a low whistle. "I didn't think Ushakii talked to anyone."

"He doesn't."

"Well, Drake," Jake said, his voice laced with murder. "You better start worrying. If your woman can get more than yes or no out of Ushakii, she can get information out of anyone."

Exchanging serious frowns, they turned in unison to see Kit joining them on deck. And each one knew the other's thoughts as well as his own.

Kit was an easy mark for someone as beguiling as Serenity.

Worse, Kit was the one person on the ship who knew the entire truth about Morgan and Jake.

"What?" Kit asked as he neared them.

"Stay away from Serenity," Morgan and Jake said simultaneously.

Under more normal circumstances it would have been funny.

"Seduce her, Drake," Jake said, his gaze returning to the source of their discussion. "A woman in love will go to her grave before she betrays her man."

Morgan shook his head. "And a woman scorned will cry out your darkest secrets from the highest mountaintop. Which is exactly what she'll do if I seduce her, then refuse to marry her."

"Then marry her," Jake snapped. "Leave her pregnant and at home to tend your brats while you're away."

It was a thought. It was definitely a thought. But he'd made that mistake before and to this day, he paid for that mistake in nightmares and guilt.

He'd left one wife to die while he was off at sea. He'd never leave another.

If only he could convince Jake of that fact.

Kit spoke up. "I don't see why you're worrying, Captain. She loves the Sea Wolf. I don't think she'd ever tell who you really are, so what does it matter if she writes her story?"

Morgan took a deep breath. "Serenity only knows that the Sea Wolf was a blockade runner during the war and that he now frees impressed sailors. What she doesn't know is who I *really* am."

"No," Jake corrected. "She doesn't know who *we* really are."

Jake looked back to where Serenity sat next to Ushakii. "The day she learns that, Drake, I'm going to cut her throat, and you won't be able to stop me."

Chapter 7

By noon the sky had turned a dark, ferocious gray. The winds whipping around Serenity felt like giant hands trying to pull her in different directions. The ship pitched, sailing over the water like a stone skimming the surface, and every time it hit the ocean, it jarred her to her bones.

"All right, men," Morgan shouted above the howling winds. "Batten down."

He moved to stand by her side. "And that also means you, Miss James. I need you to go below deck before you get swept overboard."

She looked over the side at the swelling waves that appeared to be nearly the size of the boat. "Since this doesn't appear to be swimming season, I tend to agree," she said.

Morgan guided her across the deck with one firm, strong hand at her spine. She had learned from talking to several crewmen that this was what had kept Morgan and Jake busy all day—

discussing the storm and how best to deal with it.

It didn't take them long to reach Morgan's cabin. "Will the ship hold up?" she asked, her voice cracking from nervousness.

He nodded, and she saw the concern deep in his brown eyes. "We'll be fine. I've seen much worse."

She tried to be strong. Really she did, but the sudden reality of what could happen to them hit her full force. "The *Willowood* went down this time last year," she whispered. "They were just miles off Savannah's coast when they sank from a hurricane. Pieces of the lifeboats washed ashore, but no one ever found a body." She swallowed. "Ever."

Morgan took her hand in his and gave a comforting squeeze. "Don't light a lantern, and stay in the bunk, and I promise you you'll be fine."

She gave a half laugh. "Do you always make promises you can't keep?"

Against all his better judgment, Morgan took her in his arms and held her tightly against him. She shook in his arms, and if the truth were known, so did he, only the tremors of his body weren't from fear. They stemmed from the demanding ache that throbbed through him for the warmth of her body. *I could make you forget your fear.*

If only he could.

"Believe me, Serenity, if there's one thing I know, it's how to survive."

"Then I shall trust you, Captain Drake. And I must say that I shall be terribly disappointed if you're wrong."

He laughed at her humor. "I'll be back to check on you as soon as I can."

Reluctantly Serenity let go of him and watched him leave. She took a deep breath to fortify her courage.

Oh, who are you fooling? she asked herself. *You're scared witless.*

Who wouldn't be?

Her teeth chattering from her raw nerves, she headed for the bunk and took a seat. She had barely secured herself when the door to the cabin opened.

Barney poked his balding head in and grinned at her. "Scared, are ye?"

"Terrified," she answered honestly.

"That's what the captain said, so I thought me and Pesty would come down here and see if we could help you any." He entered the cabin with a...well, it looked like a bird that had been plucked clean for dinner.

Only a few feathers remained on the poor creature. "I take it the bird is Pesty?" she asked.

"Aye. I got her back in..." He frowned and stroked his chin as if trying to recall a specific year. "Well, it was a while back, to be sure. Probably before you were born, now that I think about it. I was on the *Merry Tide* back then, and we used to ship all kinds of exotic birds to England for them rich folks to buy."

He pulled a chair up to sit beside the bunk. Pesty shifted her bare wings and made a quick squawk. "Butter beans, butter beans," the bird said.

"Sh," Barney snapped, then raised a gentle hand to touch her head. "I'm telling a story."

The bird shifted on his shoulder. "Story. Story. Whale of a tale."

Serenity pressed her lips together to keep from laughing at the bird.

Barney smiled warmly. "What can I say? She keeps me in line."

Pesty bobbed her head up and down. "In line. In line. In line and over the side, mate."

"It was nice of them to let you keep her," Serenity said.

"Oh, they didn't let me," Barney said hastily. "She caught some kind of sickness and the captain ordered me to kill her. But she was such a helpless little thing that I couldn't bring myself to do it. Instead, I took her to my cuddy and kept her safe. She's been with me ever since."

Lightning flashed, illuminating the cabin. Serenity gasped in sudden alarm.

"It's all right, lass," Barney offered in comfort.

Rain started falling, hammering a fierce tattoo against the boat. The lanterns in the room jingled and clanked as the ship tossed about. One chair skidded across the room and bumped against the far side.

"The trick is not to think about it," Barney told her.

She swallowed, trying not to think about how far away land was, and the fact that she didn't know how to swim. "H-how do you do that?"

"Me," Barney said, puffing his chest out. "I just sing. 'Course, the songs I know aren't fittin' for a lady to sing. But you probably know a few."

The ship rolled and pitched. Her stomach heaved. "I feel sick."

"Now, don't be getting sick in the captain's bed," Barney said, getting up quickly. "He won't like that none at all." He crossed the room and grabbed the washbasin out of the cabinet. "You feel the urge, you use this."

She grabbed on to it tightly and just nodded.

"Ahoy, mate," Pesty chimed.

A sharp lurch almost sent Serenity off the bed. Oblivious to the vicious bucks of the ship, Barney took her hand and placed it in a small niche carved just over the bunk. "That's a grab rail. You hang on to it and it'll keep you in place."

"Thank you," she whispered, her stomach churning even more. At the moment, she was more frightened than she had ever been in her life.

Deep inside, she wanted to run away, to find

some safe corner of the ship where no harm could befall her. But that was useless and she knew it. There was no safety at sea. The only thing that stood between her and death was nothing more than flimsy pieces of wood that could split apart at any moment and send her to the bottom of the ocean!

Serenity licked her dry lips. "How did you meet Captain Drake?" she asked, hoping it was a long story.

"I met Morgan when he was just a boy. I guess he was about thirteen back then." He smiled fondly, reminding her of a father who was thinking of his favored son. "Ah, he was tall and strong and honest. A good boy to his very core."

"What made him join the navy?"

His smile died and anger darkened his face. "He didn't join willingly. That bastard—Isaiah Winston—had done gone and sold the poor boy off to the British navy. I'd been impressed about a year afore that. Not that it mattered to me back then. Being at sea's all that I cared about. Didn't matter what ship I sailed on. But it mattered to Morgan."

Serenity took deep gulping breaths and tried to steady herself. "Why did the man sell him to the navy? Was he his father?"

"Nay, lass. Winston was no father, just an evil bastard through and through. He'd been the business partner of the captain's father. And when the boy's father died, Winston didn't want no responsibility for him. He wanted profits, humanity be damned."

Serenity knew the type of man all too well. And she despised such people. "You helped Morgan fit in?" she asked, changing the topic before she made Barney so mad he'd leave her.

"Well," he said with a sheepish grin. "I tried, but you got to understand, Morgan has a mind of his own. His own way of doing things. He has an order he expects everything and everyone to follow, and when someone gets out of line, it knocks him off keel. Those Brits don't follow that order. And Morgan was always too much of a fighter for his own good. If he thought he was right, he'd wrestle a den full of lions and not stop until they either killed him, or he had 'em tamed."

Barney shook his head. "Of course, it didn't help none that Morgan was terrified for his sister."

"His sister?"

Morgan had a sister?

"Aye, Penelope. She was a small slip of a thing. Pretty and gentle as any fawn ever born."

"Where is she?"

The light faded from his eyes. "Dead. She died about fifteen years ago." Barney stroked Pesty's head. "She was just about twelve at the time their father died. Morgan was afraid Winston would be using her in wrong ways or be selling her off to a whore..." He cleared his throat and bowed his head in embarrassment. "A place young girls shouldn't be."

Serenity frowned at his words. "Where was their mother?"

"She'd gone on to Mermaid's Paradise as well."

"Mermaid's what?"

"She was dead, too, lass," he said gently. "Morgan's mother died of a fever when Morgan was eight."

Her throat tight, Serenity couldn't imagine how horrible it must have been for them to find themselves without parents. Her mother's death had been one of the hardest things she'd ever had to face. Even nine years later, she missed her mother so much it hurt.

What would it be like to lose her entire family?

She couldn't even imagine it.

"Poor Morgan."

"Aye," Barney agreed. "It was a hard time for the captain, not knowing where his sister was. If she was safe."

"Didn't they have any family who could help?" she asked.

Barney shook his head. "His father had been a British lord who lost his title and had come to America to make his way. The only family they had was back in England. Winston swore to Morgan's father that he would send Morgan and Penelope back to England if anything should happen to him."

"And Winston betrayed them."

"Aye. In more ways than one." His look turned dark, murderous. "I was with Morgan the day he found out that his father hadn't died in an accident like Winston had said. The old bast—" He cleared his throat again. "Winston killed Morgan's father."

Serenity's mouth dropped at his declaration. Morgan's father had been murdered? "Why did he kill him?"

"Greed. Winston wanted the shipping company for himself. Morgan's father wouldn't let him trade slaves. During one of their fights over the matter, Winston stabbed him."

Serenity shook her head in disbelief. How could anyone do such a thing?

"What did Morgan do when he found out?" she asked.

"He swore he'd tear out Winston's heart."

She took a deep breath, knowing that if someone had killed her father, she'd demand no less. "Did he?"

Barney stroked Pesty's neck. "Well, life has a way of getting in the way of what we want most. It took Morgan three years before he was able to escape the navy and have a hope of ever finding Winston or Penelope."

Serenity leaned forward, entranced. Morgan had escaped the navy? This sounded like her fictitious hero.

"What did he do? How did he escape?"

Barney shifted in his chair and glanced to the door as if afraid Morgan would overhear him. "One night when we was docked in Jamaica, he skipped off the boat in the dead of night and vanished."

Ooo, definitely something her hero would have done. How exciting!

"Where did he go?"

He shrugged. "Don't know. He wanted me to go with him, but I was afraid of being caught and hanged, so he took off alone. I didn't see him again for, oh, six, seven years. By then he was his own captain and he was preying on Winston's ships. Said he'd hit the old bas—man where it hurt most, in his pockets. And when he wasn't going after him, he was going after the Brits."

"And what of Penelope?" she asked.

His shoulders slumped. "It took Morgan a long time to find her again."

By the look on his face, she knew what had happened. "Winston had put her in a bordello?"

Barney stiffened and gave her a withering glare. "It ain't fittin' for a woman to know such a word."

Adequately chastised, she whispered a quiet, "Sorry."

After giving her a fatherly scowl, Barney continued. "I can't imagine what it must have been like for Morgan. I wasn't there when he found Penelope, but I know how much she meant to him. It's probably a good thing he couldn't find Winston right away, 'cause I'm sure he would have killed him with his bare hands."

Not that she would blame Morgan for the killing. Indeed, a man like that should be horsewhipped!

"Where was Winston?"

"Butter beans, butter beans!" the bird demanded.

"Sh," Barney soothed. "I'll feed you in a bit." He repositioned Pesty on his shoulder. "Winston had caught word that Morgan was coming for him, and he took off. No one knew where he was. So, Morgan got his sister and took her to an island to watch over her. It was there she died."

"And Winston?"

"Morgan caught up with him about a year after her death. He'd already ruined the man financially, and he came damn near to killing him."

"But he didn't?" she asked incredulously.

"Just as Morgan was about to finish him off, he realized the worst thing would be to leave Winston to his duns. But as he turned away, Winston came at him, and in the fight, Winston was killed."

They fell silent for a few minutes, lost in their own thoughts, while the winds howled and the ship tossed. Lightning flashed again, and Pesty demanded more butter beans.

Serenity looked up at the ceiling, wondering where Morgan was now. He'd had such a hard life. And he'd lived it virtually alone. It was such a pity that a man so noble and kind had no one to love him.

And she wondered if a man who had lost everyone he held dear could ever love someone again.

Jake and Morgan stood at the helm, trying to stay on course in the midst of the storm. Of course, without the stars, and being buffeted around, it was impossible.

"Why don't you go below and rest," Jake shouted. "I'll take the first watch."

"I'm the captain, I should take the first watch!"

Jake laughed. "Which means the crew doesn't need you to go sailing overboard. Besides, Morgan, you don't want to leave me on your ship without you. You know what I'll do with her."

In spite of the seriousness, Morgan smiled. "All right. I'll be back up in an hour to replace you."

"Just bring me a bottle of rum when you do."

Nodding, Morgan made his way below deck. His ears roared from the winds and he felt chilled to his bones.

His limbs heavy, he opened the door to his cabin.

Serenity looked up and gasped as Barney broke off his storytelling. Morgan stood in the doorway, his hair and clothes plastered to his body as he dripped his way across the cabin. He had his teeth clenched and she was sure he was freezing.

Acting without thought, she scooped the quilt off the bed and threw it around his shoulders.

"You take care of him, lass," Barney said, jumping to his feet, "while I go get some food and ale."

"My goodness, Captain," Serenity said in awe. "You look like you've battled Poseidon himself."

Morgan didn't say anything as she led him to sit in Barney's vacated chair.

"Don't try and talk," Serenity said as she left him to go searching through his trunk. "I'll get you some clothes and we'll have you dried off in just a minute."

She pulled out a dry pair of pants, a shirt, and a jacket. As she returned to him, he was toweling off his hair with a corner of the quilt. "I *feel* like I've battled Poseidon," he said, his voice hoarse.

His hair was free from its queue. Damp and tousled, he reminded her of an impish child. Only his stern features and countenance were those a man who had lived a hard life.

"We have to get you out of those clothes before

you catch a chill." She helped him peel his jacket off, and it wasn't until he'd pulled his sodden shirt over his head that it occurred to her that she was undressing a man.

A magnificent man.

A man whose muscles rippled like a refined symphony under wet, bronze flesh. Spectacular muscles that hypnotized her and made her breathless.

Her mouth suddenly dry, she could do nothing but stare.

Morgan reached for the dry shirt she held in her hands, then made the mistake of looking at her face. Hunger, raw and wicked, burned in the blue depths of her eyes.

Instantly his body, in spite of the cold, came to life, and he remembered only too well the taste of her lips. Of her breath. The feel of her hands fisted against his back.

Without thinking, he reached for her.

"Here's the food." Barney's voice shattered the quiet as he threw open the door.

Serenity blinked, her cheeks instantly warming. Good gracious, what had almost happened?

Had she almost allowed a half-naked man to kiss her?

Aye, you did.

Another instant and she might have even let him go on and ...

Nay, she argued with herself, *you're far too respectable to do something like that.*

Or was she?

Her heart hammering, she handed Morgan his clothes. "I'll wait outside."

Morgan came to his feet, biting back a curse. His teeth clenched, he tossed the quilt to the floor. "You know, Barney, there are times when I wish I'd left you on the *Jiminy Bly*."

Barney's eyes widened. "What did I do?"

You interrupted what could have been a most pleasant distraction.

Sighing in frustration, Morgan pulled the dry clothes on. "You didn't do anything. Hell, I ought to thank you."

"For the food?"

No, for keeping me from making the biggest mistake of my life.

"Aye, Barney. Thanks for the food."

Frowning, Barney scratched his head.

As soon as he was dressed, Morgan opened the door. Serenity, her face ashen, was standing on the other side of the narrow hallway holding on to a grab rail. Feeling for her panic, Morgan took the three steps that separated them and pried her grip loose. "Everything is all right, Serenity. The worst of the storm is behind us."

"Are you sure?"

He gave her a warm, reassuring smile. "After

twenty years at sea, you get rather good about guessing these sorts of things."

Serenity nodded. The cabin door opened behind Morgan. "If you won't be needing me further, Captain, I'll be heading back to the galley."

"Butter beans, butter beans!" Pesty squawked.

"That'll be all, Barney."

Morgan had to move closer to her to let Barney pass. He stood so close, Serenity could feel the heat of his body, feel his breath fall lightly against her cheek. His still-damp hair curled around his shoulders, and she longed for the courage it would take to touch one lock.

It was so overwhelming to be this close to him, to be able to smell the raw scent of man and ocean.

Kiss me, she pleaded silently, craving the feel of his lips against hers, of his arms wrapped tightly about her.

He cleared his throat. "If you don't mind, Miss James, your fingernails are biting holes in my arm."

It was only then that she realized she had reached out for him and grabbed his biceps.

Heat flooded her face and she instantly let go. "I'm sorry. I didn't mean . . ."

Kiss me, Sea Wolf. Kiss me now!

She wanted to scream it, but her lips and mouth were so dry that she couldn't speak.

Morgan had seen plenty of come-hither looks in his time, but never on so innocent a face.

It would be so easy to sweep her up in his arms and carry her back to his bed. To peel her dress from her and run his tongue over every inch of her body until her taste was branded in his memory.

She was an innocent. And no matter how much he might want to, he wouldn't rip that innocence away from her the way it had been stolen from Penelope.

The way the Brits and Winston had whipped the innocence out of him.

No, he couldn't do it. Having been used, he refused to use another.

He could ... contain himself.

He was used to disappointment. Had swallowed that bitter taste many times in his life. It was just a little more bitter than the others, but it *would* go down.

Even if he had to chase it with a barrel of rum.

"If you'll excuse me, Miss James. I need to get back topside."

She frowned. "You haven't eaten anything. You just changed into dry clothing!"

He snorted and said under his breath, "Yes, but I feel the need for another cold bath."

Serenity sat alone in the cabin. Morgan had been right, the worst of the storm had passed, but the ship continued to creak and moan as it pitched and dipped on the choppy sea. She wasn't sure how long it'd been since Morgan left, but the sky had turned darker.

She was anxious and bored and desperate for someone to talk to her when a knock sounded.

"Enter," she called.

Morgan came in with Court, the cook's son, a step behind. The boy placed a covered platter on the table, then quickly took his leave.

"Why is it, Captain, that you always seem to be wet when you're near me?"

He muttered something about her and his wetness under his breath that she couldn't decipher.

Peeling off his jacket, he said louder, "Cookie didn't dare light a fire, so we have cold food this evening."

As hungry as she was, it could have been shoe leather and she would have been grateful. Pulling back the lid, she quickly realized it probably *was* shoe leather.

She wasn't really sure what the dried brown lump was. "Yum," she said aloud, "Hard-boiled wood, my favorite."

He grunted. "It's dried beef and onions. You'll get used to it."

Morgan grabbed more clothes out of his trunk, then went outside. After several minutes, he returned with his wet clothes dripping from his left hand.

"You can hang that up over here," she said,

pointing to the makeshift clothesline she had secured from the end of the bunk to the window. She'd found a ball of thin cord in his chest of drawers and she had used it to hang up his other clothes.

She didn't know what he thought about her ingenuity. He kept his thoughts carefully guarded as he crossed the room and added his wet bundle to her growing collection.

Morgan grimaced as his gaze swept over the articles of clothing. He recognized his own, as well as Serenity's attire from the night before.

But what caught and held his attention were the frilly intimate underthings that were also hanging up. Frilly things that made him wonder what secret delights they covered.

"Been doing laundry?" he asked, his voice nothing more than a hoarse croak.

"Well, you said fresh water on board was scarce, so I thought I'd take advantage of our sudden surplus and use it."

His hand brushed against her soft cotton chemise and his body instantly reacted. Rolling his eyes, he stifled the urge to return back to the storm. One more dousing and he was sure he'd catch his death.

That is, if being this close to her undergarments didn't kill him first.

Clenching his teeth, he turned around and purposefully kept his back to the drying clothes. Not that it helped. Serenity had brushed her hair out and left it to hang about her shoulders. The candlelight caught in the chestnut waves, adding reddish and gold highlights.

She set the food and plates on his table like a proper dinner setting. A strange feeling came over him. One he couldn't quite define.

He knew he'd never experienced anything like this in his life. It was almost a feeling of longing. But even that couldn't quite explain what he felt.

It was just *different*.

She poured them each a mug of milk, and it amazed him that she didn't make a comment about his choice of beverage. Even Barney couldn't resist nettling him every now and again about it.

Then she did it. "Where do you get the milk from?"

Clearing his throat, he pulled a chair out for her. "We have a cow on board."

"You do not!" she gasped in disbelief.

"It's not the usual thing, but Cookie insists. He claims Court, being a growing boy and all, needs fresh milk."

Her smile was enchanting. "Where do you keep her?"

"She roams below deck with the other livestock."

Cupping the mug in both hands, she took a sip of her milk, then set it aside. "Well, I'm certainly glad Cookie insisted. I love fresh milk." She wiped the traces of milk from her lips and picked up her silverware.

Morgan took his own seat across from her while she started on her food. He watched her saw at her meat until she had a bite-sized piece. No small feat that, and he had to admire her determination.

But it was Serenity that caught most of his attention. Her wrist had a delicate curve to it as she gently picked up the meat and opened her mouth for it. White, perfect teeth flashed an instant before her lips came together to cover the fork, and she slid it slowly out.

The very tip of her tongue peeped out for just an instant as she licked a tiny spot of cold gravy from her upper lip.

Never before had Morgan noticed just how arousing the process of eating could be. But with every graceful move of her body, and with every flash of teeth on her lip, he felt as though he were being tortured.

"I'm sorry it's not more palatable," he said, his voice strained.

"Oh, no, it's fine. Why, it's a lot better than what Honor made after our first cook quit. She made porcupine meatballs, and all I have to say is that the porcupine part was definitely right. I think I still have a . . ." she looked up at him and caught his stare. "Is something the matter?"

If you lick your lips one more time, I swear . . .

"No," he said gruffly. "Nothing's wrong."

"Are you sure, Captain? You look as if—"

"I said nothing is wrong," he snapped with more malice than he'd intended.

Her face fell and he felt like a bastard. "I'm sorry. It's just been a long day," he offered as an excuse.

That seemed to console her. "You know, I was thinking this morning about the fact that it really isn't right for me to take over your room. I know how men are when it comes to their territory and—"

He interrupted her with a short laugh. "Men and their *what*?"

She shrugged. "Territory. My brother and father get quite insane anytime anyone intrudes on their private sanctuaries. I'm sure you view this room as such, and I wouldn't want to put you out."

Uncomfortable with her choice of words, Morgan shifted in his seat. Well, *put out* would definitely describe that piece of his anatomy that was currently ramrod stiff.

"And where do you propose I put *you*?" he asked.

"I was thinking we could put a hammock up by the window perhaps."

"Have you ever slept in a hammock, Miss James?"

"Well no, but I'm sure it's not that hard."

It's harder than it's ever been before, he thought, shifting once more in his seat. "A hammock is no place for a woman."

Serenity stiffened at his words. Words that set a fire raging in her belly. "And why is that, Captain Drake? Why is a hammock fine for a man and not a woman?"

By his face she could tell he didn't want to explain himself.

The answer he gave her rated right up there with her father's *because I said so, and as long as you live under my roof . . .*

"It's just not fitting."

She set her fork down and eyed him with all the malice she felt. "Says who?"

"Everyone."

"Everyone?" she repeated, her eyes wide. "I certainly don't say so, and I believe I count as someone."

He had *that* look on his face, that exasperated *why can't you see reason* look that her father always got when she confronted his more ridiculous notions.

"Where do you get these ideas?" he asked after several seconds of silence.

"My ideas are my own, Captain Drake."

He snorted. "Well then, that's comforting. I would hate to think these novel ideas of yours are catching among women."

Insulted, Serenity glared at him. "I'm not the only woman to hold such views. Are you familiar with the writings of Mary Astell?"

"Never heard of her."

"What about Lady Mary Wortley Montague?"

Now, that was a name Morgan knew—everyone in polite society was aghast at her exploits. "What about her?"

Her face lighted up. "Then you know her views on women. We are not addle-pated, goose-twits who have no other purpose than—"

"Goose what?"

"Goose-twits," she repeated. "Women do have value in this world, Captain Drake. We can hold our own!"

"In case you haven't noticed, Miss James, this is a man's world. Women need protecting from it."

Serenity came to her feet and narrowed her stare on him. "I'll tell you what we need protecting from. *Thoughts like those* and men who think the only value a woman has is to be a pretty little decoration on his arm, or some trophy conquest."

She put her hands on her hips. "The day shall come, Captain Drake, when women will take their proper place in society. And I assure you, that place is not the drawing room."

His laughter rang out, and he applauded. "Bravo, Miss James. Tell me how long you have practiced that speech."

She saw red.

Ignoring her, he continued to dig himself in deeper. "And who put such ideas into your head?"

"Are you saying that I can't have my own thoughts?"

At least he had the decency to look a little sheepish. "That's not what I meant. But let's face facts, those aren't the normal ideas. You didn't come up with this mutiny on your own."

"Mutiny?"

"Aye, mutiny. You stand before me, hands on hips, and defy every time-held belief. If women were meant to be the equals of men, then why since the very day God gave Eve to Adam, has man ruled woman?"

She inched closer to him, her hands itching to strangle sense into his male brain. "Need I remind you, Captain, that God did not make Eve from Adam's foot so that he could tread upon her. She was created from his side to *be his equal*."

He crossed his arms over his chest and eyed her. "Then why are women by nature, by God's own design, the gentler sex? Women faint at the slightest scare."

Oh, how she wanted to knock the smug look off his face! He was so proud of that argument—well, she had an even better one.

"Slightest scare, Captain? I assure you, sir, that I have seen women suffer for days to bring a child into this world. And I have yet to see a woman faint during the labor of it. I beg you, show me a man who would willingly bear that much pain for that many hours, and not cry out for his *mommy*! In fact, you want to know why women have a higher tolerance for pain, Captain Drake? I'll tell you why, it's so that we women can put up with you men!"

He laughed.

By heaven, the man's audacity knew no limits. He actually threw his head back and laughed at her!

"I don't see the humor, Captain."

"No," he said, sobering—well, all except the corners of his lips, which continued to turn up in a smile. "I don't suppose you do."

Morgan tried to force the smile from his face, but she stood so proud and fierce before him that he just couldn't. She was a rare treat.

He'd never in his life met a woman who could have phrased her views so eloquently—or so amusingly. In truth, he had known a few men who did just what she said, sailors who'd been wounded and had in fact cried out for their mothers.

"You make a most convincing argument, Miss James, but it doesn't change anything."

Serenity folded her arms over her chest in a duplicate of his pose, and looked away from him.

Men! Would they ever see past their own narrow views of the world?

Suddenly Morgan was beside her. He lifted her chin with a knuckle until she had no choice but to meet his eyes. Fire and longing burned in their dark depths.

Morgan brushed the pad of his thumb against the soft underside of her chin. Her skin was so soft, so warm. She had a strength of courage that would indeed rival any man's. It must be hard for her to face the laughter of people and not give in. He admired that in her.

And he swore that he would never again laugh at her—not even if she told him that one day a woman would be prime minister of England.

"I don't want to fight with you, Serenity," he whispered.

"Then what do you want?"

To make love to you.

Morgan clenched his teeth, knowing he could never say that to her. So instead, he switched to a safer topic. One that needed to be spoken before she really did find out the truth of what he'd once been. "I want you to forget about the article you're writing. Leave my crew alone to attend their duties."

Anger sparked in her eyes, turning them a vibrant shade of blue. "Why?"

"Because everyone on this ship has a duty, mine is to run it, Barney's is to keep peace, and yours is to stay out of our way."

She knocked his hand away from her face. "I didn't realize I was in anyone's way."

He closed his eyes and took a deep breath. "This isn't a game, Serenity. You need to—"

"Mind my sewing, read some nice, sweet poetry, and do the laundry."

"Exactly."

If looks could kill, Morgan decided he would now be splintered across the far wall.

"Very well," she said, her voice ice. She moved over to where his laundry was drying. She grabbed his still-dripping coat and threw it over his shoulders. "Since my job is to sit here and keep out of the way and yours is to run the ship, I suggest you get to it!"

"But I—"

"But nothing, Captain. Heaven forbid you leave the helm for more than a minute. Anything could happen. God could toss down a lightning bolt and set fire to the ship. A sea monster could rise up from the depths of the ocean and swallow us whole. Or, dare I say it? The weight of male egos may be so great that it plops a hole right in the center of deck and we sink from it!"

And before he could protest, he found himself standing outside in the hallway, the door closed firmly behind him.

Now, how did she keep doing this to him?

Just as he turned to confront her, the door opened.

Serenity shoved his plate into his hands. "And whatever you do, don't forget your shoe leather."

Once more, she slammed the door shut in his face.

"Serenity!" he bellowed, knocking against the door with his clenched fist. "Open this door!"

"Go to the devil, Captain Drake."

Incensed beyond reason, he snarled, "That's not very ladylike!"

The door opened and she came at him, her nostrils flared, her eyes smoldering. "Then try this one. Go to hell, and . . . and rot!"

And before he could move, he once again confronted a shut door. "Serenity!"

"Oh, forgive me, Captain," she drawled in the most helpless voice he'd ever heard. "But I can't open that huge old door by myself. Why, I fear I might get a splinter. If only there was some strong, able-bodied man who could save me from my weak and helpless plight . . . "

Even through the door he heard her sad, melodramatic sigh.

He decided that it was a good thing she didn't open the door. Because right then, standing in the hallway with his coat dripping on his dry clothes, his plate in his hand, and his male ego greatly offended, he probably would have strangled her.

But sooner or later, she would have to leave, and when she did ...

.

Chapter 8

Serenity confronted the room with her wrath fully unfurled.

"Okay, Morgan Drake, if you want to see a woman keep her place, then I'll show you a woman keeping her place."

And with the taste of vengeance scalding her tongue, she set out to do her worst to his most hallowed space.

Regardless of what he said, she knew men valued their sanctuaries and any female encroachment rankled them to their core.

So, if he wanted a frilly little miss who minded her sewing, and never spoke without a man's permission, she'd give it to him! In true female fashion, she would redecorate his masculine haven.

Searching the trunk she'd found below his bed, she pulled out the yards and yards of canvas he kept stored there. It wouldn't make the best curtains in the world, but it would be enough to get her point across.

She found scissors and a needle and thread in the trunk where he kept his clothes, and took the canvas to the table.

Even if it took her all night, she would show him feminine ways.

Morgan walked across the deck, his anger still burning. The rain had all but ceased and only a light drizzle assaulted him now.

"You look like hell, Drake," Jake said as he approached him. "I thought you were turning in for the night."

"Don't remind me," he muttered.

Jake laughed. "Women," he said with a knowing smile. "What did she do to you?"

Morgan tossed his wet coat to the deck and snarled. "You won't believe what she thinks."

Propping one arm against the wheel, Jake cocked a brow. "From what I've seen of her, there's no telling."

At last, he'd finally found someone to take his side! Grateful for Jake's sanity, Morgan unloaded his burden, "She thinks women ought to be equal to men."

Jake rolled his eyes.

"That's what I thought."

"I'm telling you, Drake, bed the wench. That'll take her mind off such stupid notions."

Sighing, Morgan shook his head. "I wish it were that easy."

Jake gave him a disbelieving stare. "Excuse me, but I believe that someone must have exchanged places with you. You can't be the same man who took three whores to his bed for a week and didn't emerge until they couldn't walk."

"It's not the same, Jake."

He snorted. "It is the same."

"If you mean that, then why haven't I seen you chase after a woman in the last three years?" Morgan asked. "You, who always prided yourself on the fact that you could have any woman you saw? If it's so easy, why don't you join my men on shore when they visit a cathouse?"

"I can't do that."

"Why not?" Morgan asked. "I've seen you collect women like a beggar collects food scraps. What has made you so chaste when it comes to any attractive woman who crosses your path?"

"Because Lorelei would have my head, and I don't mean the one on my shoulders."

Morgan couldn't resist taunting him. "So you're *afraid* of Lorelei? A woman?"

Color flooded Jake's cheeks at the insult. "I'm not afraid of anything..." He looked down and said in a voice that reminded Morgan of a small peevish boy, "I just don't want another woman."

"Because there *is* a difference."

Jake shook his head and laughed. "You always have to win an argument, don't you?"

Morgan clenched his teeth. He certainly had never won an argument with Serenity.

After several seconds of silence, Jake spoke up. "I guess I just don't see why *she* makes a difference."

Morgan didn't even want to think about *that*.

Serenity was different. Everything about her.

"Go get some sleep," Morgan said with a sigh. "I've got the helm."

Jake released the wheel to him. "I think I've pretty much corrected our course. We do have one slight problem, though."

"Which is?"

He pointed up to the mizzenmast. "Even with them down, we lost the mizzen topsail and the fore topsail to the wind. I figure the repairs can wait until morning, but you will need to replace them."

"Aye. I'll have Lou and Kit take care of it."

Provided Serenity will let me back in my cabin to get the spare sails.

"Good night, Drake."

If only the night was good, Morgan thought sullenly. But right then, nothing seemed good at all.

Hours went by slowly while Morgan watched over the helm, doing his best not to think about the woman below.

In an effort to distract himself, he looked up at the damaged sails. Fate had been kind to him, he'd only lost two. The exact number he had left in his cabin. He'd meant to purchase more in Savannah, but Jake's unexpected abduction of Serenity had precluded that.

Sighing, he realized he'd have to check the sealant below in the storage rooms again lest the storm had damaged it and they lost more supplies. Blast it all anyway.

And then his thoughts turned to more discomforting matters, such as Serenity surrendering herself to him...

Not long after dawn, his crew began stirring, coming topside with lazy, tired walks. Lou climbed the mast and headed for the crow's nest while the others headed to the jardines on the poop deck to relieve themselves.

"Captain!" Lou shouted as soon as he took his post. "There's a sloop to port aft."

Morgan turned in the direction and squinted.

He could just barely make out the shape with his naked eye. "Bearing?"

"Headed straight for us, Captain."

"Can you make their markings?" Morgan asked.

Lifting the spyglass, Lou studied the ship. It seemed forever before he answered. "Aye, she flies the Stars and Stripes, Captain."

Morgan breathed a sigh of relief. At least it wasn't the Union Jack or Jolly Roger. An American ship he could deal with, but first he had to let them know he was friendly—not a pirate or privateer out to liberate them of their cargo.

Spying Barney to his right, he shouted. "Take the helm, Mr. Pitkern."

"Aye, aye, Captain."

Morgan headed to his cabin.

He tried the lock and luckily it gave way. Hoping Serenity was still asleep, he gently nudged the door open.

His luck was holding. She lay curled up on his bed like a small child. He sighed in relief as he watched the gentle rise and fall of her chest.

She hadn't bothered to remove her dress, which was now hopelessly wrinkled. But what captured and held his attention were the tiny, bare feet peeking out from beneath the hem. He'd never paid attention to a woman's toes before, but for some reason he found hers delightful.

Until he looked up and saw the curtains decorating his windows.

His stomach lurched.

Nay! Surely she hadn't...

Oh, yes, she had!

His anger igniting, he charged to his ruined sails. "What the hell have you done now?" he roared.

Serenity came awake with a small cry of alarm. She looked to him and her demeanor instantly changed to one of relief. "Oh, it's just you."

"Yes," he said, his voice barely above a whisper. "It's just me. The man who's now going to *kill* you."

Instead of being alarmed, she lifted one eyebrow curiously. "Kill me?"

Morgan clenched his teeth. This was the last thing he needed. He had an unidentified ship heading straight for him. A ship that appeared friendly, but on the open seas, there wasn't such a thing as a friendly ship. Even though it flew the American flag, it could still be pirates or anyone else flying under a phantom flag.

"Do you realize, Miss James, that the material you used for your *curtains* happens to be the canvas for sail repair?"

She gave him a huffy glare. "Are you saying

you only have two sails on board a ship this size?"

"That's exactly what I'm saying."

"You're not amusing, Captain Drake," she said in a dismissive tone. "I know for a fact that ships carry entire rooms full of spare sails. Why, you're trying—"

"Our spare sails were damaged in a storm that ripped a hole in the helm where they were stored," he interrupted. "The two in my trunk were the only two that were salvageable."

Uh-oh was written plainly on her face as she realized what she'd done.

Before Morgan could say anything more, Kit stuck his head in the door. "Beg pardon, Captain. Lou says the sloop is making haste straight for us. We be needing a flag or they're sure to think we're pirates."

Morgan's gaze narrowed as he continued to stare at Serenity. "I'll deal with you later."

He crossed the room to his desk drawer, pulled out a key, then went to the trunk he had next to the door. Morgan threw back the lid. Searching through the folded material, he located an American flag.

Morgan stopped at the door. "Keep her out of trouble, Kit. If she touches anything else in my room, toss her overboard."

Kit's eyes widened. "Aye, Captain Drake."

Morgan pinned Serenity with his hostile gaze. "I mean those words, Miss James."

Instead of being concerned, she just rolled her eyes.

Grumbling under his breath, Morgan headed topside.

"What did you do to get the captain so steamed, Miss James?" Kit asked.

Serenity pushed herself off the bunk, and pointed to the windows with her thumb. "I made curtains with the sails."

Kit's eyes widened even more. "Miss James, didn't you know better?"

"I do now," she said with a sigh. Wishing she had given her actions more thought, Serenity picked up the flags and clothing Morgan had left strewn on the floor.

She noticed Morgan had four flags—from Ireland, France, Britain, and Spain. "Why does Captain Drake have all these?" she asked as they refolded them.

Kit showed her where to place them in the trunk. "If a ship flies a friendly flag, then most approaching ships will let it pass without conflict."

"And if a ship doesn't fly a friendly flag?"

He pursed his lips and sighed. "Well, it's usually challenged. Most of the time one ship or the other will surrender after only a few rounds are shot."

"Really?" she asked. "I thought ships constantly battled each other."

"Let's just say that sea battles are hard to win. We've picked up survivors from the victory ship numerous times. It only takes one or two cannonballs in the wrong place to sink both ships."

"Then why fight?"

Kit shrugged. "Fighting is always a last resort. Unless..." his voice trailed off, and he looked as if he hadn't meant to keep talking.

"Unless what?" she prompted.

Scratching the back of his neck, he gave her a doleful look from under his brow. "Unless the ship flies the *Jolie Rouge*."

"You mean the Jolly Roger?" she asked.

"No, ma'am. The *Jolie Rouge* is a pirate's red flag of death. It means no survivors will be tolerated."

Serenity's heart pounded at his words. "How often have you seen this *Jolie Rouge*?"

He looked away, and by the slump in his shoulders, she could tell how much the questions bothered him. "More times than was ever necessary, Miss James."

Morgan was about to hand the Stars and Stripes to Lou when Jake's voice stopped him. "It won't work, Drake."

Morgan turned to face him.

Jake, his hip leaning against the side rail, nodded out toward the approaching ship and handed Morgan his spyglass. "That's Wayward Hayes's ship, *Death Queen*."

"Are you sure?" Morgan asked.

"I smell his body odor from here. Besides, I've had enough run-ins with him to know his ship on sight. Though I didn't know what he looked like until the other day, that's one ship I know as well as I knew my own when I sailed. I'd be willing to wager he's already figured out who you are."

Jake scratched his chin. "Guess you got your wish after all. You should be grateful, you didn't even have to go to the Caribbean to find him."

"Yes, but I would much rather have faced him on my own terms, and not with two ruined sails." Morgan let out a slow breath as he considered his options.

The last thing he needed was a conflict with Hayes. Especially with his current, nosy *guest*. He didn't like the thought of fighting while he had a female passenger on board. The risk to her safety was just too great.

Morgan looked up at the sliced sails. "There's no way to outrun him."

"Captain," Lou interrupted from his position in the crow's nest. "They just hoisted the Jolly Red."

Jake curled his lip. "Same Hayes. He's not going to give quarter."

Morgan turned to the helm where Barney held the wheel. "Sound the alarm, Mr. Pitkern. There's going to be a fight."

"I'll take the helm while he does," Jake offered. "But if I were you, Drake, I'd let it be known that the Marauder is still alive and well. Hayes might be smart enough to let us pass in peace. Even he has to fear something sometime."

Morgan considered the request. What would it matter to Hayes if he found out the Marauder and the Sea Wolf were one and the same? The price on the Marauder's head was four times that of the Sea Wolf. "If I do that, *she'll* know who we are."

Jake shrugged. "I don't guess the sharks'll care who we are when they're making their meal off us. 'Course, you know what Hayes'll do to your woman when he finds her. Maybe we should go ahead and cut her throat to save her the pain."

Jake was right. Hayes would never go easy on a woman he suspected was a pirate's mistress.

Morgan took a minute to watch his men hurry to their stations. They were all good sailors; some with families.

His gaze fell to Barney and he sighed. He'd never hear the end of this once Barney found out what he'd been doing those years they were apart.

And Serenity...

"Be the Marauder, Drake," Jake urged by his side.

In spite of the seriousness of their situation, Morgan laughed. "Would you stop? You sound like an old nag."

Did he have any other choice?

Not bloody likely.

Reconciled to his fate, Morgan mumbled, "I think we should resurrect Black Jack and let the Marauder rest in peace."

Jake laughed. "If you remember, it's said the Marauder killed Black Jack."

"For aggravating him, as I recall," Morgan said before crossing the deck.

For what seemed the hundredth time that morning, Morgan headed back to his cabin. He opened the door and stopped short.

He'd left his flag trunk open.

And Serenity sat on the floor with an ashen face as she held the flag he'd come for.

Kit had been speaking, and stopped midsentence when he saw the captain.

His face reddened. "I didn't know you still had it, Captain," he said by way of an apology.

Serenity ran her hand over the black flag that bore the image of a grim reaper holding a sickle in one hand and a heart in the other.

"Tell me," she said, her tone icy as she rose

slowly to her feet, "that you killed the Marauder and kept this as a souvenir."

It would do no good to lie. Government officials had plastered that flag all over the Colonies in an effort to locate its owner. That flag belonged to one of the fiercest pirates known.

The Marauder. Second only to Black Jack Rhys when it came to the reputation of ruthlessness, it was a past Morgan had done his best to bury.

But that was the thing about the past—sooner or later it always came back to haunt him.

Without explaining himself to her, he gently took the flag from her grasp.

"What are you going to do with *that*?" she asked.

"I'm saving our necks." And with that simple phrase, he headed back to the deck.

Serenity's heart seemed to crumble as reality set in. Her Sea Wolf wasn't some noble hero out to right all the wrongs of the world.

Morgan was...

Was...

Morgan was a pirate! A real-life, cold-blooded, take-no-survivors, heave-ho and kill-all pirate!

She reached out for the bunk, her legs suddenly weak. "He's the Marauder," she breathed, her vision dulling.

"It's all right, ma'am," Kit assured her, moving to help her sit down before she fell.

"All right," she repeated in disbelief. "All right! He's a pirate." Her eyes widened in sudden realization. "You're a pirate, too!"

At least Kit had the decency to blush. "It's not what you think."

Oh, it most certainly was! She wasn't on board the ship of some romantic buccaneer who saved men's lives and acted nobly. She was on the ship of a cold-blooded killer, of a man renowned for his fierce temper and quick saber.

On more than one occasion, she'd listened to men talk about the Marauder in fearful whispers, as if by mentioning his name some horrible misfortune would befall them.

"The captain retired from piracy years ago," Kit explained. "I didn't even know he still had the flag."

"Is *that* supposed to comfort me?"

"But you don't understand . . ."

Not willing to hear any more from Kit, Serenity went after Morgan.

She wanted an explanation from him. To hear from his own lips how he could be the Marauder.

How could her Sea Wolf be a killer? How could her perfect hero do something so loathsome?

On deck, she paused. Cannons had been uncovered and now stood ready with a crew of three manning each one. Atop the rigging were numerous men who had muskets and pistols at the ready.

It was eerily quiet, as if they were a painting and not a real crew. The only movement came from the pirate flag that was being drawn up the rigging.

Suddenly a rough laugh sounded. "Morgan!" Jake called. "You've got to see Hayes's face."

She watched as Jake handed the spyglass to Morgan.

"I haven't seen a man look so pale since that doctor in Jamaica told Robert Dreck he'd have to amputate his pecker."

Morgan didn't answer, he just looked out at the approaching ship.

Serenity's cheeks grew warm from Jake's crudity.

Jake turned to face her and the smile on his lips died instantly. He nudged Morgan's shoulder.

Morgan lowered the spyglass and met her gaze.

Something passed between them. Something Serenity couldn't name. But it kept her spellbound as she watched him cross the deck to her side.

"I know what you're thinking," he said to her. "I can read it on your face."

She stiffened. "What am I thinking?"

"You're judging me without knowing the facts."

"And what are the facts?"

His face turned granite. It was probably the first time in his life someone had asked him to explain himself, and by the look of him, he wasn't ready to do so.

"The facts are that we are about to be attacked by Wayward Hayes. I've warned him who I am, but I doubt it'll stop him from—"

The sound of a cannon exploding interrupted him.

"Incoming!" Jake roared.

Morgan grabbed Serenity and pulled her to the deck.

An instant later, the cannonball fell a few feet short of the ship. A huge tidal splash came over the edge, dousing the two of them.

"Attacking!" Morgan finished his sentence.

Terrified from the experience, Serenity stared at him in disbelief. He was enjoying this!

His eyes actually twinkled in merriment.

The man was mad. Insane!

"Yep," Morgan said with a sigh as he brushed his wet hair out of his eyes, "Hayes really wants me."

How could he be so blithe?

Morgan raised his voice to shout to his crew. "Retaliate. Booty only to those who earn their keep!"

She shook her head. "How can you be amused by this?"

He gave her a rakish grin. "I live for this. It makes me feel alive."

"It makes me feel like I'm going to be sick," she whispered, her stomach pitching in fear.

Morgan pulled her to her feet. "We need to get you below."

"And if they sink the ship?" she asked, not wanting to be trapped below deck where she couldn't get to a lifeboat.

"There's a greater risk of your being hit by a bullet or cannonball than there is of the ship going down."

"I don't believe you," Serenity said. Why should she, when everything about him was a lie. "Kit told me that it's entirely likely."

Remembering how his ship the *Rosanna* had been torn apart during a similar fight with the British last year, Morgan decided she might be right. "Then I want you to hide over by those barrels and don't move."

"Show me the way."

Serenity followed him to a small alcove.

Morgan squeezed her elbow to reassure her. "Don't worry."

She gave a very unladylike snort. "'Don't worry,' he says. We've only got a madman trying to blow us out of the water, and the *Marauder* tells me not to worry." She looked up and met Morgan's gaze. "Tell me, Captain Pirate, at what point should I start to worry? When I see the whites of their eyes? Or when the sharks begin to circle me?"

He smiled at her outrage. "I would say you should definitely start to worry when the sharks begin circling you."

"That's what I love most about you, you're just so comforting."

Morgan shook his head. She was a brave woman. Something inside him hated leaving her there to fend for herself, but he had too many other duties to attend.

And a vicious enemy to confront.

Serenity watched him cross the deck, checking on his men like a normal military commander. Cannon fire roared all around her with a deafening pitch and she placed her hands over her ears in an effort to protect them. Sulphur rolled across the deck in thick waves of odor that stung her lungs and brought tears to her eyes.

"What have I gotten myself into?" she breathed. She must have been insane to ever wish for an adventurous life. Suddenly her days of safety hidden behind her large desk seemed a blessing.

And yet, as she watched Morgan she realized that he really did love it. He was a natural leader as he confronted death.

She widened her eyes as one cannonball whizzed just past his head, ripping a portion of one mast. The force of the damage sent splinters over Morgan and one grazed him. Blood creased his brow, and he absently wiped it away as if it didn't concern him in the least.

But it scared her. Terribly.

It felt as if the battle raged on forever. And as every second ticked by, the explosions grew louder and louder.

Until at last the crewmen's shout went up louder than the cannons.

"That'll teach 'em to fly the Jolly Red," Barney shouted. "Shove it up their bloomin' arses!"

Morgan looked more than well pleased with them, and Serenity raised her head up to peer over the side of the ship to where she could see the sloop. Large pieces of her side were missing and her masts had collapsed, and were now lying half on board and half in the water.

They had done it. Somehow his crew had crippled the ship with very little damage to their own.

She looked to Morgan, and a strange warmth glowed inside her. He stood shouting orders to Kit and Jake. His hair curled about his neck as the wind whipped through it. He gestured toward the ship with his sword.

He turned to face her and her breath caught in

her throat. He was marvelous. Marvelous and terrifying.

This wasn't her dream pirate who never hurt another soul. This was a flesh and blood man with his own ideas—archaic ideas that clashed with hers.

A man who was powerful and dangerous.

He approached her.

Her mouth became as dry as a desert. She rose to stand on unsteady feet.

"Glad to see you survived, Miss James."

In spite of everything that had happened, she gave a nervous laugh. "I wasn't so sure you'd survive," she said, brushing at the cut on his cheek. Though his cheek was cold, his blood was warm against her fingertips.

Morgan swallowed at her hesitant touch. Something happened inside him. Something he couldn't name. Something that wanted things from her he knew he couldn't ask her to give.

He wanted her. Right now, this instant, with the thrill of victory still hot and thick in his veins.

He wanted to celebrate this conquest with an even greater one.

Before he could stop himself, he pulled her up to him and kissed her long and deep.

She hesitated only a moment before she gave in to him, opening her lips so that he could plunder the rich treasure of her mouth.

She tasted of honey and sweetness. Of innocence and passion, and he knew then that against all reason he was going to have her.

That he *had* to have her.

One way or another, he would claim her body.

Chapter 9

"Hayes is dead!"

At Jake's cry, Morgan looked up.

"What?" he asked in disbelief.

Jake nodded toward the *Death Queen* and the body two of the crew held up to show them that their captain was no longer a threat. "He must have been hit during the fight."

Morgan released Serenity, unable to believe he had at last purged the world of one demon.

Jake jumped down from the railing and came over to them. He eyed Serenity with a malice Morgan knew all too well. "I don't suppose you'll let me cut her throat."

Morgan looked at her over his shoulder. "Don't worry. I can guarantee you, Serenity will never tell this particular story."

"How? You going to cut out her tongue and take her hands?"

"Nay, I have an even better idea."

Serenity was chilled to her bones at the tone of

voice Morgan used. Not to mention the grisly image she held of what Jake had just described doing to her and her precious neck. Involuntarily she clutched at her throat.

Could Morgan really kill her?

Looking at the coldness on his face, she decided she would rather walk the plank into a shark's nest than be alone with him.

"Jake," Morgan said, "you take the helm of the *Death Queen* and the *Revenge* will tow you into port. We'll need to make repairs on the *Revenge* before we go any further."

Jake gave an evil smile as he leaned one hip against the edge of the ship's starboard railing. "Just what I need, a good pirate ship with a good pirate crew."

"Jake," Morgan said his voice full of warning. "Try to remember, Black Jack Rhys met the Marauder...and lost. Last anyone heard, he was swimming at the bottom of the ocean."

Jake smirked and folded his arms across his chest. "You take all the fun out of things."

"I certainly hope so. The last thing you need is for someone to report to the American or English government that you're alive and well." Morgan turned to Barney. "Make ready to sail, Mr. Pitkern. Our headings have changed to Santa Maria Island."

Then Morgan faced Serenity, and she realized

her hopes of him forgetting her were in vain. "You and I need to talk."

Terror consumed her. "Talk about what? How you're going to kill me?" That was certainly one discussion she didn't want to have. One she could wait a long time to have, in fact.

He didn't answer.

"How about if I stay..." her voice trailed off as he directed a look at her that made her tremble.

Very well, she thought. She would follow him, and if he made a move to hurt her, she promised herself he would long regret it.

At least she would try to make him long regret it.

Of course, the worst thing she could probably manage would be to bleed on him. Fine revenge, that.

Morgan led her to his cabin and held the door open for her to enter. Serenity tried to be brave, really she did, but her imagination was working overtime. Too easily she could envision all sorts of horrors he had planned to keep her silent.

He closed the door with an ominous thud.

She noted that his gaze drifted to the curtains and his jaw flexed.

A sudden chill skidding up her spine, she asked quietly, "You're not still angry about those, are you?"

His look would have melted an iceberg. "My anger where you're concerned runs so deep that . . ." His voice trailed off. He shook his head as if reconsidering his words, and paced along one side of the room.

She felt as though she had died and was waiting for Saint Peter to choose her eternal sentence. Time seemed to hang suspended as he paced the room, his boots clicking against the planks of the floor.

The windows to his cabin were open, and a soothing breeze ruffled the curtains she wished she had never made.

She inched closer to the door.

Maybe she could make it out . . .

"All right, Miss James," he began at last, making her jump. "I'm going to do what I've never done before."

She made ready to run. "From the stories I've heard, Captain, there's absolutely nothing the Marauder hasn't done. Why, I've even been told you eat children and infants for breakfast."

Morgan let out a low growl. "If you don't hold your tongue, I might serve *you* up to the crew for dinner." He clenched his hands into fists at his side and paused before her as if gathering his thoughts.

Her way to the door momentarily blocked, she had no choice but to look up at him and his cinnamon-colored eyes that burned with raw anger.

When he spoke again his voice was low, and yet it seemed to fill the entire space of the room. "I know what you must be thinking."

"That you're a pirate who is now going to kill me?" she asked before she could think better of it.

Her words seemed to make him relax. A little. The corners of his lips twitched and his eyes softened. "Very well, I knew half of what you were thinking."

Unsure if she should take a breath in relief or a mad dash at the door, she asked, "Which half?"

"Don't interrupt."

Serenity stiffened at his gruff command. It was foolish to goad him, but at this point, did she really have anything to lose? Besides, she wasn't one to just stand by and wait for him to hand down his judgment at *his* leisure.

She wanted to know her fate.

"Don't interrupt? I do believe, Captain Death Pirate, that I have a right to know what you intend to do to me. Or is not telling me part of the torture you use on your victims?"

He became ramrod stiff again.

"As I was saying," he began, ignoring her question. "I realize you don't know how to take in all the information you've just been given. But you have to understand exactly what you heard."

"What I heard," she said, her voice shaking with pent-up fear and heartbreak, "is that the man

I thought was an American hero is actually a low-down, thieving murderer who has no more regard for human life than . . . than—"

Morgan grabbed her by the arms, and she could tell that he wanted to shake her. "You have no idea of the things I've seen," he said, his voice so sharp it could slice iron. "I *was* a pirate—once. I'm not denying that, nor do I make excuses for it. I was young, angry, and desperate. Three things that make a most lethal combination. I wanted blood from the Brits and I wanted blood from my enemy."

"And you were willing to do anything for it."

"Yes."

Her heart shattered even more. It was true. He was the Marauder.

Still, she wanted him to deny it. To tell her that he had never harmed anyone undeserving. That he was the same caliber as her fictitious hero. That he, Morgan, would never lie, never rape, never . . .

"You killed innocent people?" she asked, desperate for him to redeem himself.

"If they got in my way."

With one sentence, he had vanquished the last of her hope.

Douglas was right. She was a dreamer, and no man could ever be as honorable as the men she imagined for her stories. They were phantoms. Horrible, wretched phantoms she had created to save her from this reality.

The death of her dream brought an ache to her chest that almost suffocated her.

She tried to push him away, but he held her fast. "My God, you're a monster," she whispered.

"No," he said quietly. His eyes darkened and she saw the regret and sorrow that filled him. "I'm simply a man who sold his soul for vengeance."

In spite of everything she'd just learned about him, an urge filled her to comfort him.

He was tortured by his past, even a blind man could see it. His regret ran soul-deep, and that wasn't an illusion.

The breeze ruffled his loose hair. Even now, he was devastatingly handsome, more so with his vulnerability laid bare before her. He was asking her forgiveness. She could sense it. But who was she that he would ask such?

She wasn't one of the men he had cut down in cold blood as the Marauder.

"I'm not proud of what I did, Serenity," he said, his voice barely above a whisper, "But I want you to understand that I *never* flew the Jolly Red. I've never killed a man who couldn't defend himself."

Did she dare believe him? "That's not what I've heard."

He released her as if she disgusted him. "Then believe what you will. I won't be held responsible for the lies of a gossiping tongue."

Serenity watched as he went to look out the windows. He braced one hand on the low overhang and leaned his head against his biceps. The waves swelled in the wake of the ship while he stood as still as a statue.

She didn't know what to say, or feel. A thousand emotions whirled through her—confusion, disappointment, fear.

He wasn't what she'd thought him to be. Maybe that was her own fault. She had built him up into a legend no man could possibly compete with.

Even though she'd dreamed of pirates and fantasized about Morgan being one, she'd never really considered him one of the loathsome pack.

Not a true pirate.

He was supposed to be Randolf. A gentleman pirate who toyed with other ship's crews, but never actually hurt them.

It didn't make sense to her. She could believe Jake was a cold-blooded pirate. He'd shown himself to be anything but merciful or kind. But that didn't fit Morgan. He could have ordered her killed to silence her. He didn't.

He could have killed Hayes's crew.

Again, he didn't.

He could have turned his back on Ushakii and

allowed him to live out his life in slavery. But he hadn't done that either. Nor did he have to free American sailors from the British.

It didn't make sense to her. How could a man capable of such goodness also be capable of such ruthlessness?

"Would you answer me one question?" she asked, moving to lay one hand on his arm. "Tell me how the Marauder became the Sea Wolf."

Refusing to meet her gaze, he sighed. "That's a long story."

Part of her begged to let it go at that. But she couldn't. She had to understand him. To know how a man like the Marauder could change—*if* a man like the Marauder could change.

With a teasing smile, she lowered herself until she met his downward gaze. "Well, I certainly have nowhere to go and nothing really better to do—except make more curtains."

He gave her a hostile glare.

She knew she should be terrified, but she sensed the danger had passed. He wasn't going to kill her. Of that she was certain. "Well?"

Morgan looked away from her and shook his head. He didn't know what to do. Fate had thrown Serenity into his life and now it had given her the knowledge to destroy him.

He had committed horrible crimes in his past, he knew that. Even now he could hear the screams of men blown to pieces while he ordered his gun crews to continue their assault.

And for what?

For peace of mind?

The irony of it all ate at him constantly. He'd sought peace and found a hell far worse than anything he'd ever imagined.

That was why he freed the Americans trapped by the Brits. He wanted to save them from making his mistake. Save them before they found a means to ruin their lives with hatred and vengeance.

"Morgan?"

She placed a soothing hand on his arm. It was the first time he'd heard his name from her lips, and it sounded like a gentle caress. Did something to him that he couldn't explain or define.

"Serenity," he said, his voice pleading. "Don't make me have to hurt you."

I couldn't live with myself if I hurt you.

He saw the fear in her eyes. If only he could make her understand. But not even he understood why he'd done all the things he had.

How he wished he could go back and change his past. To have that day back when he had first flown the Jolly Roger . . .

"Serenity," he said, letting out his breath, "If you write this story, you will destroy so many people."

He pulled her into his arms and held on to her

as tightly as he could. He wasn't sure why, but he needed the comfort of her presence, the feel of her body against his.

And she felt so wonderful. Her feminine curves molding perfectly against his front.

If he could have one wish, it would be to have met her as a different man. A land-based man who might be free to make an offer for her.

But he had ruined any chance he might have for such a life. He'd been at sea too long, and old sailors were never content on shore. Nay, they died there. Died of stagnation and boredom.

Serenity could barely breathe from his tight embrace, but she didn't mind. For some reason she enjoyed his crushing hold, enjoyed the smell and feel of him.

And in that instant, she knew she couldn't hurt Morgan. She would never write her story. Even though it was probably the greatest story she could ever relay to the public, it wouldn't be worth the cost.

Unlike Morgan, she would never sell her soul for her quest.

"Just tell me why," she whispered, "and I'll never tell a soul what I've learned."

He gave a hoarse, half laugh. "Can you honestly do that?"

"If I understand why."

Morgan leaned his cheek against the top of her

head. And then he did the most unbelievable thing, he actually explained himself to her.

"I didn't set out to be a pirate, Serenity. I want you to know that. Never in my wildest imaginings did I see myself committing the crimes I've done in my life."

He toyed with a shiny lock of her hair, trailing it between his fingers. "After I escaped from the British navy, I signed aboard a small French sloop and worked like a dog for close to a year. I was saving up money, trying to pay investigators to find my sister, trying to save enough money so that I could take care of us when I found her.

"But it wasn't enough. It was never even close to enough. I could barely afford to pay the investigators, and what little was left . . . "

Serenity's heart ached for the agony she saw on his face. She had seen firsthand on board this ship just how hard sailor's work was. Morgan had been scarce more than a boy when he started his life at sea.

He released her and stepped away. "One day we were in the Caribbean when a ship attacked. It was Black Jack Rhys."

"But he didn't kill you. Why?"

Morgan shrugged. "I don't know. Just as Jake was going to cut my throat, he changed his mind. He said I would make a fine addition to his crew."

Serenity nodded. Deep down she knew she

couldn't fault Morgan for joining Jake's crew. No doubt, Jake would have killed him instantly had he refused. "So, you became one of them."

He stopped and gave a short laugh. "Not at first. Like you, dear Serenity, I thought they were repugnant."

She had never said repugnant. Just cold-blooded, vile, loathsome...

"What changed your mind?"

He gave a deep, bitter laugh. "Greed. Once I found out how much money there was to be made as a pirate, I couldn't resist. I had tried honest labor and all I had to show for it were blistered hands and a striped back. But as a pirate..."

At least he looked embarrassed about it, she thought.

"In less than six months I had enough money for my own ship."

"And you became the Marauder."

"The scourge of the seas," he said with a hint of humor in his voice.

"How can you joke about that?" she asked, aghast.

He sobered. "It's not a joke. I know that. But I consoled myself that I wasn't lining men up and killing them either. I preyed solely on the Brits and Isaiah Winston's ships. To me at the time, it was all justified. Especially once I found my sister."

Serenity thought about what horrors his sister

must have faced. "Barney told me what Winston had done to her."

His eyes tormented, he looked away. "You can't imagine what she looked like when I found her. The things that had been done to her. I pray God that you never know the terror she was subjected to."

Serenity reached out to touch him. He covered her cold hand with his warm fingers and gave a light squeeze that sent a chill up her arm.

"I went after any Brit I could I find," he said with a sigh. "I goaded them into fights, forced them to face me even when all they wanted was to flee. I'm not proud of what I did. At the time, I couldn't see past my rage."

Shaking his head, he continued. "I know now that each one of them had a family as well. A family I pray to God every night didn't suffer as much as Penelope because of my actions.

"But Penelope was so broken by the experience," he whispered. "All I wanted from that moment on was blood. I blamed the Brits for buying me and keeping me from protecting her. I blamed Winston for his selfish greed, and I blamed myself for not finding her sooner. You can't imagine how much hatred I carried with me. The weight of it was enough to crush every decent or merciful impulse I'd ever had. And it was then, in that instant of my rage, the Marauder you've heard of was born."

She took a deep breath to fortify herself. So, the stories *were* true.

"Then you did—"

"Yes, I was ruthless," he said, cutting her off with his lethal, hate-filled tone. It felt as if he were trying to impart his feelings to her, as if he were reaching out to her in a way that was alien to him.

Her fingers tingled from the pressure of his hold. Still, she didn't withdraw.

"When did you stop?"

"During the war. By then I had made a sizable dent in Winston's company. My anger and hatred had been dulled by the uselessness of my personal quest, and I began to crave freedom from my past. I wanted to bury the Marauder and so I petitioned the Colonies for a letter of marque against the Brits."

He fell silent, his hand still crushing hers. Emotions played across his face and bitterness burned bright in his eyes.

"It's ironic really," he said, his voice hoarse. "In the end, I didn't change my actions, just the reason. Instead of attacking ships for my own personal gain, I split the profits with the new government."

"But I thought—"

"I know what you thought." He reached up and gently stroked her cheek. His gaze softened as he looked into her eyes, and she noted the hint of admiration in the hazel depths of his eyes.

Something hot flickered deep in her stomach, an ache in a part of her she'd never before known existed. She wanted something from this man— something she didn't even know how to define or explain. It was just a deep, soul-wrenching ache.

"You, my dear Serenity, are a dreamer. Reality is a far cry from the legends you write. The only difference between a privateer and a pirate is that a pirate makes more money."

"Nay," she said with a shake of her head. "The difference between a pirate and a privateer is modus operandi. A pirate takes no prisoners, leaves no survivors."

"Not from what I've seen, and I don't think you've known enough of either category to make that judgment."

"Maybe, but still—"

He placed a finger over her lips to silence her protest. "Listen to me, Serenity. You can't go around holding people up to some kind of imaginary measuring stick. No one could live up to the man you wrote about in your story. Especially not me."

In that instant, he seemed more like her Sea

Wolf than ever before. This man, haunted by his past and searching for . . .

Peace of mind?

Redemption?

She frowned as she realized she had no idea what it was he truly sought. He had said his fury was dulled. He'd destroyed Winston. So what was left for him?

When all was said and done, what then would become of the pirate turned patriot?

"What is it you want out of life?" she asked. "Will you spend the rest of your life wresting Americans away from the British? Or is there something more you want?"

Morgan sighed. "I've never given it much thought. I suppose I'll be like Barney, an eccentric old man walking around with a bald old bird."

She smiled in spite of herself.

He looked down at her. "What about you?"

Her smile fading, she sighed as she thought about her useless wants. Other than writing, there had only been one other thing in her life that had seemed important. Something that was every bit as illusive and impossible as her wish for a career. "I always wanted children," she confessed past the lump in her throat. "Two boys and two girls."

"Then why did you never marry?"

She gave a bitter laugh. "Who would marry me?

What with my ludicrous ideas of mutiny, what man could ever put up with it?"

Morgan smiled gently at her. Any man with an ounce of common sense would put up with her.

But he couldn't say it out loud. Confessing that might give her hopes about them. After all, she was a reckless dreamer who already fancied him as some sort of mythic legend. He didn't dare say anything that might make her think she could win him over.

He'd already made that mistake with a woman, and he wasn't the type of man who repeated his mistakes.

Unlike Serenity, he was a realist who had banished foolish dreams along ago.

Even so, he stroked her soft cheek with the back of his fingers, wishing that things were different. That *he* was different.

"I have your word then?" he asked her. "You'll never write one word about my identity?"

Her eyes twinkled mischievously, and deep inside he cringed. "Only if you promise me one thing."

He realized he had no choice. "Anything."

"I want you to take me up to the crow's nest."

Chapter 10

"What?" Morgan asked, shocked by her unexpected demand.

"You heard me, Captain Crook," she said saucily, removing his hand from her cheek. She tilted her head up to look at him. "I'll keep your story to myself if you'll take me up the rigging to the nest."

Before he could stop himself, he laughed. "That's the most ridiculous thing I've ever heard. Next, you'll want to be captain! Own your own ship." He snorted in derision. "Why stop there? Why not be president of the Colonies?"

Her eyes narrowed in warning, "Need I remind you, Captain, that there have been women who have sailed as well as any man? Why, Anne Bonny and Mary Read were both said to have fought like a man when they and Calico Jack were taken. And when Anne Bonny went to see him in prison, she told him that if he had fought like a man, he wouldn't die like a dog!"

He laughed even harder. "Where did you hear *that*?" he asked.

"I read it in one of my father's books," she said triumphantly.

Morgan continued smiling that annoying little smile that made her blood boil. "Well, should you ever meet Jake's wife, you better not let her hear that or she'll have your head."

His words confused her. "Why?"

"She happens to be their granddaughter and she's very defensive when it comes to those types of lies spread about her beloved grandmother, especially the rumors that say Anne Bonny was ugly."

His smile fading, he cleared his throat. "However, though it galls me to admit it, you're right about women donning men's clothes and becoming sailors.

"But," he said before she had a chance to gloat. "They weren't well-bred ladies who had been reared in genteel homes. They were prostitutes or hoydens. Do you really want be added to their *prestigious* company?"

Serenity stepped away from him and looked out the windows and let the sea air caress her. The ocean air smelled so sweet and she wished for so many things that she knew would never be hers.

Longing swept over her so fiercely that she ached from it. "You've no idea what it's like, Captain Drake, to be a woman. To be told all your life that everything you want is foolish and that you're useless except as a broodmare.

"First it was simple. 'Don't climb that tree, Serenity. Ladies never do such.' Then it was, 'Don't run, it's not ladylike. Don't raise your voice. Don't speak your thoughts. Don't laugh too loudly, don't eat too much, don't cut your hair, don't wear those colors.'"

Unshed tears stung her eyes. "My whole life is *don't*."

Morgan watched her as she leaned her head against the glass. The wind whipped the tendrils of her hair out from her body and she looked so frail, so lost.

No, he couldn't imagine what it must be like for her to want things and be told no at every turn. Once he'd escaped the British navy, his life had been his own. He'd done as he pleased.

"Now I'm too old to even be a broodmare."

He barely heard her whisper.

Without thought, Morgan moved to stand behind her. He reached out to touch her soft hair.

She looked up at him from over her shoulder and he saw the raw pain inside her. "Can't you understand—I want to know what freedom is like," she breathed. "I want to climb the rigging and look out at the sea."

"You are insane."

"Probably," she said, once again becoming the no-nonsense woman he had come to know. "But that's my offer. Take it or leave it."

Morgan smiled at her audacity. "You know, you're not really in a position to argue. I could have you cut up into shark feed and no one would ever know."

"Yes, but if that was your intention, then you wouldn't have brought me down here. You said it yourself, Captain. You never harm an unarmed person."

"Damn," he teased. "Just my luck."

She turned to face him, completely serious now. "Do I have your word?"

At the moment, he wondered who was the craziest between them. Certainly there was a bed in Bedlam with his name on it. "Aye, you have it then. But be warned, I'll treat you just as I do my men. You'll be expected to lift yourself up the rigging."

"That's all I ask."

"No pity for you."

She lifted her head up and stiffened her spine. "I ask for none."

Morgan smiled wickedly. Here was his chance to prove to her why women were best suited for home life. And he wasn't about to let it pass. Nay, one trip up the rigging and she'd be content with her woman's role in life.

Aye, whether she wanted to admit it or not,

women were the weaker sex and thus it was his duty to point that out to her.

"Very well then, Miss James, put your brother's trousers back on. I'll wait in the hallway while you dress."

As soon as she was ready, she opened the door and smiled at him. "All right, Captain, I'm ready to face my greatest challenge."

"You want to break your neck."

She lifted her chin and gave him a saucy glare from the corner of her eye. "I want to climb up there and see the high seas."

Morgan laughed. "Very well, but if you get killed, I'll not take the blame."

Her laughter joined his. "Don't worry, I'll just haunt you forever."

His laughter dying, Morgan realized how true her words already were. He knew the image of her bright smile and laughing eyes would stay with him until the end of his days. Indeed, how could he ever forget the way she looked just now, standing before him in those black trousers, molded to perfection on her rounded hips. Her black shirt was knotted at her slender waist while her nipples protruded ever so slightly in the fabric. She was not the type of woman a man easily forgot.

Not the type of woman a man could have near him and not touch.

Get ahold of yourself.

But what he really wanted to get ahold of was her.

Taking a deep breath to steady himself, he led the way to the deck.

Morgan decided he was most definitely the one insane as he showed her how to hoist herself up the ropes that led to the crow's nest. She hung above him, her hips undulating in a most provocative way as she shifted her weight.

His body strained against his seams and he damned himself for not leaving her in her dress.

Indeed, as if the sight of her garters and other things above your head would have been better than this!

"Make sure you keep your grip tight," he said to her as she lifted herself up through the ropes. All in all, she was doing a great job of climbing up. She'd only slipped once.

"Don't look down," he heard her whisper as she reached up over her head and grabbed another line, and it was only then that he realized she was terrified.

"Are you okay, Miss James?"

"Fine."

Funny, the curt word sounded more like a prayer than an answer.

"We can go back to the deck any—"

"No, no," she assured him. "I'm getting along just fine."

Morgan positioned himself directly under her. "Don't worry, I won't let you fall."

Serenity glanced down at him. "Could you really catch me?" she asked.

"Absolutely. Besides, Barney would have my head if I let you make a mess on the deck."

"Oh, thanks," she said, smiling. "I'm glad chivalry is alive and well on the high seas."

Her courage renewed, Serenity finished the climb to the crow's nest.

She wasn't sure how to climb into the small circle, until Morgan came up behind her and helped her in. She stood to one side as he squeezed himself in next to her, and she could feel his body bulging against her hip.

Her face flaming at the closeness of their bodies, she averted her gaze to the deck far below while he moved away from her.

The ship rocked and she grabbed the small rail that ran around the tight circular space. "How does Lou do this every day?" she whispered.

Morgan stepped out of her line of vision. "How can he not?"

Mesmerized, she stared off into the far horizon where the fading light of day met the waves of the ocean. The two of them blended together into the most wonderful symphony of harmonious color. "It's beautiful."

"Yes, it is," Morgan breathed in a strange tone that made her take a look at him. It was then she realized he wasn't talking about the sea.

Suddenly shy, Serenity looked back at the horizon. "Have you spent much time up here?" she asked in an effort to keep herself from noticing how handsome his face was, how dark the fading sun made his eyes.

The red highlights in his loose hair. Hair she was sure was soft and . . .

"I haven't been up here in a long time," he said, removing the spyglass from where he'd clipped it to his waistband.

After extending it, he handed it to her.

Then his arms surrounded her as he held it up for her to see. "Look through here," he directed.

Serenity tried to focus on the sea, but all she really noticed was how pleasant he smelled, how warm his chest was against her back.

"I can see Jake," she said as she swung the spyglass over to the *Death Queen*. "Captain Hayes's crew doesn't seem to mind his leadership at all. They actually look . . . dare I say, happy?"

Morgan smiled at her shock. "No doubt it's because Jake tossed the captain's daughter overboard as soon as he took over."

Frowning, she looked at him over her shoulder. "He did *what*?"

"The lash. I'm sure he tossed it overboard as soon as he took over. Jake has never been one to whip his men into shape, if you'll pardon my cliché."

"Oh," she said. "My brother wrote an article about such discipline. One of the captains he interviewed said it was the only way to keep order on board a ship. That it was no different than locking people in the stocks."

"Jake showed me there's better ways of dealing with your men. When it comes to finding punishment to fit the crime, I doubt Solomon himself could have equaled Black Jack's justice."

She gave an odd half laugh. "Who wouldn't obey Black Jack Rhys? I'm sure he just kills whoever offends him and tosses him overboard."

"Don't be so harsh, Serenity. Jake has a lot of reasons to act the way he does."

"Such as?"

Morgan sighed as he remembered some of the childhood stories Jake had imparted to him over the years. Terrible stories that defied belief. "His own mother tried to poison him twice when he was a boy to get rid of him. When that didn't work, she sold him off for two bits to a tavern owner who wanted someone to clean out slop jars and spittoons."

"What?"

He nodded, his heart heavy for his friend. "His mother was a prostitute who didn't take kindly to the fact he didn't die. She did things and allowed things to happen to him you can't even begin to imagine in your worst nightmare. If you find any kindness in him at all, I assure you it is there by way of a full miracle."

Serenity looked back at Jake as he directed men to swab the decks of the *Death Queen*. "What of his father?"

"No one has any idea who his father is."

"Is that why he became a pirate?"

"I suppose. He once told me that if he was going to be accused of being the devil's own, then he would give people a reason to believe it."

Serenity shook her head in pity. "What made him stop pirating?"

He smiled. "A woman."

"His wife?"

"Aye."

"So, he gave up his life for her."

"Nay, she gave him a life. Until Lorelei, he never knew kindness or love. She gave him back his soul."

"And what of you?" she asked quietly. "Could a woman give you back yours?"

Could I be the woman who gives you back your soul?

He gave a half laugh and she flinched, half-afraid he'd heard her silent plea.

"Nay, I'm not like Jake. I actually tried to settle down years ago with a wife. But it was a mistake. A costly mistake."

"You were married?" she gasped, her chest tightening at the knowledge.

He nodded.

"Did she die?"

His eyes turned dark, sorrowful. "While I was at sea."

"I'm sorry, Morgan."

He sighed and she ached for his loss, wished for a way she could ease the agony etched into his brow. "As was I. I thought I could be the type of man who could settle down and have a family. What I learned was that the call of the sea was more than I can deny. I can't stay landlocked."

By the look on her face, Morgan realized he should have kept his mouth closed. He had just put a wall between them that he didn't want to build.

It's for the best.

Yes, it was for the best. He knew he could never settle down. He belonged to the sea.

It was home.

"I think it's time we headed back down."

Serenity nodded.

No sooner had they returned to the deck than Barney approached him. "Might I have a word with you, Captain?"

Morgan watched as Serenity excused herself, and part of him longed to follow after her and try to bridge the sudden gulf that had sprung up between them.

Thinking better of it, he turned to his quartermaster. "Sure, Barney, what do you need?"

"I wanted to know why you kept such a secret from me. Why you never once told me you were the Marauder."

First one, now the other. He was getting really tired of explaining himself to people. "It's not something I'm proud of, Barney, nor is it something I wanted people to know."

"But I thought I was different. We've been through a lot, you and me. And you let me just babble off about being pirates when you knew the truth. Made me look like a blooming ninny, you did."

Morgan placed a hand on his shoulder. "That's not true, Barney. You're the closest thing I have to a father, and I didn't want you to know that about me, any more than I'd want my real father to know."

Barney nodded. "You're still a good lad. Pirate and all. 'Course, I won't be saying nothing else 'bout being a pirate. At least now I know why you were always so squeamish."

Thank God Barney didn't hold it against him, Morgan thought.

It shouldn't bother him that Serenity did. Yet for some reason he couldn't fathom, he wanted to regain her respect. It mattered deeply to him that she not hate him.

He glanced over to where the *Death Queen*

sailed, and smiled. He knew what Jake would say if he were here. And for once, he agreed with the surly pirate.

Aye, he'd bed the wench. One way or another.

Chapter 11

Late that night Serenity came awake with a start. "Who's there?" she whispered, her heart thumping against her breastbone as she strained to see into the darkened room.

"It's all right, Serenity. It's just me."

She calmed as she realized Morgan stood just to the side of her bunk, his lean body silhouetted by the faint moonlight that spilled in through the windows. His faced was masked by shadows, but she could feel his gaze on her like a physical touch. It was as if he searched her features for something.

"Is something wrong?" she asked, wondering what had brought him to her bed in the middle of the night.

"No, I just wanted to show you something."

There was a hint of mystery to his voice, and if she wasn't mistaken, there was also a note of playfulness. A playfulness that she'd never before heard from him.

Grateful she was still dressed in her brother's clothes, she climbed out of bed. Morgan lit a small lamp and held it up over his head so that she could see.

"I thought I told you to lock the door," he said in a chiding tone.

"I honestly forgot."

Instead of the glower she expected, he smiled. "For once I'm glad you didn't listen to me."

Then he took her hand. A strange warmth fluttered in her stomach at the gentle pressure of his callused hand wrapped around hers.

The only sounds she could hear were the gentle lapping of the waves, and the thundering of her own heart.

Morgan led her topside. He blew out the lamp and pointed up to the sky.

Following the line of his hand, Serenity gasped. Above her head a thousand stars twinkled. But more surprising than that was the shower of sparks in the sky. It was as if a hundred stars were falling at once. Never in her life had she seen anything so miraculous.

"It's incredible," she said breathlessly.

"I thought you would enjoy it."

"What is it?"

"Old sailors call it the star dance. It doesn't happen often, but when it does ..."

"Oh, thank you," she said. "I'm glad you woke me."

His smile widened.

Serenity stared up at the stars that twinkled and fell. They were breathtaking.

Morgan pulled her by the arm and led her over to where he'd placed a blanket on deck along with a small midnight picnic. Serenity laughed at the sight. "What is all this?" she asked suspiciously.

He shrugged. "Who says we can't enjoy a quiet evening alone?"

"The town gossip, Mrs. O'Grady, were she here. I say, Captain Crook, but it looks like you've got more than the stars on your mind."

"And if I admitted that I did?"

Her heart stilled at his deep voice.

How easy it would be to succumb to him. And how disastrous. Biting her lip, she reminded herself of Chatty, of the horrible things people had said and done to her after she'd been caught alone at the lake with her beau. She'd done absolutely nothing and yet everyone in town had treated her like Jezebel.

Even so, Serenity couldn't quite silence the nagging voice in her head that told her a night in Morgan's arms would be well worth the price.

If only it were that simple.

She gave him the only answer she could. "Then I would have to say you're wasting your time."

He blew the lantern out, then set it down on the deck and bent close to whisper in her ear. "Am I, Serenity?"

The seductive tone of his voice sent shivers through her.

Kiss me, Morgan! Please, just one small kiss, then I shall return to my room and have sweet dreams of you in a safe world where no one can harm us. Where no one can mock me.

"You are an incredible woman." He brushed her braid off her shoulder.

Run, Serenity. Run back to your room now before it's too late!

But it was already too late.

She couldn't move. Like a lamb trapped by a deadly wolf, she was hypnotized by his voice, held spellbound by his touch.

"A curious woman." He moved to stand behind her, and she could feel his breath fall against her throat as he ran one long tapered finger down her cheek. "I'm quite sure you've wondered what lies between men and women. Why it's forbidden for them to be alone."

"Never."

His rich laughter filled her ears. "You're a terrible liar."

His arms came around her suddenly, and holding her tightly against his chest, he rested his chin on her head. Ribbons of pleasure spiraled through her at his touch, and she wanted to lose herself in this one moment in time.

He raised one hand up and gently stroked her cheek. Never in her life had anything felt so wonderful.

If only this could last forever.

But her feelings were just the enchantment of the night. The sight of the stars dancing, of the gentle rippling of the waves, the music of the wind caressing her body in time with his hand. This wasn't real. It was an illusion. The same kind of illusion that she'd had about him to begin with.

The Sea Wolf wasn't her noble prince. He was a man with a black past. A past that would mean Morgan's life if he were ever caught.

Aye, that was the argument she would use to safeguard her heart. The argument she would use to drive him away. "You are a crooked pirate, Captain Drake. I could never give myself to a man who killed for pleasure."

"And if I told you I never killed for pleasure?"

Serenity closed her eyes, trying to squash the part of her that took delight at his words. She mustn't listen to that part of herself.

She needed to push him away. To make herself seize her denial.

But the dreadful thing was, she couldn't lie to herself.

"I don't know if I could believe you."

But she wanted to. Desperately. It hurt so much to learn that her prince was a bandit.

He tilted her face toward him and splayed his fingers along her neck. Over her shoulder she looked up at him, and the intensity and need in his eyes took her breath. Never had a man looked at her with such raw, unbridled longing. She was at a loss as to how to deal with him.

With a terrifying need of its own, her body leapt to life under his skillful hands.

"Haven't you ever done something wrong that you later regretted?" he asked, his voice thick and deep. "Something that made others think terrible thoughts about you?"

"Yes," she whispered, her voice breathless. "I ran away with a pirate."

His deep laughter filled her ears, quickening her blood as his smile softened the hard edges of his face. "And is that the worst thing that ever happened to you?"

"Nay," she said, her throat tight. The worst thing that had ever happened to her was being held right now by a man she knew she could never have. Feeling things for him she knew she shouldn't feel.

Morgan felt her pulse race beneath his fingertips. Her fear reached out to him, but more than that he felt her hunger. The same hunger that throbbed through his body as he battled himself to keep from taking from her what he wanted most.

She needed seduction. He would have to move slowly. Hold her for tonight. Kiss her. Introduce her to her body's delights one step at a time.

Slowly.

You're a selfish bastard, Drake. This is wrong. You have nothing to offer her except a broken heart.

And as wrong as it was, he couldn't stop himself. Maybe it was because he'd been too long at sea without a woman, or maybe it was her unique charms. He didn't know the reason, he just knew he had to have her.

He bent his head down and nuzzled gently at the soft flesh of her neck while wisps of her hair teased his cheek, his lips.

Serenity moaned in pleasure and buried her hand in the soft curls of his hair. Never in her life had she experienced anything like this. Her entire body burned and ached. Her breasts swelled and her nipples grew taut.

His lips were so warm against the flesh of her throat, felt so incredible. His tongue stroked the fold of her ear, and her legs turned to jelly. His arms tightened around her, and she knew they were the only thing that kept her on her feet.

"Oh, Serenity," he breathed in her ear. It was half a curse, half a caress.

His hand slid inside her shirt and cupped her

aching breast. Her breath caught in her throat at the intimate contact that was half pleasure and half torture. Her breathing rapid, she bit her lip as an aching need thrummed through her body, pooling itself between her legs.

Then he moved his hand away from her breast, and just when she thought she was safe, he cupped her between her legs. She moaned in pleasure as his hand did the most incredible things to her body.

Tell him to stop! her mind demanded. But she didn't want him to.

He had been right, she was too curious for her own good. And this just felt too wonderful to stop.

Then he moved in front of her, his lips claiming hers. Serenity opened her mouth to taste the full essence of him. She buried her hands in his hair.

He slid his hand down into her pants and touched the most intimate part of her body. Her legs collapsed and only his arm around her back kept her from falling.

Morgan pulled back from her lips and ground his teeth. His entire body burned until he feared he'd go mad from it. All he could think of was burying himself where his hand played. But he knew he couldn't. Not yet.

He wanted her as he'd never wanted any other woman, and the best way to have her as hot and ready for him as he was for her would be to show her what pleasure her body held. Let her hunger for him as much as he did her.

He returned to her lips and drank of the only pleasure he knew he would have tonight, as he quickened the strokes of his fingers against her tender folds.

Serenity didn't know what was happening to her body. All she could focus on was the rhythm of his touch. The burning heat of her body as he teased her with his fingers. As he gently stroked and probed her body, his fingers sliding in and out of her, faster and faster.

She gripped his hair in painful need as her pleasure built and built until she was sure she would die from it.

And just as she could stand no more, her body burst. A thousand tendrils of pleasure rippled through her and she cried out in ecstasy.

And still his fingers continued their exquisite assault.

"I can't take it," she begged, her entire body convulsing and trembling.

He removed his hand and leaned against her, trapping her back against the ship's railing. It was only then she realized he was covered in sweat, his body shaking as much as hers.

"That is only one small taste of what I can show you," he whispered hoarsely in her ear.

And then he left her.

"Morgan?" she called softly, her body still pulsing. "Where are you going?"

"To take a long, cold bath, then get drunk."

Morgan threw back another shot of rum. His stomach burned, but not nearly as much as his loins. At this rate, he was sure he was going to die from the pain.

I could have had her!

She'd been his for the taking. He had given her release, and given himself hell.

Well, it's what you deserve.

It was, he knew that. He had no right to take from her what he had. After this night, she'd never be the same. Now she knew the rewards of desire, knew what pleasures her body could achieve.

He growled at himself. He never should have sought her out. Never touched her the way he had.

In all honesty, he hadn't meant to touch her. His intentions had been honorable enough.

Well, not completely honorable. He had intended to kiss her. To hold her.

Ah, face it, Drake, you'd meant to seduce her! Who do you think you're lying to? You know the truth.

He cursed and cupped his head in his hands.

"Captain?"

Morgan tensed at Barney's voice. Straightening up, he glanced to where Barney stood in the entrance of the galley. "What is it, Mr. Pitkern?"

"Mr. Pitkern, is it?" said the quartermaster with a hint of humor in his voice as he entered the room. "You must be suffering much to be so formal when it's just the two of us."

"Two? You mean you're out and about without Pesty?"

Barney joined him at the table. "Well, I was thinking of having a bit of rum, and she don't like it much when I drink."

"She's a true woman then."

Barney plopped his mug down on the table and poured himself a liberal amount of drink. "In some ways she's a greater nag than my sweet Bertha."

Morgan frowned at the mention of Barney's wife. The old man seldom spoke of her. "Is that what has you up?"

Barney heaved a weary sigh, lifted the mug from the table, and took a hearty swallow.

"Today be her birthday," he said after a few minutes of silence. "I was just trying to think about what she'd want for a gift, if she were still here." Barney sat down across from him and smiled sadly. "She so loved lilies. We had a yard full of them. I was just thinking that we spent the first month of our marriage planting those lilies in her garden. It was too early in the year, I thought, but she proved me wrong." He gave another sad laugh. "Funny, she often proved me wrong. Even when I was right!"

Morgan smiled, thinking about Serenity and her knack for doing the same to him. "Do you ever miss living on land?"

Barney cleared his throat and shook his head. "Never. 'Tis Bertha I miss."

They sat in silence for a while, each lost in his own thoughts. Each longing for something they couldn't have. Aching for something that was useless to want.

Barney poured himself another mug full of rum. He finally broke the silence. "Funny how love can make you happy no matter where you live. I could have had nothing more than a tin shack and dirt to eat when I had Bertha, and life would have been as good as if I lived in a palace."

Morgan contemplated his words.

For some reason, they made him think of his mother. He could barely remember her most of the time, but the one memory he carried of her most clearly was an image of her with his father. They'd been laughing together as she played his father's favorite song on the pianoforte. His father had stood just behind her, his hand lovingly placed on her shoulder. They had looked so happy that day that Morgan had stared at them until they realized he was in the room.

It was an image he could never forget.

Nor could he forget the terrible sadness his father had felt at her death. The years he had heard his father crying alone in his room when he thought no one could hear him. The lock of black hair his father kept concealed in his fob watch.

Even now, he could hear his father telling him that losing his wealth and titles had been nothing compared to losing his precious Beatrice. Money could be regained, but people were irreplaceable.

Morgan sighed as he realized he would never know such love. He would live out his life alone with no one to comfort him. No one to care what happened to him.

And in that moment, he made a startling discovery about himself—deep down in a part of his heart that he had long ago shut away, he wanted to know what it felt like to want to live and die for one person.

What would it be like to hear a woman whisper she loved him, whisper that she'd never want another man?

He ached for it.

And to his deepest mortification, he realized he wanted to hear it from Serenity.

"What the devil?"

"Morgan?" Barney asked, his brow raised. "What be the matter. You look as if you're about to meet your maker."

"It's nothing. I just had a bad thought." A terrible thought, really.

Why, he could barely stand being in a room with her without wanting to strangle her.

They were as ill suited as any two people could possibly be. He was a realist, she a romantic dreamer. He believed women should mind their place and she thought women should take their place wherever they wanted to.

Just imagine what she'd teach their children! Mutiny. Sheer mutiny. He'd have daughters running around wanting to be sailors and dressed in pants like hooligans.

Of course, Serenity looked awfully good in pants, his mind reminded him. She felt even better in pants.

That thought brought another painful ache to his groin, and he lowered his head to his hands and growled low in his throat.

Barney gave a raspy laugh. "You've got flaming britches, don't you, boy?"

He looked up with a puzzled frown. "Flaming what?"

"Britches." A wide smile split his face. "That little girl done gone and made you as horny as a herd of rhinoceroses."

"Don't be ridiculous," he snapped, not wanting to hear the truth spoken aloud. "I have no idea what you mean."

Barney gave him a knowing grin. "Sure you do. I've seen the way you look at her like a babe eyeing a peppermint stick. The way your gaze lingers on her, how close you stand when she's next to you. I may be old, but I'm not blind."

Why did he bother to deny it?

Yet he'd been doing it for so long, he couldn't bring himself to stop. "I've just been too long without a woman," he said, half to convince Barney and half to convince himself. "You know what that's like. I'd be aching after anything in skirts at this point."

By the look in his eye, he could tell Barney didn't believe a word of it.

Aloud Barney said, "Well, Cap'n, you can always take matters into your own hands." He gave a sideways glance down at his own pants. "If you know what I mean."

Morgan cleared his throat. The thought had occurred to him more than once, but he knew it wouldn't satisfy him. Not in the least. "I'd rather *she* take matters into her hands."

Barney's laughter rang in his ears. "Well then, it's a good thing we're going to Santa Maria. I'm sure you can find a willing woman to ease your pain."

With that said, Barney got up and took his leave.

Morgan sat quietly, thinking over Barney's

words. There were lots of attractive women on Santa Maria. Some of whom he knew intimately. But even as he thought of them, imagined them writhing beneath him, he felt nothing.

Until he thought of Serenity.

Instantly he burned.

This was turning out to be the longest voyage of his life!

Serenity stood before the open windows, watching the dark sea swirl behind the ship. Moonlight reflected off the waves, giving them a mysterious aura of beauty. Still, she couldn't really focus on them. Instead, her thoughts were held captive by what she'd experienced.

She didn't know what Morgan had done to her, it was sorcery of some kind. Of that she was certain.

No wonder it was forbidden for young ladies to be alone with men. Good gracious, who would have thought such pleasure could be found?

Guilty and ashamed, she wished she had never gone topside with Morgan.

What must he think of her now? Surely no decent woman would have allowed him to take such liberty.

Yet her body tingled from the memory of his touch, and she felt heat sting her cheeks.

What was she going to do?

Avoid him!

Yes, that was all she could do. Lock herself in this cabin and make sure that she never went near him again. Then at least she wouldn't have to face him and have him remember her wild abandon, her shameless murmurs.

Under no circumstances would she open the door. Not even if the ship caught on fire and sank!

Days passed slowly as Morgan tried his best to see Serenity again, but each time he ventured near his cabin, he was met by solid resistance.

And a locked door.

A locked door he was beginning to despise with a vengeance.

If not seeing her wasn't bad enough, he'd been forced to borrow clean clothes from his men, since she refused to even allow him entry long enough for that.

Only Kit and Court were allowed to see her.

"Court!" he called, spying the boy making his way across the deck with a tray of food.

The boy stopped and turned to face him. "Aye, Cap'n?"

"Are you taking that to Miss James?"

"Aye, sir."

"Then please see to it that she receives this note." Morgan pulled the sealed letter out of his pocket and handed it over to him.

What the hell, it was worth a try. Heaven knew, it'd worked for Jake on more than one occasion.

Besides, she couldn't stay locked up forever.

Just what was she doing in there anyway? Making more curtains? He shuddered at the thought.

Serenity recognized the timid knock. "Is that you, Court?" she called just to verify what she already knew.

"Aye, mum."

She opened the door and met Court's beaming smile. She'd learned much about him these last few days, including the fact that his father was much like her own—loud, but semi-indulgent.

Cookie wasn't the beast Morgan portrayed him to be. He was a good man who just got tired of being stuck below deck all day while everyone else got to see the daylight. It was his envy that drove him to be gruff with the others. That and the fact that he was a shy man who liked to be left alone.

But not Court. He loved people and he loved to talk as much as Serenity. She looked forward to his visits.

"How have you been?" she asked as Court came into the cabin and set her platter on the table. "Is your burn still bothering you?"

"Just fine, mum, thank you for asking. Your idea about onion juice worked just fine, it did.

Why, the blister be almost gone." He held his hand out to show her where he had accidentally touched a hot pan.

Serenity took his hand in her own and traced the spot where only a red place marked what had been a bad burn just days before. "I'm so glad Dr. Williams was right. He's said such strange things in his column that I was never certain if they were right or wrong. I guess now we know."

Court smiled. "Pa said it was a foolish thing you suggested, until he saw the results. He wants to know if you have any cures for his toothache. It's been givin' 'im a hard time to be sure. Why, he even yelled at the captain yestereve."

Her eyes widened. That was the one person Cookie never confronted. "He did not!"

"Aye, mum, 'e did. Thought the captain would have his head, I did."

She smiled at the image. She almost wished she'd been there to see Morgan get his pride nipped. But she had given up on that quest. At least it was nice to know someone was taking her place.

"Your father wouldn't happen to have any small burnet on board, would he?"

Court's brow furrowed. "Never heard of it meself, so like as not we don't."

"What about chamomile?" she asked as she

lifted the lid off the platter and set her food on the table. "Do you have any of that?"

"Barney takes it in his tea ever' now and a'gin. I'm sure he might be in the mood for some sharing."

"Oh good." Serenity handed him the platter and lid back. "All you need do is make an oil of the flowers and place about three drops on the tooth. That should hold him until he gets to a dentist."

"You're a saint, mum. A blessed saint."

She reached out and brushed the lock of hair from out of his eyes. "I'm nothing of the kind."

His smile lost some of its luster as he looked at her. "You remind me of me own mum. Pa thinks so, too. Said she was a real lady like you, not one of those types what meets us on land wanting some money for her favors. She had genteel ways."

Her throat tightened at the sadness that burned in his eyes. "You must miss her a lot."

"Aye," he answered, his voice thick.

"I miss my mother, too. She died when I was just a girl, but some days it feels like it was just yesterday."

Court sniffed. "I suppose I'd best be going, afore we both end up in tears."

He moved to the door, then stopped. "I almost forgot, mum. The captain sent this note for you."

He took a piece of sealed parchment from his pocket and handed it to her.

"Oil of chamomile flowers. I'll tell me pa," he said before turning around and opening the door.

Serenity barely heard the last of his words as he made his way out of the cabin. Instead, her attention was on the quick, clean strokes of Morgan's writing. It amazed her that a pirate would be literate. Especially one sold so young to the sea.

She broke the seal.

I feel like a weed in the midst of Winter. 'Tis the sunshine of your smile that will bring back the Spring of my days. We arrive in four days. I hope you will grace me again with your presence.

Yours,
Morgan

She traced the flowing letters with the tip of her finger and couldn't suppress a smile. A poetic pirate no less. Who would have thought?

Stay away from him! her mind warned.

She knew she should listen. Still, she saw the flowing script and felt the thrill of excitement run thick through her veins.

What was it about such a tiny note that made her breathless?

She crumpled the note and made to toss it out the open window.

Her arm drawn back, she watched the sea and faltered.

I feel like a weed in the midst of Winter. 'Tis the sunshine of your smile that will bring back the Spring of my days.

No one had ever written such to her before. Never. It was the type of note most women waited a lifetime to receive.

How could she toss it away?

And before she could stop herself, she opened her hand and did her best to straighten out the wrinkles.

After all, what would it hurt for her to keep it?

Chapter 12

Two days went by as Morgan waited for some sort of acknowledgment of his note.

None came.

He'd pushed her too far. No doubt the entire incident had embarrassed and shamed her. He should have never touched her—he knew that. If only he could apologize. Make some sort of restitution.

Sighing in frustration, he headed to the galley for a quick bite to eat to tide him over until dinner. Maybe a good run-in with Cookie would distract him from his guilt over Serenity.

As he approached the galley, he could hear Court speaking, then the gruff rumble of Cookie. At first he couldn't make out the words, but as he drew nearer, something odd happened. Something that defied belief.

"Now, tell me again about this rosemary."

Frowning, Morgan stopped just outside the door, stunned immobile. Was that Cookie's voice?

Surely, it couldn't be. He'd sounded almost... well...friendly.

"The doctor said that if you add a sprig to wine it'll help with digestion and cure a headache." Serenity's voice was like a symphony to his ears and it brought a warm rush to his blood. "What I've found is that it helps your head best when steeped in boiling water."

Cookie snorted. "Who would have ever thought?"

"Court?" Serenity asked with a tender note in her voice. "Would you please bring me the milk?"

"Aye, mum."

Morgan walked forward, keeping himself to the shadows so that he could spy on them.

Sure enough, Serenity stood before the stove, stirring something inside a large iron kettle while Cookie leaned over the table, rolling out dough. She wore the pink and white striped dress, her hair coiled neatly around her head. There was a quiet grace to her as she tapped the spoon against the side of the pot and wiped her hands on the white apron pinned to her skirt.

A rich, sweet aroma filled the air, making his stomach rumble.

Court handed her the milk. "Would you be needing the potatoes now?"

"Yes, please."

Her smile brought a surge of pleasure to Morgan's chest, but still he was too stunned to know what to do. Never before had Cookie tolerated anyone other than Court in his galley. Never mind someone to actually help him *cook* in the galley.

"Now, Mr. Rodale," Serenity said, and it took Morgan a few seconds to realize that must be Cookie's real name. She added the potatoes and milk to the pot, moving back slightly as some of the boiling water splashed out. "You never finished telling me your story."

Cookie chuckled as he cut biscuits out of the dough and placed them on a pan. "That's right, where was I?"

"There was a young pirate in a tavern," Serenity supplied for him as she returned to stirring her pot.

"Aye," Cookie said with a laugh as he balled the dough up again and began kneading and flouring it. "A young lad of about twenty or so had just sat down and got his mug of ale when this old pirate comes hobbling up with a peg leg, a hook for his right hand, and a patch over one eye."

He paused as he picked up the rolling pin, coated it with flour, and once more rolled the dough out across the floured table top. "This young fellow looks him up and down like a young fellow would and is impressed by what he sees. 'How'd you lose your leg, old man?' the boy asks. The old pirate snorts at his impertinence. 'I got this peg leg the day me crew and I attacked the largest port in Portugal. We sailed in and fought like the devil hisself and while we was fighting, the captain of the flagship jumped onto me ship and I fought him too. But while we was fighting me foot got coiled in some rope and as I was trying to get free, he swung his sword and lopped off me leg at the knee. So I grabbed a plank from the railing, stuck it in me bloody stump, and that's how I got me peg leg.'"

"How dreadful!" Serenity gasped, picking up spare dough from the table. She pulled off little pieces and added them to the pot. "The poor fellow."

"But wait," Court said, his face beaming with enthusiasm. "Pa's just getting to the good part."

"Mind your chores, boy," Cookie snapped in his usual distemper. "Now, where was I?"

"The pirate had explained his peg leg," Serenity said, stirring the dough into the pot.

"Oh, aye. Well now, the younger pirate was awed to be sure so next he asked, 'What about the hook?' 'Arrrrr,' said the old pirate, 'the hook came when we were firing our cannons at the fort in St. Augustine. I'd just loaded a cannonball and lit the fuse when a blast jarred me ship and the cannon swung around toward our hull. Without thinking, I reached out and pulled the cannon around— saved me ship, but the cannon went off and took me hand with it. So I picked up a hook from the riggings and jammed it in me bloody stump, and that's how I got me hook.'"

Serenity visibly cringed and made an awful face. Morgan bit his lip to keep from laughing. She made an adorable sight. One that made his mouth water even more than the delicious aroma that was coming from the pot she stirred.

Court picked up a broom and started sweeping the floor around the stove and table.

Cookie continued, "'Incredible!' said the young fellow. 'So how'd you get the patch?' 'That was the most grisly of all, boy,' said the pirate. 'It was after the battle, later that very same day, while we was pillaging the port. I grabbed me a feisty woman, had a bag of gold over my shoulder, and was headin' back to me ship when I heard a strange noise overhead. I looked up, and there was a huge seagull flying over.'"

"A seagull?" Serenity asked.

"Aye," Cookie said with a rare smile. "The old pirate had looked up at it and it capped him right in the eye."

She frowned. "Capped him?"

"Well, Miss James, it unloaded itself, if you know what I mean."

By her blush, Morgan could tell she understood.

"So, the young lad looks at the old pirate and says, 'But that doesn't explain the patch.' 'Aye, matey,' he said. "Twas me first day with the hook.'"

Morgan bit his lip to stifle his laughter. However, Serenity gave a delightful, hearty laugh that filled his ears with music.

"That's so terrible!" she gasped with a fake shudder. "Wherever did you hear such?"

Cookie began wiping the table clean. "You hear a lot of jokes from the sailors while they're eating." A frown settled down on his brow and it was obvious the matter bothered him for some reason.

Serenity placed a hand on Cookie's shoulder and in spite of the ridiculousness of it, a stab of jealousy whipped through Morgan. She wasn't supposed to comfort a man.

Come to think of it, why, she was down here against his orders!

"You should tell the captain how you feel, Mr. Rodale," she said quietly. "Let him know that you'd like to have more help so you can go topside during the day."

Cookie scoffed. "What, and turn them surly oafs loose in my galley without me? I shudder to think what they might do. Just my luck, they'd use gunpowder for pepper and then we'd all be in a fine fix."

Smiling, she rolled her eyes and turned back to check on her pot.

Court stopped his sweeping, his face beaming with a smile. "I've got a joke, Miss James!"

Serenity tapped the spoon twice against the pot and added the lid. "All right, Mr. Court, let us hear yours." She moved aside to allow Cookie to place the biscuits inside the oven.

Court went back to his sweeping. "There was once this brave captain whose ship was in danger of being boarded by pirates. So the good captain looked to his cabin boy and shouted, 'Bring me my red shirt!' The cabin boy quickly ran to his cabin and brought back the captain's red shirt, which the captain put on posthaste. The battle raged on all day, but in the end, they were victorious and the pirates were punished."

He paused to cuddle the broom in the crook of his arm and scratch his nose before continuing. "Two days later they spotted three ships of pirates and the captain, just as calm as ever, again called for his cabin boy to bring him his red shirt. Again the battle lasted all day and again the captain was victorious. Well, later that night, the crew was re-counting their war stories about the pirates when the quartermaster asked the captain why it was he always wanted a red shirt to wear during battle. So the captain, giving the quartermaster one of those looks that only a captain can manage to give, said, 'I wear me red shirt in case I get wounded in bat-tle. That way no one will know that I am hurt and the rest of you will continue to fight without any worry over me. His crew was much impressed by his words." Court stopped sweeping and nodded at her. "It's a brave thing to be wounded and not let it show."

Serenity nodded in agreement, her face sweet and indulgent like a proud mother's. "Go on."

"Well," Court said, "About a week later, the lookout called down to the captain that there were *ten* pirate ships headed their way. Every man-jack on board quivered in his boots and they all looked to the captain for guidance. The captain stood just as proud as ever and called calmly to the cabin boy, 'Boy, bring me . . . my brown pants.'"

Serenity's eyes bulged.

Cookie bellowed in rage. "Now, what kind of joke is that to be telling a lady? I raised you better than that, boy!"

And just as Cookie reached for Court, Serenity grabbed his hand. "It's all right, Mr. Rodale. He meant no harm."

Court looked like he'd been struck already. "I'm sorry, Pa. I just wanted to make her laugh, too."

Serenity gave Court a reassuring hug. "It was a fine story to tell other boys, but your father's right. You shouldn't tell such jokes in mixed company."

He hung his head and the broom dropped to the floor. "I'm sorry, Miss James."

She gave him another squeeze before she retrieved the broom and returned it to his hands. "Nothing to apologize for. You were just trying to make me happy and that is a wonderful thing. Isn't it, Mr. Rodale?"

Cookie's eyes narrowed. "Not as fine as me tanning his backside for such."

"Mr. Rodale," she said with a warning note in her voice.

Something happened to Morgan as he watched her comfort Court while scolding one of the worst-tempered men he had ever known. Something scary and unfamiliar.

A tenderness came over him for her.

A strong desire to make her laugh just as they'd done. A desire to hold her close and watch her . . .

Watch her what?

Comfort his own children?

It was there, just a spark of an idea. A quick flash of remembered longing so deeply buried within him that he'd forgotten its existence. But yes, long ago, before he'd made the mistake of marrying Teresa, he'd wanted children and a family. A wife who would stand by his side. Someone who would love him for himself and who would never let him go.

But his image of that bride hadn't been a strong-minded, irritating woman who locked him out of his own room. A woman who challenged every idea he held.

He wanted to run away from these strange feelings, to find a safe haven and never again think about them. But he couldn't. Cowardice was one crime he'd never committed, and it went against every part of him to turn tail and run.

Especially from her.

"Miss James?" he said, moving forward into the light.

She looked up and the color drained from her face. "Captain," she said coldly.

Cookie appeared somewhat embarrassed by being caught with her. Court quickly ran from the room, his broom trailing along behind him.

Morgan watched the boy's scampering and then turned to face Serenity. "I wish a word with you, Miss James."

"Well, I'm afraid that's not possible," she said, lifting the lid on the pot and stirring the contents. "I'm in the middle of helping Mr. Rodale with—"

"Cookie won't mind sparing you for just a few minutes."

She slammed the lid back on the pot.

Then the most unbelievable thing happened, Cookie moved between them and directed a warning gaze to Morgan. "Seems the lady doesn't wish to be alone with you, Captain."

Flabbergasted, Morgan stared at the man. No one had ever in his adult life defied him, especially not a member of his own crew.

"Do you know what you're doing?" Morgan asked, his voice lethal.

"Aye, Captain. I'm protecting the girl. It ain't proper for her to be alone with you and you well know it."

Serenity felt the anger bleeding from Morgan. Unwilling to let her new friend be harmed, she quickly moved forward. "It's all right, Mr. Rodale. I—I can speak with him."

Cookie's eyes narrowed on Morgan with dire warning burning bright. "I can trust you to mind your manners?"

Morgan stiffened and his nostrils flared.

Instead of being frightened by his captain, who had life-and-death control over him, Mr. Rodale looked at her. "If he offends you, lass, you let me know and I'll be serving him up a purging concoction for his supper."

She smiled at Mr. Rodale's threat.

Until she faced Morgan, and then her smile died upon her lips. "After you, Captain."

Her reluctance burned through Morgan as he led her back to his cabin and the privacy it offered.

Be gentle with her, he reminded himself. *Take your time. Remember she is still embarrassed and shy. Give her time to get used to you all over.*

But what he really wanted to do was strangle her for turning his crewman against him.

How did she do it? How in the world did she get

near the surly cook when no one else had been able to get so much as a how-do-you-do from the man?

Confrontation will get you nowhere. You know that.

Easy, Morgan.

Moving to stand in the center of his cabin, she turned to face him.

He started to shut the door, then thought better of it.

Easy.

"How long have you been sneaking to the galley to be with Cookie?" he asked before he could stop himself.

She arched her brows incredulously. "Is that jealousy I hear in your voice?"

He disregarded her jibe. "I thought I made it clear that you weren't to go alone to the galley."

"You also made it clear that I could trust you with my person, and you breached that trust. How can I trust anything you say?"

He flinched at the anger in her voice and the truth of her words. "You *can* trust me."

"Ha! You've lied to me from the start. Let me believe you were some noble gentleman with my best interest at heart and instead you make free with your hands the first moment we're alone."

He had expected her to be embarrassed, not outraged. Instead of the fearful, delicate flower he had expected to comfort, she was a hellcat spitting and hissing at him. Blaming the whole event on him.

Well, it wasn't his fault solely! Who did she think she was, looking so delectable, wearing men's clothes and stealing his breath.

She never should have agreed to go to the deck with him in the first place. She should have known better.

Aye, a woman knew not to let a man get her alone! It was her fault as much as it was his.

His own temper flying, he moved to stand before her. "Well, you didn't seem to mind my touch."

Her eyes narrowed and she advanced on him without warning.

Too stunned to think, he took a couple of steps backwards.

"You are low," she accused, poking her finger in his chest.

He backed up a few more steps.

"Vile!" she continued. "Only a blackguard would say such. Who do you think you are, sir? No, wait, allow me to answer. You're a black-hearted pirate who takes what he wants."

He wanted to answer her insults, but his mind was too stunned to think of an appropriate response. No one had ever confronted him thus.

As she stood before him, her legs braced wide apart and one hand on her hip, she looked like a savage lioness about to tear its prey into pieces.

He backed up until the wall prevented him from any further withdrawals.

"Well, sir," she said, again poking her finger into his chest to emphasize her words. "I suggest you find another way to occupy yourself, for this miss isn't to be had by the likes of you."

His eyes narrowing at being trapped, Morgan slid from between her and the wall.

Again she advanced on him, backing him up as she railed. "We have two more days until we reach Santa Maria and Mr. Rodale has assured me that there are several trading ships that dock there whose captains are willing to take passengers. I intend to be one of those passengers. So do us both a favor and stay away from me until then."

It was only then that he realized she had backed him out of his cabin.

Before he could blink, she stepped back into the room and slammed the door in his face.

"Woman!" he bellowed as he heard the lock click into place.

He saw red. Instinctively, he tried the handle.

Oh, it was locked all right.

This was it!

He'd had enough.

His anger coursed through his veins like fire and without thinking, he stomped to the storage room down the corridor where the tools were stored.

The room was tidy and orderly, with several axes secured against the far wall. Grabbing the one nearest him, he retraced his steps back to his cabin.

The wooden handle chafed the flesh of his palms as he gripped the ax tightly in both hands. It was time Miss Serenity James learned he wasn't some lapdog for her to command.

No one told Morgan Nathaniel Drake what to do or where to go.

No one!

He paused before the door, listening to her tirade on the other side.

"Ooo, he makes me so mad. *I thought I told you not to go to the galley alone,*" he heard her say in a mocking voice. "Really! As if he's afraid some nice man would harm my reputation after what he did."

She spoke louder, as if she knew he was on the other side. "I wish I were a man so that I could pound you to dust, Captain Drake. A sound thrashing is what you deserve."

A thrashing! his mind snarled.

Aye, that sounded like a good idea to him. Thrash the little vixen. Show her who was in charge!

Before he could think twice, he raised the ax and brought it down upon the door.

* * *

Just as she started disrobing, Serenity heard the sound of wood splintering. Her heart pounding, she watched as pieces of the door broke apart and the shiny silver head of an ax shredded the wood.

The lock gave way and the door thundered back on its hinges. Morgan stood in the doorway, a dark ominous look on his brow as he held the ax down by his side. "Don't you ever lock another door against me."

She should be terrified, she knew that. Yet he stood there with death itself etched on his face, holding the ax like a great woodsman as he glared his rage at her.

Every fiber of his body was tense, and the tattered door swung back and forth with the rhythm of the ship.

It was a ridiculous sight.

All this because she'd locked the door?

In spite of herself, she laughed. Deep and loud. She couldn't stop.

Until she remembered what she wore. Or more to the point, what she didn't wear. With a cry of alarm, she rushed to the bed and pulled the quilt off to wrap around her shoulders.

Morgan couldn't move. His ears were still ringing with her laughter as he watched her sprint to his bed, wearing only her thin camisole that emphasized every sweet feminine curve she possessed.

"What the blazes were you doing?" he asked, dumbfounded to have caught her in the midst of undressing.

"That's none of your business."

And then he saw it. Her laundry was once again strung out across his cabin.

"Laundry?" he asked, his brow knotted in confusion. "You were doing laundry?"

She stiffened her spine. "I was about to take a bath, if you must know," she snapped. "It seemed a good way to vent my anger. At least more practical than destroying doors."

He tightened his grip on the ax handle, wishing it were her neck he grasped. "I thought I told you water was scarce."

"You did, but Mr. Rodale and Court brought me a barrel of rainwater this morning so that I could have a bath and wash my clothes. Rather than insult them, I thought I would respect their kindness. But had I known you would throw a tantrum, I assure you I would have waited."

Now it was his turn to see the humor.

He *had* thrown a tantrum. There was no other word to describe what he'd done.

He drew a deep breath to calm his racing heart. What was it about this woman that made his emotions so volatile?

He'd always prided himself on his even moods.

On his ability to handle even the most difficult situation with calm dignity and rationality.

But when it came to her, his iron control melted like butter.

Was there any way to make a graceful exit from this fiasco? He glanced around at the remnants of the door strewn about the floor and Serenity standing by his bunk, draped in his quilt.

There was definitely no way to make a graceful exit.

"Gather up your clothes," he said in a low voice. "I won't be able to repair the door until we get to Santa Maria. You can dress in Barney's room and I'll..."

"Clean up the room?"

He nodded.

She gathered her clothes and stopped by his side. Her gaze darted along the pieces of the door before she looked back at his face. "I guess I won't be locking the door tonight, will I, Captain?"

He growled a low warning in his throat.

Serenity decided it would be best to make a hasty retreat. She practically ran down the hallway until she reached Barney's room and knocked on the door.

"Who is it?" Pesty asked.

"It's Serenity. Is Barney in there?" she asked before she realized how foolish it was to have a conversation with a bird. She waited a few minutes and when no one said anything, she eased the door open. The room was empty except for Pesty.

With a sigh of relief, she entered and shut the door firmly behind her. Only then did she allow the horror of what had just happened wash over her.

The man was insane! He had come after her with an ax!

No, her mind quietly chided. He had come after the door with an ax.

I have never in my life known a girl who could push a man to the limits of his sanity, she heard her father's voice in her head. *But you, gal, you take it all. I'll never know what your sweet mother was thinking when she named you Serenity. It must have been wishful thinking on her part. If I had my way, I'd have named you Incense!*

Really Serenity, her brother had once said, *what is it about you that you have to push people when you can plainly see they're ready to kill you?*

It was a terrible flaw in her personality. One she'd never understood, but it was true. She did so love to aggravate people. Especially arrogant men.

A small smile hovered at the edges of her lips as she again pictured Morgan standing in the room with the ax in his hand, his face etched with fury. It had been a funny sight.

But it was definitely one she never wanted to see again.

"Just two more days and then you're safe," she said to herself as she began dressing.

"Two more days," Pesty repeated. "Two more days."

Yet for all the safety, a tiny part of her hoped the end of those two days would never come.

Later that night, Serenity was just about ready to go to bed when she heard approaching footsteps.

Footsteps that heralded the approach of Morgan.

As he had promised, he had cleaned up the remnants of the door from his cabin. She had spent the rest of the day in the galley with Mr. Rodale and Court.

By unspoken, mutual agreement she and Morgan had avoided each other all day. Especially once word had gone around the crew about what had happened between them.

At first she'd thought Mr. Rodale would have Morgan's head, but she and Court had finally talked sense into him.

Now Morgan stood in the doorway with a bedroll hanging from his left hand.

"Is there something you need?" she asked, her voice frigid as she stepped away from the bunk.

He shook his head and without a word to her,

began unrolling his blanket and pillow. He stretched out on the floor just outside her door.

"What do you think you're doing?" Serenity asked, arms akimbo as she approached him.

Morgan pulled the blanket up around his chest and looked up at her. "I'm about to go to sleep for the night, if you don't mind."

"Well, I certainly do mind your sleeping in my room."

His gaze traced the outline of the door frame, then he looked directly into her face. "I believe I am outside the cabin."

"Inside, outside, what difference does it make now that there's no way to bar your access to my bed? Do you think me foolish enough to sleep with you so close by? You forget, Captain. I know what manner of man you are."

He gave a tired sigh. "I'm in no mood to fight, Serenity. Go to bed. I'm here simply to make sure no one disturbs you."

Did she dare believe it?

As if sensing her doubt, he rolled over and gave her his back. "Go to sleep, Miss James."

Hesitant, she returned to her bed and carefully crawled in, making sure to keep her eyes on him all the while.

He never moved.

* * *

All night, Morgan listened to Serenity toss and turn in his bed. Every time she moved, his body reacted, aching for hers. Too easily, he remembered the passion of her embrace, the sound of her ecstasy.

She's killing me, he thought sourly.

Slowly but surely she was absolutely killing him with want.

Sighing, he realized he wouldn't get any sleep this night, and from the sounds of it, neither would she.

Determined not to yield to his body, Morgan said quietly, "I'm sorry about the door. I shouldn't have overreacted."

There were a few seconds of silence before she responded to his apology. "I'm sorry I goaded you to such anger."

Well, it was a start, he thought. At least she was able to see her own part in his idiocy. "You certainly have a way of doing that."

"So I've been told. My father claims it's my greatest talent."

They fell silent for several minutes.

Serenity thought about the fact that once they got to Santa Maria, she would never see him again.

Why did that thought bring such a surge of pain to her breast? She should be delighted to go home, yet she couldn't stand the thought of not seeing his face every day.

But that was the way it must be. She had to go home sometime, and the sooner, no doubt, the better.

"Morgan?" she asked.

"Yes?"

"Just before you came, I was remembering how alone I felt after my mother's death. My father was so grief-stricken that he almost completely forgot about us."

She gave a sad half laugh. "You probably wouldn't have liked my mother very much. She's the one who taught me my mutinous ideas."

"What did your father have to say about her views?"

"While she was alive, he was very supportive of her. They had a few memorable fights, but all in all he found her unorthodox views . . . tolerable."

Tolerable, Morgan thought with a smile. Now, that was an appropriate word. Especially if the woman was anything like her daughter.

Of course, he found Serenity more than tolerable.

When she wasn't making him furious, he actually liked her a great deal.

At times she was downright irresistible.

"Did she want to be a writer?" he asked, wondering if that was what had prompted Serenity's interest in working for her father's paper.

"Nay, she actually wanted to be an explorer."

For a moment he was stunned. "She did not!"

"Yes, she did. She said that would be the greatest challenge she could think of. She wanted to be like Sacajawea and go west across the French Territories."

"Did she ever get to?" he asked, knowing that if Serenity wanted something like that she would do it regardless. He doubted if anything could stop her from doing whatever nonsense she set her mind to.

"Nay," she said with a sigh. "She never got to travel beyond Charleston and Marthasville."

"What made her decide to give up her dream?"

"My father. She said living with him and running after her children was enough of an adventure for her. She didn't need any more than that."

Morgan laughed at the image he had of Serenity as a small child. He just bet she was indeed a huge handful.

"My mother was the type of lady who never raised her voice," he said quietly. "I don't think she ever had an opinion that my father didn't give her."

"I think that's what every man dreams of having," she said, and he could hear the bitter disappointment in her voice.

"I don't know," he said in an effort to cheer her

melancholia. "I think some men, like your father, appreciate a challenge."

Silence descended and hung between them until he thought she'd gone to sleep.

Finally she spoke, "And what type of man are you, Morgan?"

Chapter 13

Morgan had never answered her question. Not that night, nor the next night. Serenity had waited and waited, but he'd never spoken.

The silence had dragged on until she couldn't take it, and when she'd prodded him for an answer, his words had been clipped. "Goodnight, Serenity."

Even now, his rejection stung her. Either he was the type of man who did like a challenge and he didn't want to encourage her, or he didn't like her at all and was trying to be tactful.

Either way, she lost.

Either way meant he had no use for her and that hurt her so much more than she'd ever thought possible. It hurt way down deep in her chest and soul.

Serenity promised herself to think no more of it. Soon they would part and that would be that. She would go on with her life, regardless. And she would be strong. Never would she let anyone see her pain, most especially not Morgan.

Her will reaffirmed, she stood alone on the deck, staring at the exotic island of Santa Maria as they drew near it. In truth, she'd never seen anything like it. The land rose up out of the ocean and a fine mist enshrouded it with an enticing veil that added mystery and softness to it.

"Are we in the Azores?" she asked Kit as he approached her.

"No, Miss James," he said, laying down the rope he held in his hands. "This is a relatively unknown island that's inhabited by . . ." He rubbed the back of his neck and avoided her gaze. "Well, the types of folks I'm sure you wouldn't want to be alone with."

His words gave her pause. "But Mr. Rodale told me that I could buy passage from a trade ship here."

"And he's quite right. Trade ships stop by often, looking for information and other, less respectable, things."

Kit left her and went to join a group of men who were lowering sails.

Serenity watched the shoreline drift closer. She was almost homeward bound back to Savannah.

The thought should have thrilled her, and yet ...

What was the use in wishing for what could have been?

Sure, she'd had a couple of nights of quiet conversation with Morgan. She'd learned much about his parents, about his sister. He had even told her some of his adventures as a pirate, and though she knew she should hate that particular part of his past, she couldn't quite muster up that emotion.

Maybe she was just too curious after all.

But one thing he never spoke of were his years in the British navy. No matter how she phrased her question, he would deftly turn their discussion to something else.

Looking to where he stood by the helm, she felt a flutter in her heart. He was such a handsome man.

A thoughtful man, she realized. Even though his views didn't always mesh with her own, he had at least thought them out and was able to defend his ideals under fire.

And deep down inside, she admitted that she loved to verbally spar with him on those ideas. Even when hers weren't contradictory to his, she couldn't suppress the urge to rankle him and make him fight to convert her to his views.

But that was soon to end.

A few more hours and ...

She sighed.

The ship came around a huge mountain, and there on the other side was the most beautiful sight Serenity had ever beheld. Sunlight danced on the waves that pounded against sand as white as snow. Three ships had weighed anchor just off-shore and she could see a small settlement of homes not too far from the shoreline.

A large pier jutted out into the ocean and several children scurried along its edge, playing some sort of dodge game with two chickens. A myriad of flowers and plants bloomed all around. It looked like paradise.

"It's breathtaking, isn't it?" Morgan said in her ear.

He must have moved up behind her while she studied the area.

How could the mere sound of his voice give her chills? Banishing the thought, Serenity nodded. "Why do they call it Santa Maria?" she asked.

He smiled that smile that never failed to turn her legs to mush. "It's a joke, really. It was named after the same island in the Azores where a number of ships from the Spanish Armada are kept. At the time this island was founded, it was the pirate equivalent to the real Santa Maria."

"And now?"

"Now you'll find a lot of retired pirates who

wanted to escape their past before the authorities found them. Here they can live in peace and talk about the old days when pirates ruled the seas and they still held their youth." He came around to stare at her. "There's actually a lot of trade that goes on here nowadays, thanks to Robert Dreck."

"Who is he?"

"An old friend of mine." He looked over her head to where Barney stood at the helm. "Bring her about, Mr. Pitkern, and weigh anchor."

"Aye, aye, Cap'n."

Raw emotions hovered in Morgan's eyes as he looked back at her. "I suppose you'll be wanting your things from my cabin...now."

Did she really hear the note of sadness in his voice? Looking up at him, she wondered if she could really leave.

You have to!

She nodded. "Yes, I better go get my things."

Morgan watched as she crossed the deck, his heart heavy. He wanted to call her back, to beg her to let him take her home.

Why?

He didn't want to think about the why. It scared him to think about it. All he knew was that he would give what little soul he had left for another week with her.

Let her go, Drake, he mumbled to himself. He must let her go.

Serenity sat quietly in the rowboat as Kit rowed her and several other members of the crew to shore. Morgan was up ahead of them and would reach the shore first.

Half the crew had been left on board while the other half were all shouting and singing, exuberant over their island excursion. Not that she could blame them. The place was enchanting.

Islanders had come out to meet them, including a group of ladies whose low-cut sleeveless blouses and hiked-up skirts left very little doubt as to what they did for a living.

But in truth she did envy them their clothes. The heat here would rival Savannah's August weather any day. She patted at her sweat-dampened hair and wished she could loosen her stays.

Kit rowed her as close to shore as he could. Immediately sailors began jumping overboard, rocking the boat as they splashed toward the shore like excited children after a favorite toy.

"I'm afraid you're going to get wet, Miss James," Kit said in an apologetic voice.

She smiled at him. "Nothing to fret over. I'm sure I'll dry out in no time in this heat."

She stood up, and just as she started to climb out, she met Morgan, who was standing knee-deep in the water. "May I lend you my assistance, Miss James?"

Serenity hesitated. They hadn't touched since *that* night, the mere thought of which brought an unholy amount of heat to her cheeks. "I—I . . . "

And then against her will, her body leaned forward.

Morgan scooped her up in his arms and held her tightly against his chest. It felt sinfully good to be this close to him, to smell the raw scent of his skin, feel his hands cupping her body in a protective manner.

"I believe I can walk now," she whispered, her heart hammering.

"No need in ruining your dress," he said, his voice slightly hoarse, and she wondered if he felt the same desperate longing she did.

It was so wrong, and yet she couldn't stop herself from wanting another kiss.

From wanting . . .

No more, she snapped at herself. A man wasn't supposed to touch a woman like that. Not without wedding vows, and even then she wasn't sure if they were supposed to do what he'd done to her that night.

Still, she let him carry her to shore with only the tiniest edge of her hem sweeping against the waves.

When he finally stopped and set her down, she

wasn't sure she could hold her own weight. Something about his touch had made her breathless and weak.

"Morgan!" a rough voice called out.

She turned to see a man of about fifty or so years rush toward them. Years of squinting against the island sun had made deep lines around his eyes, but even so, he was very handsome and distinguished-looking. His white hair still held a strand or two of the black it had once been. He wore a flowing white shirt that was open at the neck, and a long, light blue waistcoat. His tan breeches and white stockings looked crisp and unbearable in this heat.

"It's so good to see you." The man took Morgan's hand and pumped it giddily. "Or are you still going by Marshall? Damn, boy, if I ever know what to call you."

Morgan smiled. "It's been a long time, Robert."

The man named Robert turned to Serenity then and gave her a measuring stare that she was sure took in more than just her appearance. There was a sageness to him that led her to believe he could size up her very soul.

"Allow me to present Serenity James. Miss James, this is Robert Dreck, the governor of the island."

Robert laughed. "Governor, indeed. What he

fails to tell you, Miss James, is that I won this island in a card game." He lifted her hand, bowed low before her like a true noble lord, and placed a gentle kiss on the backs of her fingers. "It is an honor to make your acquaintance."

Morgan cleared his throat, and she didn't miss the warning stare he directed to Robert.

Robert's smile grew wider. "Tell me how such a lady came into your surly presence, Drake."

Serenity answered for him. "Fate and misfortune laid me at his door."

Robert started to respond, and then his gaze looked past her and he saw Jake wading ashore.

"My God," he gasped. "It's Jack. I don't believe my eyes!" He rushed forward to greet Jake.

"Jake once saved Robert's life," Morgan explained. "I know Robert didn't mean to leave you so rudely, but he hasn't seen Jake in a long time."

"No need to explain. How is it you know Robert?"

His jaw flexed and he became rigid. At first she didn't think he'd answer and then after a pregnant pause, he said, "I married his daughter."

After greeting Jake, Robert had led them to waiting coaches which had taken Morgan, Serenity, Jake, and Barney up to his Grecian-style plantation home named *La Grande Maison*. Robert had introduced her to his wife, Martha, and his youngest daughter, Kristen, before the men had retired to his study.

Martha, who was probably a good ten years younger than Robert, had laughing blue eyes and light auburn hair. She was short and plump, and vivacious. But there was something more than that, a cheery happiness that ran so deep in Martha's personality that all a person had to do was look at her to feel happy.

And Martha had an uncanny ability to read people. She'd no more than just met Serenity before she ordered a bath be drawn and urged Serenity upstairs to rest.

Now Serenity stood inside an upstairs bedroom looking out on the weeping willows and Spanish moss that lined the drive.

Kristen, who was around Serenity's age, directed the servants to fill the tub and prepare her bath like a military drill instructor. Though slight of stature like her mother, and with the appearance of a fragile china doll, Kristen was not a woman to be taken lightly. Once she donned the cap of commander, Serenity doubted if anyone possessed the backbone to stand up to her.

Serenity tuned out Kristen's commands while she thought about Morgan's disclosure of being married to Robert's eldest daughter, Teresa.

This had once been Morgan's wife's home, and Serenity couldn't help wondering how much he had loved Teresa. What they had shared, and what memories this house stirred within him.

"Miss James," Kristen called, "your bath is ready and we're waiting to help you undress."

"Thank you," Serenity said, pulling herself away from her thoughts.

A light blue cambric dress had been brushed and was lying on the bed.

"I thought the color would bring out your eyes," Kristen explained. "It was part of a shipment that Father purchased just last week."

"It's beautiful. Thank you."

"Miss James?" Kristen asked as she moved closer to her.

"Call me Serenity, please."

Kristen nodded. "Serenity, I know we just met, but I can't help noticing that something seems to be the matter. Would you like a sympathetic ear?"

How could she possibly broach this topic with Kristen?

"It's about my sister and Morgan, isn't it?"

Serenity chewed her lip, not really wanting to talk about this. Yet she needed to. "He loved your sister very much, didn't he?"

Kristen gave her a comforting squeeze. "Do you want the truth?"

"Please."

Kristen dismissed the servants and quietly shut the door before she turned back to face Serenity. "Teresa was in love with another man," she confessed in a low tone. "He was a local farmer's son, and she used to sneak out every night to meet with him."

Serenity gasped. That was the last thing she'd expected Kristen to say.

Kristen's eyes turned dark and sad, and tears misted in her eyes. "My parents didn't know at the time, and I had promised her I wouldn't tell. You've no idea how many times since her death I wished to God that I had told them. That I had stopped her from doing something so terribly foolish."

Kristen looked away from her. "They saw each other for a few months and then Teresa learned ... well, she was in the family way."

Serenity frowned. "I don't understand."

Kristen bit her lip as if debating something. She finally continued, "I guess I should explain everything from the beginning. All this mess started with Morgan."

"With Morgan?"

"Aye. When Morgan found his sister, he didn't know where to take her. Penelope had caught a terrible disease and she would fly into fits of rage. Morgan brought her here because my mother was the only person he knew who had experience dealing with people like her. But it was too late. The disease was incurable and so my mother and Teresa did their best to make her comfortable."

Kristen swallowed. "Teresa befriended her, loved her like a sister, and she helped Penelope live out her final days in quiet dignity. So later, when Morgan found out what had happened to Teresa, and the fact that the man who did it had run off to sea and abandoned her, Morgan insisted she marry him."

She met Serenity's gaze. "You can't imagine how upset Teresa was. She knew Morgan didn't love her and she didn't love him, but she agreed for the baby's sake."

Her face sad, Kristen folded her hands in front of her. She went to stand in front of the open windows and looked out across the lawn. "Morgan, bless his heart, tried to settle down here with her. He used to sit out on the dock for hours at sunset watching the tide come in. You could read on his face how much he missed the sea. How much he wanted to return to it. But he stayed here, by Teresa's side, until she begged him not to worry over her. She told him that she would be fine and that he should go back to sailing. He didn't want to at first, but my father also encouraged him. When he left, he promised Teresa he would be back in time for the baby's birth."

It was all starting to make sense to Serenity. "He didn't make it."

"No," she said with a shake of her head. "She died shortly after giving birth."

"And the baby?"

"Stillborn."

"Oh, Kristen, I'm so sorry." Serenity moved to her side and hugged her close.

Kristen patted her on the back. "It's all right. I like to think that Teresa finally found peace. She was so unhappy those last few months. Every night she would cry herself to sleep and I could hear Morgan pacing the floor outside their room. He had no idea how to make Teresa feel better. Broken hearts are hard to heal.

"I just wish Morgan could find peace as well," Kristen whispered. "He blamed himself for not being here with her when she died."

Kristen pulled away and went to place towels around the bathtub. "But I'm glad to see him happy with you," she said, looking up, her eyes sincere. "So tell me, when do the two of you plan to marry?"

Serenity was so startled that she couldn't even speak for several seconds.

When she finally found her voice, it came out as a small croak. "I beg your pardon?"

Kristen smiled. "Don't be so alarmed. I loved

Teresa, but I love Morgan too, and all I want is for him to be happy. I'm glad he found you."

"No, no, no," Serenity said hastily, wondering what had made her jump to that conclusion. "We aren't planning marriage. In fact, I plan to buy passage from this island back home while he continues on."

Kristen straightened up from the tub with a deep frown creasing her brow. "But I thought—"

"Morgan and I barely get along," Serenity said in a rush. "We fight over everything."

A knowing smile curved her lips. "He makes you insane, doesn't he?"

"Absolutely."

"And you love to irritate him? Live for it, in fact?"

Now Serenity frowned. Did Kristen possess second sight? "How did you know?"

Her smile widened and she gave a light laugh. "I feel the same way about my husband."

"I didn't know you were married."

"For six years now," she said. "It was love at first sight. The moment I saw George, I knew he was the one for me. You feel the same for Morgan. I saw it on your face downstairs when you arrived."

"Nay, really, I couldn't love Morgan. He's a pirate."

Kristen shrugged as if the matter was completely unimportant. "So was George. So was my father. Men do many things that they later regret. Even at his worst, Morgan was never as bad as many others I've met. In fact, I've known so-called privateers and naval officers who were far more cruel than even Jake. And believe you me, there are times when Jacob Dudley could give the devil himself a run for his money."

That was a statement Serenity didn't doubt.

Kristen moved to her stays and started unlacing Serenity's dress. "What's in a man's past doesn't matter nearly as much as what's in his present, and most importantly, what's in his heart. Morgan loves you," she said, stepping around to where Serenity could see the bright earnestness of her gaze. "I've never seen him stare at a woman the way he does you. His hand even lingered at your waist before you followed me up here."

Serenity laughed. "You don't miss anything, do you?"

"Not much. My mother calls it my own special curse." She circled around Serenity. "Tell me, if he had never been a pirate, how would you feel about him?"

Serenity bit her lip as she thought the matter over. "He is handsome, isn't he?"

"As sin itself."

"Charming," she said with a wistful sigh.

"Absolutely. Don't forget debonnaire, kind."

Serenity barely heard the words as she continued to tally Morgan's finer points. "He makes me laugh when I'm not angry at him."

Kristen *tsked*. "Oh, sweet. It's too late for you. It's true love if ever I've seen it."

Serenity shook her head in steadfast denial. "Oh, I don't know if I believe in true love anymore," she said with a sigh. "There was a time, not long ago in fact, that I believed in romantic fairy tales, but these last few weeks I've learned that life—that people, aren't the way I want them to be. They are the way they are, and no amount of wishing will change that."

"Yes," Kristen said lifting her brows, "but we don't choose whom we love with our heads, we choose with our hearts." She lightly touched the area on Serenity's chest where her heart pounded in spite of her denials. "We love in spite of faults and sometimes because of them. Correct me if I'm wrong, Serenity, but when you're around Morgan do you feel breathless?"

"Oh, yes."

"Jittery?"

"At times."

"Do you find yourself begging for his mere touch?"

Serenity's face flooded with heat. How could she ever admit *that* out loud?

"So you do."

"Well, what has that got to do—"

"It means you're in love, Miss James. The next question is, what are you planning to do about it?"

Chapter 14

What was she going to do about it? That was the question that had haunted Serenity throughout her bath.

Kristen should have been an interrogator or a solicitor, with her ability to strip back delusions and reveal the truth.

What could she say? The woman was incredibly sharp of mind. And the only way Serenity had gained peace was by pleading a headache.

Now alone in the room, dressed in the blue cambric and sitting on the fainting couch in front of the open windows, Serenity allowed her thoughts full rein.

She was in love.

The truth of it had hit her hard, and yet she wondered how she could have been so blind to the truth all this time.

Why else would she have even cared about his past?

It certainly wasn't because she'd written a silly old legend only to learn that legend was a man.

It was because she felt deceived by the man she had given her heart to.

"What am I going to do?" she murmured to herself.

She toyed with the purse of money that rested in her lap. Mr. Rodale had given it to her to buy safe passage home. The faded brown leather pouch was threadbare and ragged around the edges. From the moment he'd given it to her, she'd felt guilty. But at the time, she'd been desperate to leave. And she'd promised to get his money to him as soon as she returned home. Of course, she didn't really know how to do that, since he would be at sea.

But she would have been home.

Home.

The word was so sweet. She would see Honor and Jonathan and her father. Douglas.

She smiled.

But she would never again see Morgan.

Closing her eyes, she remembered the feeling she'd had the day in the shop when he'd swept into her life like the phantom she'd written of in her story.

The feeling she'd had the night he'd shown up at her party to seek her out.

But most important, she remembered the feeling she'd had that night after he left her in the library—that she'd slammed the door on some kind of opportunity.

Morgan.

He was her knight in shining armor. Her dashing pirate prince who...

Who could break her heart by refusing her love.

It should be easy! she lamented to herself. She should be able to go downstairs this instant and say, Morgan Drake, pirate or not, I love you. I want to spend the rest of my life with you.

But it wasn't that simple.

Nothing in life was ever that simple.

"Good Lord, what if he laughs in my face?" she whispered.

He might. And who would blame him? Here she was, some boyishly framed miss who needed glasses to read and who spoke words of social reform. A woman who made him mad enough to chop down his own door.

He'd probably had lots of women throw themselves at him. Lots of beautiful women. Sophisticated, know-their-place women.

And not one of them had ever been able to hold on to him. Their failure gave her little hope.

"Oh, Morgan," she whispered to herself. "If only I knew how you really felt."

* * *

La Grande Maison had been fashioned after the large homes of Virginia that Robert had admired in his youth. After years of fruitful piracy, and his winning hand of poker, Robert had decided to settle down on Santa Maria, and set his sights on the daughter of a local official.

Once Martha's father had seen the house Robert was building, he'd quickly given his daughter over for a hefty slice of Robert's wealth. She had been less than pleased with her father's choice of husband.

Luckily, Martha's upset at her father hadn't lasted. In no time, Robert had won over his new bride.

In all the years Morgan had known them, they had always been happy with each other.

The only thing Robert valued more than this house and his wife were his two daughters.

Morgan sighed at the memory of Teresa. She'd been a beautiful girl with long blond hair and a sweet, docile disposition. Like her mother, she had never said a cross word, and she'd had an enchanting smile.

But her smile had never made him quiver the way Serenity's did.

And in spite of his best intentions toward Teresa, Morgan had never loved her. The truth of that cut him deeply.

In spite of his heart, he had tried to be a good husband to her, but the lure of the sea had been too much.

Now, full circle, he stood in this same house waiting for the rustle of a feminine hem to herald the approach of a woman he was desperate to see. Twelve years ago he had been nervous to propose to Teresa. The words had even hung in his throat. It had only been by sheer will that he'd finally uttered them.

Now he wanted to see Serenity.

Morgan looked up the stairs for what seemed like the millionth time. For half an hour he'd been waiting in the large, open foyer. A split staircase curved up to the next floor. A floor where she waited.

Where was Serenity?

He grunted at the unintended double entendre. His serenity had left the moment he met *her*. Just what sort of name was "Serenity" for a woman who brought him anything but peace?

Fate was surely laughing at him.

"Morgan? Are you all right?"

He turned at Kristen's voice as she entered the foyer from the French doors that led out to the gardens.

"I'm fine."

"Then why are you pacing?"

"I'm not pacing."

She cocked an amused brow.

Forcing himself to stop, he crossed his arms over his chest. "Don't you have something more important to do than spy on me?"

A calculating look darkened her eyes. "Well, as a matter of fact, I do. I was actually on my way to tell Miss James that a trade ship just came into port that is bound for the Colonies."

He felt his face blanch, and if he hadn't known better, he'd have sworn Kristen enjoyed seeing it.

"If you'll excuse me . . ." She picked up the hem of her dress and started up the stairs.

"Wait!" he snapped before he could stop himself.

She turned about, her eyes wide with innocent questioning. "Yes?"

Morgan debated what to say. He wanted to go upstairs and beg Serenity not to go. He wanted her to stay with him.

His mind hurriedly searched for a logical reason for him to feel that way. A reason he could accept. One he could live with. And he finally realized what the reason must be.

It was his duty to see her home safely.

Yes, that was it.

It was his duty!

Why should she buy passage when he could transport her for free?

Then another thought struck him. "Where did she get money for passage?"

Kristen shrugged. "Maybe she pirated it."

"You're not funny, Kristen."

"That's a matter for debate. Now if you'll excuse me, I really must deliver my news. Unless . . . "

"Unless what?" He prayed the desperate hope he felt wasn't etched onto his face.

"Oh, never mind." And with that she turned around and flounced up the stairs.

Kristen paused on the second floor and peeked back to where she'd left Morgan. He looked so angry that for a moment she thought he might actually come up after her.

"You're a stubborn, stubborn man, Morgan Drake," she whispered. "And I pity poor Serenity for having to put up with you."

Of course, her own mother-in-law had said the same thing to her when she married George.

Men were never easy, especially not when you loved one. As her mother had told her on her wedding night, the first two years of marriage a wife will want to devour her husband. After that, she'll wish she had.

Kristen snickered. There were times when that was definitely true, but she also knew the pain of letting go someone you loved and the fear of never finding them again.

She'd loved George the first time she'd met him at sixteen. She had known then that she would never know happiness without him. And though she knew he loved her too, he refused to acknowledge it.

"Your father would have my head, among other things," he'd told her. "I'm not a fitting husband for you." And he had left her island.

Well, it had taken her four years of searching for him to get him to the altar, and neither one of them had regretted it since.

She didn't want to see Serenity and Morgan go through the terrible nights she and George had known wondering where the other one was... whom they might be with.

And worse, the regret for those lost years that could never be recaptured. Years when they should have been together.

Nay, she wouldn't see them suffer.

With that thought foremost on her mind, she went to wreak her havoc.

Serenity jumped at the light knock on her door. "Yes?" she called.

Kristen came in with a bright smile. "Is your head any better?"

She blushed at Kristen's concern, especially since she'd lied about the headache to begin with. "Yes and no."

"Well, I have some news that might help," Kristen said, moving to stand between the couch and the windows. "There's a ship at the docks that's headed for the Colonies."

"Oh," Serenity whispered, her heart heavy. "I suppose I should send for the captain."

"No need," Kristen quickly assured her. "Father already told him about you, and the captain said there wouldn't be any problems returning you home."

Kristen twirled her hair with one finger and asked innocently, "There aren't any problems, are there, Serenity?"

Yes, she wanted to say. There was one big problem.

How to leave Morgan behind.

"No problem," she lied again, her conscience biting her over the deception. "Do you know when they plan to leave?"

"In three days."

Three days! Her heart sank. Just three more days and then she would never see Morgan again.

Kristen leaned over and whispered softly. "But you know, a lot can happen in just three days."

"Yes," Serenity said with a sigh. "The world could come to an end. I could get knocked sense-less, or—"

"Or you could make Morgan fall in love with you and propose."

Serenity burst out laughing. She didn't mean to, but the very idea was so ludicrous she couldn't help herself.

Kristen slowly folded her arms over her chest and eyeballed her. "You don't believe me?"

Sobering, Serenity shook her head. "Morgan has made it clear that marriage is the last thing he wants."

Kristen cocked her head. "What a man says and what he really wants are seldom the same. Trust me. When it comes to manipulating men, I doubt if Helen of Troy could top me."

Kristen moved closer. "Think about it, Serenity. If Morgan marries you, then you'll never have to listen to the gossips in your hometown. Sure, they'll talk about Serenity James who ran off to sea to *marry* her true love. But they'll never say the vicious things about you that they will if you return home alone."

Kristen bent down so close her lips almost touched Serenity's ear. "Think about it," she whispered before crossing the room to stand in front of the open windows to where she could look out on the sea.

Serenity did.

It would definitely be a solution. "But what if all he wants to do is go to sea?"

Turning around, Kristen's smile grew wider.

"Let him. He'll only go once and it won't be for long."

Serenity arched a brow in doubt. "What makes you so sure?"

"Do you see George here?" she asked.

"Your husband?"

"Yes. He loved the sea as much, if not more than Morgan. He swore I'd never keep him dry-docked." Kristen looked more than pleased with herself. "Well, three months after we married, he headed out. Any idea for how long?"

Serenity shook her head.

"Two days." Kristen held up two fingers to emphasize her words. "Two days, and he ran back swearing he'd never leave me again."

"But he's not here now."

"True," Kristen admitted. "But had I so much as poked out my bottom lip, he wouldn't have left. In fact, I had to beg and threaten him to before he would go."

All this sounded good to Serenity. Imagine taming a pirate! Wrapping Morgan so tightly about her finger that he would never want to leave her. Oh, she definitely liked the sound of that.

But it just seemed to good to be true.

Did she dare trust Kristen?

On the other hand, Kristen had known Morgan a long time, and in the short time Serenity had known the young woman, Kristen had realized truths about her that stunned her. Kristen was definitely observant. And she knew how to read people.

If anyone could be right about Morgan other than Morgan, it would probably be Kristen.

Lord, what if she failed?

"I don't know, Kristen."

Kristen shrugged. "All right. Then, think about it. But do it quickly. Time isn't on your side."

Chapter 15

Serenity wondered if listening to Kristen was the wisest thing to do. For nearly an hour Kristen and her maid had pinched, pulled, and plucked until they had finally approved Serenity's appearance. She felt more like the Christmas goose than a woman.

Still, she was pleased with the results. They had actually managed to give her a becoming hairstyle that curled around her face and shoulders, showing off her hair. The light blue dress was every bit as kind to her eye color as Kristen had predicted.

"Just wait until Morgan gets a look at you," Kristen had whispered in her ear before they had descended the steps.

Even so, her heart had been in her throat the entire way down the winding staircase.

Pausing in the doorway of the drawing room, she saw Jake first. He was talking to Robert. Morgan had his back to her.

Somewhat disappointed, she followed Kristen

to where her mother waited for them on the stuffed sofa. "My, Miss James, aren't you the fetching one," said Martha. "Why, Robert," she called to her husband. "I do believe we'll have to keep Miss James as far away from the townsmen as possible."

Serenity blushed at her kind words.

Morgan turned in her direction with his usual composure. But once his eyes focused on her, they grew larger, then seductive as a slow, appreciative smile curved his lips. Chills shot through her. Never in her life had she received such a wonderful compliment.

"Well then," Martha declared. "I believe we are all ready to sup."

And by the look in his eyes, Serenity already knew what Morgan wanted to feast on. A thought that thrilled her even more.

Maybe Kristen was right.

Maybe, just maybe, she would listen to her newfound friend. Because if Kristen knew anything at all about men, then she knew one hundred times what Serenity knew.

Dinner was lovely. The dining room was as grand as the rest of the house. Two crystal and gold chandeliers hung over the long mahogany table on each side of an enormous fan that was set in motion by a chain pulled by a crisply dressed servant.

Martha had broken out her best china, silver, and crystal goblets. Never in her life had Serenity beheld such splendor. And the meal—gracious, not even the Christmas bounty could compare with the meal before her.

Stuffed goose, roasted pork, candied fruits, and meat pastries were served with great flair.

She listened quietly as the men told their sea stories. Morgan sat at the opposite end of the table from her, to Robert's right, while Jake sat to his left with Barney by his side. Two seats were vacant, and then she, Martha, and Kristen sat at the opposite end.

"I know the seating is a little unorthodox," Martha said as she placed a serving spoon full of gravy on her plate. "But I thought the men might enjoy more time together to reminisce."

Embarrassed that her thoughts were so plain, Serenity fiddled with the napkin in her lap. "You needn't explain to me."

"Try the goose, Serenity," Kristen offered as the servant brought the platter to her side. "It's Carmen's best dish. You've never tasted goose until you've had hers."

"Thank you," she said with a smile, taking a few slices. "I'm sure it's wonderful."

There were several seconds of silence before Martha spoke again. "Morgan tells me you're a writer?"

Serenity lifted her head with pride. "Yes, ma'am."

"What a noble profession. I've never met a writer before. It must be difficult for you though, being a woman."

"It's certainly not easy." She cast a glance down to where Morgan sat and noted that he was staring at her. Swallowing, she quickly looked back at Kristen, who gave her a knowing smile.

"I always wanted the courage it would take to make the world stand on its ear," Martha continued. "To make men appreciate me for something more than my looks."

"Oh, Mama, Papa loves you for more than your looks."

"Now he does, but it took thirty years of marriage and an aging body before he saw me as something more."

"Oh, Mama."

"So tell me, Serenity, have you ever read Mary Wollstonecraft?"

"Avidly."

"Scandalous!" Martha cried. "She writes the most scandalous things I've ever seen. But between us, I admire her views, especially on the education of women. Why, I only learned to read by raw determination. I remember my father tanning my backside when I was thirteen because he caught me reading. Like many men, he thought book learning would fill my head with the devil's notions."

And so the dinner passed with Martha's enthusiasm and Kristen's humorous cries of alarm, and Morgan passing looks to her.

When they had finally finished dessert, the men headed back toward Robert's study, and Martha started leading the women toward the drawing room.

"Serenity?"

Serenity paused at the sound of Morgan's voice. "Yes, Captain?"

He walked toward her with a masculine swagger that made her breathless. The candlelight played in his eyes, making them dark and shiny. There was an amused tint to them as well, one that was beguiling and warm. "I was wondering if we might have a walk outside in the garden. It's a pleasant night."

She lowered her voice to keep Martha or Kristen from overhearing her. "I remember what happened the last time it was a pleasant night, and I allowed myself to be alone with you."

He gave her a devilish grin. "I promise it won't happen again. I shall be on my best behavior."

Then he leaned closer and whispered in her ear. "Unless you *wish* for it to happen again. In that case, far be it from me to disappoint a lady."

Her heart pounded. Part of her was delighted by

his words and the knowledge that he did in fact want her.

Still, it was improper for her to encourage him. "You're a sly one, Captain Drake. And you're certainly mistaken if you think you can get me where you want me. I dance to no man's tune. Most especially not yours."

He covered his chest with his hand and feigned a wound. "I've been cut down, my lady. Now and in the prime of my life. You have fatally wounded me with your words." His grin returned, just as wicked as before. "But tell me, what would it take for you to join me in the garden?"

He looked past her to where Kristen and Martha waited. "Tell her, Kristen," he said, raising his voice to where they could hear. "She'll be safe with me for a few minutes. You know yourself what an honorable man I am."

Kristen laughed. "You mean a cad. Aye, I know all too well what a cad you are, Morgan Drake." She approached them. "Go ahead, Serenity. Mama and I will leave the doors open. If he so much as kisses your cheek, just gasp and we'll come running."

Morgan directed a warning glare Kristen's way. "Shall we?"

He held his arm out to Serenity, and before she could stop herself, she tucked her hand in the crook of his arm and allowed him to lead her outside.

It really was a beautiful night, she thought as she looked around the carefully manicured garden. Roses and ivy were entwined around trellises set off by tall hedges and carved marble benches. Kristen had told her earlier that this garden was Martha's pride and joy, and it showed in every aspect of the carefully planned and tended area.

A soft breeze caressed her cheeks as she turned to face Morgan. "So what is it you wished to talk to me about?" she asked.

He looked away for a second, as if collecting his thoughts. When he spoke, his voice was deep, thick. "I was thinking that maybe you shouldn't buy passage on that colonial ship. You have no idea what kind of captain is in charge."

Her heart soared at his words.

Could he possibly be saying what she wanted him to say?

Dare she even hope it?

"Are you asking me to stay with you?"

"No," he said so fast that it brought an ache to her chest. So much for her wants.

At the moment, she wanted to strangle Kristen for encouraging her!

"I wasn't saying that at all," Morgan continued, dashing all her hopes with each word. "I just think that you should think twice—"

"Think twice before what?" she asked, her voice sharp and edged.

Who was he to dictate to her? He didn't even want her around!

"Think twice," she continued, "before I head off in the middle of a night on a ship full of men who can't be trusted? Hmm, where have I seen this scenario before? At least I know the captain of the new ship isn't a pirate, wanted by—how many governments?"

"Just two, but that's not the point."

"Then what is the point?"

Morgan bristled at her tone and the way she kept twisting his words around. Making him say things he wanted to say, but didn't want her to hear. "Where did you get the money to buy passage anyway?"

"I don't see how that's any of your business."

"Everything about you is my business."

Her mouth dropped and she looked at him incredulously. "How do you figure that?"

"I got you into this and—"

"I believe I am the one who got me into this, and therefore I should be the one to get myself out."

"Yes, but as a man it is my duty—"

"Oh, please," she said, throwing her hands up, "must we have this tiff again?"

Torn between the desire on one hand to kiss her, and on the other to strangle her, Morgan chuckled. She was a challenge, most definitely.

But that was one of the things he liked most about her. With a woman like her, a man would never be bored. "Can we ever have a moment when we're not arguing?"

Serenity smiled and reached out to carefully pluck a yellow rose from a nearby bush. He watched as she gently stroked the delicate petals between her fingers and the moonlight played against her profile. "We do seem to do that a lot, don't we?" she said.

"Yes, yes we do." Morgan became quiet while he tried to think of some way to keep her on board his ship. Some way she wouldn't find arguable.

Then it occurred to him. "You know, if you let me take you home, I'll teach you how to be a sailor."

She sighed and sat down on one of the marbled benches. "I no longer wish to be sailor, and I promised you I wouldn't write any stories about you, Jake, or your crew. All I want is to go home."

He walked over to where she sat, her arms braced on each side of her.

"But why?" he asked, looking down at her as she dipped her head to study her feet. "Surely you know what waits for you back there. The gossips, the—"

"I know," she interrupted, her voice filled with pain. "I know firsthand how vicious people can be." She looked up at him with the moonlight sparkling in her eyes. He saw her soul there. A soul of need, of longing.

And he wondered what he could do to ease the pain that flickered in the center of her cobalt eyes.

"I have to go home sometime," she whispered. "The longer I'm gone, the harder it will be for me to return."

He wanted to argue with her, wanted to know what words would make her stay with him, but for his life he couldn't think of a single one.

Hell, he wasn't even sure why he did want her to stay. Only that if she left, he knew it would give him more agony than he wanted to experience.

Sitting down next to her, Morgan gently cupped her face in his hands. She was so beautiful in the moonlight with the shadows and light playing across her face. Her light eyes were shining, and he would give anything to stay like this with her.

"Are you going to kiss me, Captain Drake?" she asked in the same forthright manner he'd come to expect from her.

"And if I said yes?"

"I would remind you of your promise."

"Is that what you want me to do? To walk away?"

Serenity swallowed at his tone, at the longing she saw reflected in his eyes.

Was it there, or was it just her desire for him to want her that she saw?

"No," she answered honestly. "I don't want you to walk away."

She held her breath, half-afraid he would indeed release her. Instead he leaned forward.

She parted her lips.

"Captain Drake!"

She felt his hands tense a moment before he pulled back and glared at Kristen, who approached them. He lowered his hands from her face.

"What?" he snarled.

Kristen blinked her widened eyes and lifted her brows. "Don't yell at me, *Mister* Drake. You're the one who wanted to know as soon as the carpenter came. I'm merely following *your* orders."

"What the devil is the man doing here at this hour?" Calming, Morgan sighed before looking back at her. "Another time, Serenity?"

She barely nodded before he walked away.

Kristen approached her like a cat stalking a mouse. "Rule number three, *always* leave him wanting more."

"Excuse me?"

Kristen inclined her head toward the direction Morgan had gone. "Give me your decision, Miss James. Do we bring the good captain under your heel, or do you return home on the colonial ship?"

It must be the full moon, Serenity decided, because right then with the heat of his touch still burning her skin, she made the decision her heart cried out for.

"All right, Kristen. What do we need to do?"

Chapter 16

Unleashing Kristen was like turning loose a cyclone. Serenity wondered what she'd done to deserve all this!

The two of them spent the next morning in the drawing room, with Kristen tutoring Serenity on what Kristen considered the fine art of coquetry.

And what Serenity dubbed the fine art of foolishness.

Really, Serenity wondered, who had thought up all these ridiculous mannerisms and flirtations? And were men really so gullible?

Biting her lips, Serenity realized that yes, men really were that gullible.

"Now, stand up straight, Serenity," Kristen ordered, pulling her shoulders back. Kristen walked around her. "Lower your eyelids. No," she snapped suddenly, "don't close them, just lower them a little . . . perfect."

"I can barely see."

Kristen shrugged. "You're not walking through

a nest full of vipers where you need to know where you're going. You're trying to steal a heart. Remember, love is blind."

"So am I when I hold my eyes like this."

"Serenity."

"Forgive me."

So the morning went, with Kristen showing her how to walk, speak, and perform all the other odd mannerisms Serenity had never mastered.

"Now for the best part!" Kristen warned, and Serenity gulped in apprehension. After all the bizarre and uncomfortable things Kristen had shown her, she shuddered to think what new torture Kristen was about to employ.

"What?" Serenity asked apprehensively.

"It's time to learn the fatal stoop."

"The what?" Serenity asked with a frown.

"The fatal stoop," Kristen repeated. "It's guaranteed to bring a man to his knees."

Serenity pursed her lips. "It sounds dangerous. What am I supposed to do, knock him over the head with something?"

Kristen rolled her eyes. She grabbed an apple out of the silver bowl on the table that was set just inside the French doors.

She dropped the apple on the floor. "Pick that up."

Serenity did, and all she got out of Kristen was a sharp *tsk*.

"Now watch me." She dropped another apple. "Oh my, look what I've done," she declared in an exaggeratedly sweet voice.

"Now," Kristen said in a normal tone, "this is where he'll stoop to retrieve it. And you must make sure to stoop at the same moment."

"Why?"

She smiled. "Pretend you're Morgan for a moment and I'll show you. Go on," she urged, "pick up the apple."

As soon as Serenity bent after it, Kristen was there in her face.

Well, rather, Kristen's ample bosom was right in her face. And from where Serenity was, she had more than just a little glimpse of Kristen's cleavage.

Heat flooded her cheeks.

"Oh, that's ridiculous," Serenity said. "I couldn't possibly do—" she hurriedly moved the apple back and forth between her own breasts—"that. Besides, he would know that I did it on purpose."

Kristen shook her head. "Honey, I assure you, that man won't *think* a thing. His mind will be on other matters. You could chop off his head and he wouldn't notice."

Serenity laughed. "We shouldn't be talking about this. It isn't proper."

"Well," Kristen said saucily as she wiped the apple against her sash. "You know what I have to

say, proper has its place, but it sure doesn't warm
your bed."

Ignoring Serenity's gasp, Kristen tossed the apple into the air and caught it. "Now back to our
lesson. After he gives back the apple, or whatever
you drop, make sure you keep his attention on
your body by taking the object and trailing it
across your décolleté." Kristen demonstrated by
rubbing the apple across the tops of her breasts.

"But I don't have a dé—"

"You will tonight."

Later that afternoon they were in Kristen's bedroom, where they had picked out a gown for that
evening. Now Serenity sat at the vanity while
Kristen experimented with her hair.

Dutifully Serenity listened to Kristen's instruc-
tions for her dinner behavior, wondering how she
could ever remember all of them.

However, the worst idea was yet to come.

As soon as Kristen's eyes darkened and she put
on an impish smile, Serenity knew she was in for it.

Kristen drew Serenity's hair up into a topknot.
"You know, what we need to cinch this tight is
competition."

Serenity just looked at Kristen in the mirror.
"Competition?"

"Yes," she said as she added a few hairpins.
"We need to get you a man."

"I thought that's what we were trying to do."

"Well, yes," Kristen said, fluffing hair around Serenity's face. "But we need a man other than Morgan. Nothing makes a man want a woman more than when he thinks another man is interested."

Was that true?

Serenity didn't know for sure, but by the light in Kristen's eyes, she could tell her friend definitely believed it.

Not that it mattered. There was no other man interested in Serenity. No man other than Hopping Hands Charlie had ever been interested in her.

"Well, we'll have to forgo that, since—"

"Actually," Kristen said, picking up the brush and looking at Serenity in the mirror. "I know someone who will have Morgan stewing in his jealousy. Someone absolutely perfect for the role. Someone who owes me a favor and would..." She screwed up her face in thought for several seconds.

Finally Kristen shook her head and looked at Serenity determinedly. "I'm sure I could convince him to do it."

Serenity was skeptical, but she agreed to follow Kristen into what turned out to be a wonderful excursion.

They rode into town in an open carriage so that Serenity could see just how beautiful the island was.

It wasn't far to the small village, which was a model of efficiency. It held all the shops needed for a thriving community—butcher, baker, smithy, and more.

Serenity was amazed at how charming the place was. Shops had been built up, much akin to the style of Savannah or Charleston. Women dressed in modest fashions like hers and Kristen's, of elbow-length sleeves and light cotton, blended in with the shameless daring clothes of the island women who wore short skirts and bared their arms.

But all that faded from her thoughts as Kristen led her into the smithy.

Serenity stopped in the doorway, momentarily stunned.

The smith stood before his forge with his bare back to them as he pounded a piece of iron with a huge hammer.

Never in her life had she seen the like.

Long blond hair was pulled back into a queue that hung between tanned muscles, which bulged and flexed while he struck a piece of red-hot metal with his hammer. His entire body glistened with sweat.

"Stanley!" Kristen shouted.

The smith paused and glanced over his shoulder. A slow smile spread across his face. "Kristen, my love," he said before burying the metal piece back into the coals. He placed the tongs in a bucket of water and pulled his large leather gloves from his hands.

"Oh, my...goodness!" Serenity whispered.

He was gorgeous. Incredibly gorgeous.

His chest bare, she could see every well-defined, bulging muscle and vein. He looked like some half-naked mythic god emerging from battle.

Not even what she'd seen of his back had prepared her for coming face-to-face with this perfect piece of maleness.

He had a beautiful face with laughing blue eyes and wide dimples that cut deep moons into his cheeks.

"Stanley," Kristen said as if immune to his looks. "I'd like for you to meet a friend of mine. Serenity James. Serenity, this is Stanley Fairhope, the most handsome man ever born."

Stanley gave a charming smile that showed off his two huge dimples. "And still it wasn't enough to get you to marry me," he said with a wounded sigh. "Why, you would never even allow me to call on you."

Kristen rolled her eyes.

Stanley turned to Serenity. "It's nice to meet you, Miss James."

Serenity couldn't speak.

His smile grew wider. "Take your time. Women do that a lot around me."

He glanced back to Kristen. "Except for that one. I never could get more than a ho-hum out of her."

"As if *I* would add to your overgrown ego. Besides, I know the real you, and you're not half as charming as you think you are."

He snorted. "Do you talk to your husband this way?"

"Absolutely. It's why George married me and it's why *you* can't forget me."

He shook his head. "I know you didn't come all this way to pester me. Nor did you bother me for a friendly visit. Tell me, squirt, what's the latest scheme you're going to try and get me to take part in?"

Kristen grinned like the cat about to take the cream. Joining her hands behind her back, she rocked back and forth on her feet. "Very well, Stanley. I want you to court Serenity."

His stunned look was almost comical, but at least it gave Serenity back her tongue.

"This is ridiculous, Kristen. Morgan would never believe that this man would be interested in me."

Stanley cocked an eyebrow. "Morgan Drake?"

"You know him?" they asked in unison.

"Aye, I owe the man my life. I was on board the first English ship he attacked as a pirate."

Serenity frowned. "Then how is it you owe him your life? I thought he took no prisoners."

"No, ma'am, that's not true. He whipped the English like the dogs they were, but he was kind to the rest of us who had been forced to serve them. Brought some of us here, while some stayed on board and became part of his crew."

"Oh, drats," Kristen's aggravated voice intruded. "Then he would know who you are. It'll never work now."

"Nay," Stanley corrected. "I doubt he'd remember me. It's been at least eleven years. I was only fourteen and he wasn't much older."

Her face brightened. "Oh, good. Then he'll have no idea who you are."

"I doubt it."

"Well then, fair Stanley, I dub thee Captain Fairhope of the *Sea Princess* bound for Charleston."

"Excuse me?"

"Tonight, you'll be a colonial captain who is instantly attracted to our Miss James," Kristen said, sweeping her arm toward Serenity in a theatrical move. "A captain who will try and get her to join him on his way home."

He frowned. "Why?"

"Because our good Morgan Drake is in love with her, but he refuses to admit it."

Stanley gave a most undignified snort. "You're not about to drag me into the middle of this. I'll not do anything to hurt Captain Drake."

Kristen sidled up to Stanley and folded her

hands into a steeple up under her chin. She looked up at Stanley from under her lashes, and Serenity watched in awe as Kristen wound the man around her finger.

Indeed, the mesmerized Stanley watched every move Kristen made like a starving man eyeing a feast.

"I'm not asking you to hurt him," Kristen purred as she traced one finger down the length of his bulging biceps. She flicked her finger off his forearm. "I'm asking you to *trick* him."

Blinking as if he just woke up, Stanley gave her a doubting glare. "Only a woman would see that as a difference."

Kristen made a grand showing of folding her arms over her chest and narrowing her gaze on him. "Correct me if I'm wrong, but didn't someone whose name I won't mention try to tell George that I swore I'd never marry a sailor?"

Stanley stiffened. His jaw turned to steel. "You did say that."

"Be that as it may, you did try to trick him into leaving me, did you not?"

"That was different."

"Why?"

"All's fair when it comes to love," he said.

"And this is love. For Morgan and Serenity."

He looked askance at Kristen. "Are you sure?"

"Never been more positive."

"All right," he said with a sigh. "For you, chick-pea. I'll do it. But you owe me."

Kristen's smile grew wider. "I'll have your suit delivered to you. I believe my maid knows where to borrow one."

Kristen looped her arm through Serenity's. "Come, fair maiden, we must now add more spice to the pot."

Chapter 17

Morgan had no idea what he was in for that night. He'd spent most of the day with carpenters, trying to make repairs to his ship. But if the truth were known, all he really wanted was to see Serenity.

He missed her lively, infuriating conversation almost as much as he missed her presence. He couldn't imagine what she'd found on the island to keep her amused. In truth, he'd half expected to see her on board his ship, trying to take the hammers from the carpenters and make the repairs herself. Or join the boatswains who were repairing the sails.

But that hadn't happened.

Well, the last thing you need is her poking her head in while you've got a ship to repair. You've got impressed sailors to free, that's where your thoughts should be, not on the doings of some virginal miss.

Tightening his cravat, he promised himself to

put her out of his thoughts. She would be going home soon and he'd never again have to worry about his sails, or confront frilly underthings in his cabin.

He was glad of it, too.

Really, he was.

"Morgan!"

He paused at the dock as he heard Jake's voice. His friend sprinted to catch up to him. "Please give my apologies to Martha. I'll be late to dinner."

"What are you doing?"

"I'm trying to find positions for Hayes's crew in town. About half of them are through with the sea. And I'm..." His voice trailed off and Jake looked out at the sea with a wistful gaze.

"What?" Morgan asked, wondering what thought had cost Jake his tongue.

"Well, I was thinking that I'd be heading back on the ship for Charleston."

Morgan nodded. He would be sad to see Jake go, but he understood. "You're going back to Lorelei?"

"Don't start—" Jake snapped, his voice full of warning.

Morgan held his hand up in silent surrender. "I'm not."

"All right, then," he said, slapping Morgan on the back. "I'll see you up at the house later."

Morgan turned around and headed for the stable where he'd rented a horse. For the first time he actually understood Jake's impatience. He himself couldn't wait to see Serenity.

It had been a long, long day and all he wanted to do was share it with her. She'd get a good laugh out of Barney's bird attacking one of the carpenters when he made the mistake of hammering too close to Barney's room.

Aye, and the fight Cookie and Kit got into over the last roll.

And he desperately wanted to hear her laughter.

With that thought, he set his heels into the horse's flanks and took off for Robert's home.

It seemed forever had passed on a snail's shoulders before he entered the yard. He paused just outside and wandered into the garden.

Serenity liked flowers. He vividly recalled the way she looked holding the rose.

As carefully as he could, he picked her a rose bouquet. Aye, this would bring a smile to her lips, and maybe a little warmth to her heart.

Holding that hope close, he went back to the front door and entered the house. He swept his hat off his head and handed it to the waiting servant.

The first sound he heard was the laugh he sought. It rang out, reaching deep inside him.

She would be in the drawing room on his left. Heading that way, he halted in the doorway.

Serenity sat on the settee, wearing a breathtaking gown of white satin trimmed in lace. Her bodice had been cut dangerously low, showing off the tops of well-rounded breasts he longed to sample. The entire length of her chestnut hair had been swept up into a beautiful style that exposed the creamy smooth skin of her neck.

His mouth watered.

Her face was bright, and she reached one graceful hand over to pat...

To pat the arm of the *man* by her side!

The smile faded from his lips.

His eyes narrowed.

Who was this interloper who dared intrude on his...

Your what?

Territory?

He balked at the thought. She wasn't his territory. She wasn't his anything. He had no right to her, yet watching her laugh with another man made him furious enough to punch the fellow in his arrogant face.

Yes, his face was arrogant. His shoulders too broad. And his pants, they were cut so close that they were obscene! Who did he think he was, wearing breeches cropped like that in mixed company?

Morgan squelched the voice in his head that reminded him the pants fit about the same as his own.

That was entirely different.

"Morgan," Martha greeted him with a smile. "Are those for me?"

Well, two could play Serenity's game. He bristled under Martha's too-direct gaze and handed her Serenity's flowers. "Why yes, yes they are."

Martha took them from his hand and gave them to the waiting servant. "Why don't you come in and meet Captain Stanley Fairhope."

There was a twinkle in Martha's eyes, and if Morgan didn't know better, he'd suspect her of some sort of foul play. But that was ridiculous. Martha, unlike Kristen or Serenity, was level-headed and trustworthy.

The so-called captain and Serenity rose to their feet, and Morgan didn't miss the fact that the man's hand lingered on her elbow.

Nor the fact that the imbecile's gaze kept drifting to her cleavage.

He inclined his head to Captain Fathead. "Captain Fairley," he said, his voice deep and strong as he battled the urge to rip the man's eyes out.

At least the fellow had the God-given sense to remove his hand from Serenity's elbow.

"My name is Fair*hope*," he said, flashing a pair of those dimple things that were appealing in a woman, but looked ridiculous on any man.

This man was definitely a fop. Only a fop would have dimples.

Kristen offered Morgan a drink. After he declined, she returned it to the servant's tray, then moved to stand beside Serenity.

"I've heard so many things about you, Captain Drake," Fairhope said. "Allow me to shake the hand of the man who defeated Wayward Hayes."

So, the interloper thought he could pander to him. No chance, that.

Reluctantly Morgan extended his hand. "I heard from a couple of sailors you had a run-in with pirates on your way here."

A light of humor sparkled in Captain Fathead's eyes. "Why yes, as a matter of fact I did. Devilish beasts, those pirates. Why, some good captain should obliterate each and every one of those repellent—"

"Captain Fairhope . . ." Kristen began, interrupting the man's idiotic tirade and looking meaningfully at Morgan, "has graciously agreed to escort Serenity home personally to her family's door."

Now he truly hated the man.

Graciously offered, indeed. He had little doubt about what motivated the man to make such an offer.

Well, no one was going to lay a hand on his Serenity.

Not without a fight.

"How nice of you, Fairley," Morgan ground out. "But I have already made that offer."

"Yes, and I told you no," Serenity said.

She linked arms with Stanhope, or whatever his name was. "I'd hate to be a burden to anyone, but the good captain here has made such a compelling case that—"

"She'll attempt to take over your crew," Morgan blurted out like an imbecile.

The man gave a milksop smile to Serenity. "Fine then, she's already taken over my heart."

Serenity blushed.

Had her cheeks always been that rosy?

Her smile so stunning?

"Why, Stanley," Serenity cooed, "you say the most scandalous things."

Morgan saw red. How dare she speak to that man like that.

He wanted blood. Captain Fathead's blood.

Stanhope Fairley looked offended.

Good. Let her shred him the same way she shredded Morgan. That would teach him not to trespass on a man's woman.

"Miss James," he said in a breathless voice, "I assure you, I'm most committed to you. Would you have me declare my feelings for the benefit of all?"

Serenity stepped back with a frown. "Excuse me?"

Fairhope looked positively moonstruck. "I mean what I say, Miss James." He took her by both hands and knelt upon one knee before her. "I wish for you to marry me."

Her eyes widened and her mouth flexed.

Morgan waited, knowing his little vexation wouldn't disappoint him.

Aye, she would send the interloper packing with a few choice insults. His little vixen wouldn't tolerate such ridiculous stupidity.

"Captain, I don't know what to say."

"Well, you've never been at a loss for words before," Morgan snapped before he could stop himself.

Serenity turned to face him with eyes of fire. "Fine then. Captain Stanley Fairhope, I accept your offer."

"You what!" Morgan roared.

The fop stood, holding her hand like some treasured object against his chest. He stroked her wrist. "Miss James, you've made me the happiest man in the world. I knew the moment I saw you that you were the only woman for me."

"He's a fop!" Morgan snapped. "You can't marry a fop. Why, you're more of a man than he is."

The room fell as silent as a crypt.

It was only then that Morgan realized what he'd said.

Serenity's face turned the color of a bright cherry an instant before she let him have her wrath fully. "Just who do you think you are, Morgan Drake? How dare you say such a thing to me! You don't own me, you don't even want me. All you've done is cry out what a burden I am to you, and now that I've found someone who can make me happy, you dare stand there and make insults. You're vile, Captain. Loathsome. But then, I suppose I'll forgive you your rudeness, since you're only being yourself."

Enraged to the point of murder, Morgan looked at Fairhead. "See!" he said in triumph. "Generally speaking, she's always generally speaking."

He should have taken warning the moment he saw her eyes narrow, but he didn't.

Instead, he blurted out, "Do you really want to spend the rest of your life with *that*?"

Her shriek of outrage could have splintered glass. As it was, it made an indelible impact on his eardrums.

"If I *were* a man, I'd call you out," she snapped before gathering her skirts and storming from the room.

And it was only then that Morgan realized he'd seen tears starting in her eyes.

Tears, he thought, momentarily stunned. From Serenity? Surely he was wrong.

"You are a pig, Morgan Drake," Kristen said, rounding the settee to stand before him. She looked at him as if he were the vilest creature alive. "I'm ashamed to have ever called you brother."

Before Morgan could respond, Robert and Jake entered the room.

Robert paused an instant and stared at Fathead. "Stanley? Why on earth are you wearing that getup?"

Color stained the man's cheeks.

Suddenly everything became clear. Serenity's dress and acquiescence. Fathead's declaration of love.

Kristen's manipulative personality.

The look in Martha's eyes...

"You mean he's not a captain?" Morgan asked.

"No," Robert answered. "He's the local smith."

"Kristen!" Morgan bellowed, moving toward her.

With a squeak, she ran from the room.

"Congratulations, Captain Drake," Fairhead said with a snide grin. "You've managed to clear the room."

Morgan turned on the menace who had ruined

his night. "At least I wasn't a dupe for a knotty-pated scheme."

"No," Fairhead said, picking an imaginary piece of lint off his cuff. He looked up at Morgan, his glare hostile. "You were a royal jackass. Between the two, I think I'd much rather play the dupe."

Serenity maliciously pulled the pearl-tipped pins from her hair, taking comfort in the pain as she walked through the garden with no destination in mind. She just needed to get away. Be alone for a while until she could assuage the wounds of her heart.

"This was so stupid," she snapped, wiping angrily at the tears on her cheeks. "You knew he didn't care for you. You should have never listened to Kristen."

Hurt beyond her heart's tolerance, Serenity reached into the pocket of her dress trying to find a kerchief.

Of course one wasn't there.

"Oh, bother anyway," she sobbed, wiping her face with her hand.

"Here."

She froze at the sound of Morgan's deep timbre. He stepped out of the shadows with a crisp linen kerchief dangling from his right hand.

"What do you want?" she asked, her voice harsh. "Haven't you insulted me enough?"

Taking the extended cloth, she dabbed her eyes.

Morgan cleared his throat and looked away as if embarrassed. "I never meant to hurt you."

"Well then, if you do this much damage unintentionally, I hope to goodness you never set out for harm."

He reached for her. "Serenity . . ."

"Go away!"

Morgan took a step back and stopped. He couldn't leave her like this. She looked so frail in the moonlight with her white satin dress and her hair hanging about her shoulders in delicate curls. She'd laced her dress up tightly and worn a corset that lifted her breasts high. She wasn't as endowed as the women who typically drew his notice, yet he found her figure breathtaking.

Delectable.

Had she done all this just for him?

In one way, he was flattered. In another way, he wanted to strangle her for putting him through the whole charade.

In one night she had turned him completely inside out. Had made Morgan Drake, pirate captain and man who knew the world and how to tame it, a babbling, bumbling jackass.

And for what?

Because she'd dared touch another man?

He flinched. That was ridiculous. What did he care if she touched someone else?

What did he care if she *did* run off with Fathead?

But the truth was, he did care.

He couldn't deny it. The truth stood before him, just like the stone wall of the garden.

It was then he realized he loved her.

He felt as though he'd been struck.

Nay, he argued, he couldn't possibly. She pushed him to the brink of murder. He couldn't love a woman who delighted in tormenting him.

And yet he did.

He loved the challenge of her. Matching wits against a woman who could hold her own.

He loved her intrepid spirit.

He loved her lips, her humor, and especially the look she got in her eyes right before she started one of her infamous tirades.

Part of him wanted to cry it out, but for his life he couldn't bring a single word past his lips.

Nay, he was a man of action, not words. He would show her his love.

He scooped her up in his arms and headed toward the stable.

"What are you doing?" she gasped.

"What I should have done a long time ago."

Serenity stiffened in his arms. "Where are you taking me?"

"To my ship."

"Why?"

"Because that's where I want you."

Morgan stared at her as they entered the stable and he headed toward his horse. The look he loved so very well darkened her eyes and he knew he was about to receive a scalding lecture.

"You, sir, don't—"

He stopped her words with a kiss.

She fought for just a moment and then surrendered to him. Morgan groaned in pleasure as she opened her lips and let him taste the sweetness of her mouth.

Aye, tonight she was his.

But not in a stable.

After setting her down, he reached for his horse. He didn't even bother to saddle the stallion. Instead, he quickly bridled the horse, then swung himself up.

He leaned down over the horse's back and extended his hand. "Come with me, Serenity."

He held his breath in expectation of her answer.

Serenity hesitated. She knew what he wanted. Had listened to Kristen go on at great lengths about what happened between a man and a woman.

If she went with him, she would be forever changed.

Nay, she corrected herself. She was already forever changed. He'd already shown her things she never thought she'd see. Made her feel things she'd never known existed, and there was only one thing left.

Walk away, Serenity.

But she couldn't. Let the gossips hound her forever. Tonight there would be no shame. Tonight there would be only them.

Swallowing the fear in her throat, she reached her hand out to him.

Chapter 18

Morgan wanted to shout in triumph as Serenity's soft hand closed around his. She felt like warm velvet and smelled of delicate roses and night mist.

Without hesitation he pulled her up in front of him and set his heels to the horse.

At long last, she was his. This was a night he would savor like no other.

A woman he would savor like no other.

Serenity sighed as she leaned her head back against him and listened to his heart race beneath her cheek. The sweet ocean air mingled with the scent of Morgan, and she felt as helpless against him as a damsel confronting a dragon.

His arms held her close while the horse thundered across the beach, raising water in their wake. High overhead hung a full moon that cast mystical shadows against Morgan's face.

He was beautiful, her pirate. And for this one night, he would belong to her and her alone.

The nagging voice in her head warned that to-morrow would separate them.

But she didn't listen. She would deal with that on the morrow.

Tonight she would listen to her heart. Her heart that wanted him more than it had ever wanted anything.

When they reached the small rowboat, Serenity giggled.

"What?" he asked, reining the horse to a stop.

"You're certainly going to a lot of trouble."

His face serious, he stared down at her. "You're worth every bit of it."

"That's not what you told Stanley."

He slid to the ground, then pulled her from the horse. His hands bit into her waist as he slowly slid her down the front of him.

Her body burned in response, tingled all over.

His look was dark and deadly. "I don't *ever* want to hear another man's name on your lips."

"But Stan—"

Again he kissed her.

Serenity smiled while they kissed. She had just learned a trick. Say Stanley's name and Morgan would kiss it away.

She filed that away in the back of her mind. It could definitely come in handy.

With a groan, Morgan tore away from her lips and carried her to the rowboat. He set her carefully down before setting it adrift, jumping in and picking up the oars.

"This is the longest trip of my life," he murmured.

She laughed at the desperate note in his voice. Her body throbbed from her longing and she watched his muscles ripple as he began rowing them out to his ship.

Moonlight danced across his face, shadowing his eyes. Even so, she could feel him looking at her. It made her body even hotter.

Morgan stared at her and listened to the magic of her laughter. With her dress tucked primly around her and her hair in wild abandon, she looked like some captured nymph. A nymph he would devour fully before this night ended.

He rowed faster.

When he reached the boat, he carefully helped her climb the ladder to the deck. And this time, he enjoyed the sight of her garters and other underthings as they swayed above his head and undulated in a rhythm that made him ache all over. Soon he would taste that part of her.

He couldn't wait.

He helped her over the side, then swung his legs over.

Ushakii came out of the corner of the poop deck, where he'd been posted to watch over the ship. "Who goes there?"

"Captain Drake." He swept Serenity back up into his arms.

"Welcome aboard, Captain, Miss James," Ushakii called, then returned to his post.

"You can put me down, Morgan," Serenity said as he began carrying her across the deck.

He tightened his grip on her. "If I did that you might run away."

She trailed her fingernail down the length of his stubbly jaw, raising chills all over him. His shaft grew even harder, pulsing with his need.

"I have a feeling you would catch me," she said softly, her voice doing the most wicked things to his body.

"Be that as it may," he said in a ragged whisper, "I'd much rather have you where I want you than have to worry."

He carried her to his cabin.

He positioned her to his left, then opened the door.

Serenity smiled as they entered his cabin. It looked just as she remembered it, clean, cozy. And her lopsided curtains still hung where she'd placed them.

Embarrassed, Serenity averted her gaze and realized the door had also been repaired. "You fixed the door."

Without a word, he leaned back against it and closed it.

This time when his lips met hers, she could taste the passion, feel the heat of his longing.

He allowed her feet to slide to the floor, but her legs were so weak from his kiss that she could barely stand. Instead, she clung to him, needing to feel as close to his body as she could.

There was heaven in his touch, she'd known that since the first time he'd kissed her.

He brushed his hands through her hair. "You are so beautiful," he whispered against her ear.

Serenity smiled. It was the first time in her life a man had said that to her, and it was worth the wait to hear it from Morgan. Her pirate.

He dipped his head and pressed his lips against the skin of her breasts while his hands lifted her skirts from behind. His hands ran over her bare buttocks, pressing her hips closer to his so that she could feel just how swollen and ready he was for her.

Chills shot through her, and deep down her little voice told her this was wrong. They weren't married.

All her life she had been told to save herself for her husband. But at her age she knew that day would never come.

She wasn't a young miss waiting for her husband to deliver her. She was a woman full-grown whose heart had been stolen by a pirate.

And now she had a choice to make. Walk away

from him right now, virtue intact, or follow her heart where it led.

Tonight it led her to Morgan's arms, and that was exactly what she wanted. If this was to be her mistake, then let it. She'd been a dutiful, practical daughter all her life. For once she would do as she pleased and face the consequences, whatever they might be.

He moved his hands to the back of her gown and began unfastening the long row of buttons.

"Are you afraid?" he asked.

"Terrified," she answered honestly.

Morgan's gaze burned her with its intensity. "I won't hurt you."

Serenity bit her lip to stifle the comment that he already had; that he could only hurt her more tomorrow.

He'd been jealous over Stanley, there was no denying that. He might even, in his own way, love her. But he would never commit to her, and that knowledge cut her straight to her soul.

"Hold me," she whispered, needing to feel him close.

Suddenly she wanted to see him as vulnerable as she felt. With a boldness that astounded her, she unbuttoned his waistcoat and pulled his shirt free from his breeches. She tore his shirt off so fast that the cravat stayed wrapped about his neck. Morgan laughed before he untied it and added it to the growing pile of clothes on the floor.

His chest bare before her, she drank in the warm sight. His refined muscles rippled with every move he made. There was one jagged scar about three inches long that ran along one collarbone. Reaching out, she traced its path, her fingers brushing against his warm skin.

Morgan lifted her fingers and placed a gentle kiss on her palm. Serenity smiled at the tenderness in his eyes and sighed happily.

He trailed his kisses up her arm, bit by bit until he reached her throat. His lips were soft and firm as they played upon her flesh, raising chills and turning her will and body into mush.

Closing her eyes, she leaned her head back, savoring the feel of him, the scent of him.

He was a man like no other.

Morgan drank in her sweetness. Never in his life had he tasted anything better than the salt of her skin. She ran her hands over the flesh of his back, raising chills in their path.

Groaning, he picked her up one last time and carried her to the bed, where he carefully laid her down.

He stared at her, her hair spread out over his quilt. Never before had he taken a virgin, and if he admitted the truth, he was afraid.

He didn't want to hurt her. Didn't want to taint her, but there was no way he could walk away from her now.

He needed her as much as he needed to breathe.

He would deal with whatever repercussions on the morrow. Tonight there would only be them.

He removed his pants.

Serenity gulped at the sight of him. Her face flaming, she couldn't stop staring at his . . .

"It's huge!" she gasped before she could stop herself.

Morgan gave a low rumble of a laugh. "Only for you it is," he whispered, crawling onto the bed beside her.

He took her hand then and placed another kiss on her fingers before he led her hand down . . . there.

Serenity gulped at the hard velvety feel of him in her hand. Closing his eyes, he let out a half growl, half groan, and she reveled in her power over this man who feared nothing. Who answered to no one.

Bold from the knowledge, she moved her hand lower. Morgan sucked his breath in sharply. "Careful, Serenity. You keep that up and we'll both be disappointed."

With a wicked grin, he lay down on the bed and pulled her on top of him. He lifted her skirts until her bare belly touched against his hard hips. She moaned at the strange feel of him between her legs, of his short hairs teasing her nether parts.

She stared at his eyes, which glowed with a deep warmth, and ran her hands over his chest while he loosened her stays.

"Kiss me," he commanded.

Leaning forward over him, she let her hair fall around them, forming a canopy. Morgan nipped her lips as he removed her corset and chemise, and with one swipe over her head, her gown.

Serenity shivered as the cool night hair hit her skin. She was bare before him. Self-consciously she pulled back, covering her small breasts with her hands.

"Don't," he whispered. "Don't hide your body from me." He removed her hands and raised up. He covered her right breast with his lips, and chills shot the length of her body as he suckled her gently.

Heat tore through her body, pooling into an inferno between her legs. Instinctively she rubbed herself against his hardness. His shaft pressed against her core.

They moaned in unison.

Morgan pulled back and gave her a desperate look. "You've no idea how much I want to savor your body, but if I don't have you now, I swear I'll die from it."

She didn't understand what he meant.

He gave her a desperate kiss, before laying her

down against the bed. He ravaged her mouth as he separated her legs with his thigh.

Burying one hand in her hair, he ran his left hand down her body to the core of her aching. When he touched her at the apex of her thighs, her eyes flew open and she gasped until his fingers began a gentle assault on her body.

She couldn't stand the remembered pleasure. He plunged his finger deep inside her and whispered in her ear. "You feel so sweet," he murmured. "So tight and ready."

And then he slid into her. Serenity tensed at the unexpected feel of him inside her body.

"Did I hurt you?" he asked.

"No," she answered honestly.

He smiled and dipped his head down to nuzzle her breast. She moaned as he flicked his tongue first over her right breast and then her left. Without thought, she brought her legs up and wrapped them around his waist, plunging him deeper into her.

Morgan moaned as if in great pain.

Slowly he began to move against her hips. She bit her lip in pleasure. Never had she felt the like. He surrounded her and filled her.

With each thrust of his hips against hers, her pleasure built until she was sure she could stand no more, and still he continued his exquisite torture.

"Oh, Morgan," she gasped, running her hands

down his back, to his hips, to urge him faster and deeper into her.

Then just as she thought she would indeed die, her body burst again, just as it had done that night on deck. Serenity screamed out in release as her entire body shuddered and quivered.

A few seconds later, she heard Morgan groan and shudder over her.

They lay abed for hours, exploring each other's body.

For the first time since he could remember, Morgan felt sated. At peace.

There was no fear, no nagging regrets.

He shook his head and gave a short laugh.

Serenity lifted herself up on one elbow and stared down at him. "What?" she asked, her brows knitted.

Morgan reached up and rubbed away the crease in her brows. "I was just thinking that for the first time in my life I have serenity."

Her frown returned.

"Never mind," he said with a smile. "It was a stupid thought."

She looked as if she doubted his sanity. "Where did you get all the scars on your back?"

He brushed his hand through the soft tendrils of her hair and sighed. "They're a souvenir from my days in the navy."

"You'll never be able to forgive them, will you?"

Something inside him felt freed by her question. As if something had been trapped and her question had released whatever it was. Whatever happened, he no longer felt angry or vengeful. It was like he'd just let go of it all. Like none of it mattered anymore.

"Kiss me and I'll forgive them all."

Smiling, she leaned forward and obliged him.

Though it pained him, he pulled away from her. He pushed himself off the bed and held his arm out to her.

She offered him her hand and he pulled her from the bunk. "What are you doing?" she asked.

"Something I've dreamt of since I brought you on board." He led her across his room, to the open windows.

Serenity stared out at the moonlight rippling across the sea. The waves rolled in and out and the ship tilted in a sensuous rhythm of its own. Morgan came up behind her and placed her hands against the frame of the window, then he moved to stand behind her.

"Morgan?" she asked, her face flooding with heat. "What if someone should see?"

"No one can see us," he assured her. He swept her hair over her shoulder and nibbled against the flesh of her neck. "I want to take you, Serenity. Like this with us looking out at the sea."

"Morgan—"

"Sh," he whispered in her ear. "Listen to the music of the night. Of the waves and sea."

She did.

His arms came around her, covering her own, and he took her hands in his. He pressed himself tightly against her back and she could feel him growing against her buttocks. His warm laugh sounded in her ear.

"Say my name," he demanded.

"Why?"

"Because I want to hear it from your lips. I want to hear you tell me you need to feel me inside you again."

"But Morgan—"

His lips covered hers and he ran his hand over her bare breasts, teasing them with his fingers. Her body erupted, her breasts swelled with need.

And then he trailed his hand lower, down her stomach and back to the core of her.

Her body on fire, she pulled away from him long enough to whisper, "Now, Morgan, I want to feel you inside me now."

With a groan he tore himself from her lips and entered her from behind. Serenity gasped as he buried himself deep inside her, raising her to the tips of her toes.

And while he moved against her buttocks, his hand continued to play its magical harmony against her.

She moaned as he moved in and out, until he made one long deep thrust within her and paused.

"Show me, Serenity," he whispered in her ear. "Show me what you like."

At first she didn't understand him, but as his hand continued to tease her nether place, she knew what he wanted.

Morgan closed his eyes in sweet torture as she drew her body tight around him and slid down his shaft. Reaching the tip, she loosened herself and took him full again.

He matched the strokes of his fingers to the strokes of her hips as she moved up and down him. The sea roared in his ears as he rubbed his cheek against her silken hair.

She was every bit as wonderful as he'd expected. More so, in fact.

Serenity heard him gasp her name an instant before he took control again. His thrusts came hard and fast, his fingers stroking ever quicker until she erupted with pleasure.

She screamed out as he spilled himself into her again. Joined, neither could move as they leaned against the window, drained and sated.

Once his breathing returned to normal, Morgan withdrew from her. He turned her to face him. "You are the most incredible woman I've ever known," he said, touching her cheek.

Serenity said nothing.

After a few minutes, she pulled away from him. She moved to stand in the center of his cabin, wringing her hands. She stared at him, and he could tell by the light in her eyes that she was grappling with something terribly important.

"Morgan, I want you to know that I won't ever regret what we've done."

He was glad to hear her say that. He moved to stand in front of her and pull her back into his arms. "Neither will I."

She rubbed her hand over the hairs of his chest, lifting them with her fingernails. She looked down at her hand, refusing to meet his gaze. "I hope you'll always remember me fondly when I'm gone."

"Where are you going?" he asked, his heart hammering at the thought of her leaving.

How could she, after all that had happened?

After all they had shared.

"Home," she said with a wistful sigh. "The colonial ship leaves tomorrow and I plan to sail with it."

"What?" he roared.

"Don't get angry, Morgan. You know as well as I do that we can't go on like this. Especially not now."

"You can't leave," he insisted. *"Especially not now."*

"You're being ridiculous." She left him standing there naked and began pulling on her clothes.

"Me?" he said, grabbing her by the shoulders. "I'm not the one thinking of leaving."

"Aren't you?" She took his hands one by one off her arms and stared deeply into his eyes.

He could see the pain inside her, the fear. But worse than that, he saw her determination. The raw determination that she always got once she had set her mind to something.

"Don't try and tell me that even as you stand there you're not thinking about going back to sea and to your life."

"Yes, I am," he admitted, "but you'll be on board this ship with me."

"As what?" she asked, her voice laced with bitterness. "Your mistress? Your whore?"

His jaw tensed with anger. "Don't ever say that word."

She looked away from him and shook out her dress. "I'm not trying to drag you to the altar, Morgan. I could never hurt you. But if I stay here, I'll never be able to return home."

"So don't," he said, taking the dress from her hands. "Stay with me."

With a low, warning growl in her throat, she snatched her dress back and placed it on the chair.

"I can't do that," she said, retrieving her

camisole and corset. "I've seen how you live. I've seen how you fight. What if one day you're killed in the middle of battle?"

She turned to face him. "What would happen to me then? Would your men respect me?"

She pulled her camisole on and moved to stand directly in front of him while he searched his mind for something he could say to make her change her mind.

"Or what if you're taken prisoner by your enemies, Morgan? I've heard tales of what happens to the captain's whore, and believe me, I don't want to be passed around a British crew."

He was aghast at her words. "Where have you heard such stories?"

"It's not important."

"I would never let you get hurt."

"But you can't guarantee me that. Ever," she said quietly. She reached out and laid her hand against the stubble on his cheek. Her eyes searched his and he ached for a way to settle this, but deep in his heart, he knew the truth.

"Anything can happen at sea," she continued. "Kit told me that it's hard to win a sea battle, that you've often picked up survivors from the victory ship."

Damn her for telling the truth and damn her for being reasonable this *one* time!

He hadn't been able to protect his sister because he'd been at sea, and he couldn't guarantee Serenity that he would never lose a fight.

Grinding his teeth, he saw an image drifting before his eyes of his ship the *Rosanna* sinking last year. Just like she'd said, they'd won the fight, but in the end the damage to his ship had sunk her. He hadn't lost many men to the sinking, but he had lost some.

She dropped her hand from his face, her eyes wistful. "We both know you can never settle on land. The sea is in your blood. It's who and what you are. I would never ask for you to give more than we both know you can."

She stepped away from him. "I have to go."

And with those softly spoken words, she finished gathering her clothes, dressed, and left his cabin.

Nay! his soul screamed.

He couldn't let her go.

Grabbing up his pants, he began jerking them on.

"Where be you headed, *majana*?"

Morgan paused as he listened to Ushakii talking to Serenity just a few feet from his door. Ushakii's watch had probably just ended and he was no doubt headed for his bed.

"I'm leaving, Ushakii. 'Tis time I went home."

"You can't be thinking of heading out alone, child. It's the middle of the night. You might get hurt. Why, you can't even row yourself ashore. Let me escort you back before something terrible happens to you."

Morgan could imagine how she must look, the tender smile that was no doubt curving her lips as she gazed up at Ushakii with doleful eyes.

"Thank you. I would deeply appreciate it."

Then their voices drifted off.

She was gone.

He let his pants fall to the floor as the significance hit him squarely in the chest.

Chapter 19

Morgan didn't sleep at all that night. He lay quietly in his bunk, one arm raised above his head, as he stared up at the ceiling lost in torturous thoughts.

Over and over he saw Serenity before him, her eyes flashing, her body writhing beneath his.

The look on her face as she'd walked gracefully out of his life.

He drew a deep breath against the pain that lacerated his chest. It felt as though his heart had been torn out.

She was gone.

And he had let her go. He had just turned his back and let her walk out of his life.

"So," he whispered to himself. "I'm a coward after all."

But deep inside he knew it was for the best. She'd been right. Even if they married and she traveled with him, sooner or later she would become pregnant, and then what?

He couldn't raise a child on board a ship. He didn't even want to try.

God forbid, what would happen if they were attacked and the ship went down with both Serenity and their child on board with no way to save them?

What if they were lost at sea and he was forced to watch them starve in a lifeboat while they waited for a rescue that never came?

No, he could never stand that.

He must let her go.

He would survive. He always survived, and pain was nothing new to a man who'd lived most of his life with it.

Morning came too soon to Serenity. She watched the sun creep up over the island from the windows of *La Grande Maison*. Downstairs, she could hear the first stirrings of the staff as they set about opening windows and preparing breakfast.

Kristen had been good enough to donate several gowns to her for the trip home, and a valise, which now was set on the bed packed and ready to go.

When she'd returned in the wee hours, Kristen had been waiting up for her, and Serenity had confided to her new friend what had happened between her and Morgan. And the fact that she was determined to leave.

Kristen had done her best to change her mind,

but one thing about Serenity—her stubbornness knew no equal. Somewhere in the early morning hours, Kristen had finally given up and retired.

A soft knock sounded on the door. "Miss James?"

She recognized the voice of Kristen's maid. "Come in," she called.

The maid opened the door a crack. "The coach is waiting for you, miss."

"Thank you." Serenity forced herself away from the window, and on trembling legs, she walked to her valise. This was really it, she was going home.

Picking it up, she left the room.

Kristen was waiting at the foot of the stairs, her face sad, her arms wrapped around her. "I didn't think you could really go through with this. Even after our discussion."

Neither did I.

Serenity's grip on the balustrade increased as she took the last four steps that brought her even with Kristen. "I have no choice."

"Pity. I thought you were more of a fighter."

Serenity laughed bitterly, and looked at a picture across the hall to keep from meeting Kristen's sharp gaze. A gaze she knew would see through her and strip bare the depth of her feelings. "I guess I know this is one fight I can never win. Even my stubbornness has its limits."

Nodding, Kristen forced a smile to her lips.

"Well then, I wish you all the luck in the world. It's been fun getting to know you." Her smile turned sincere. "Tweaking Morgan's nose ... "

Serenity smiled at her teasing tone. "Thank you, Kristen. If you ever come to the Colonies ... "

"I'll make sure I find you. Who knows, I may yet demand George take me to see you."

"I would like that."

Kristen pulled her into a hug.

Serenity held on to her friend, knowing that once she returned home, she would never again experience this kind of female companionship. The women of Savannah would never be as forgiving or as kind as Kristen.

Time to go, Serenity.

Now, before you change your mind.

Reluctantly Serenity pulled away and headed out the door without looking back.

She refused to look back. Only regret waited there, and she didn't want to regret knowing Morgan.

Loving Morgan.

She climbed aboard the coach and watched as Kristen came out to the steps to wave good-bye. Returning the gesture, Serenity was thrown back into her seat as the driver whipped the team into motion.

She listened to the early morning noises as the coach wound its way down the dusty dirt road to the shore. This island had been a wonderful experience, one she would treasure forever.

All too soon, the coach pulled up to the dock and the driver got down to help her out. She took his outstretched hand and descended. The driver reached in behind her and removed her valise from the seat, then handed it to her.

With a knot in her stomach, Serenity headed toward the small boat that would row her to the colonial ship.

In spite of her resolve, she found herself looking over at *Triton's Revenge*. It stood proud in the water, like Morgan himself. The early morning sunlight glinted off the skeletal masts, and the ship swayed and dipped against the waves as the serpent masthead glared at her.

Gulls flapped and called loudly overhead. The ship looked deserted.

Was Morgan still asleep? Or could he see her now as she made her way quietly back home?

Not wishing to think about it, she waded to the boat. The boatswain helped her to her seat, then began rowing them out.

As they crossed the narrow distance to the ship, she tried to banish the image of Morgan rowing her out the night before. The incredibly handsome look on his face as he watched her with desperate longing.

Dear Lord, how she wanted him. Needed him more than she needed the very air she breathed.

Gripping the side of the boat until her knuckles burned, she fought the urge to jump out of the boat and swim to Morgan's ship.

She didn't want to leave him.

She would give anything in the world to stay.

Stop the boat! her mind screamed.

But they could never be happy. She wanted a home with a family and he loved the sea.

She remembered her father's old saying, a bird and a fish can fall in love, but where do they live? If they make their nest at sea the bird will starve and if they make their nest on land . . .

"Good-bye, Morgan," she whispered to the early mist.

Morgan stood on the poop deck, watching the small boat moving steadily closer to the colonial ship. Even from this distance, he could make out Serenity's form.

An ache so fierce it was almost crippling consumed him.

If not for the netting that his crew had put in place the day before, he would launch himself overboard and swim out to her.

But that was ridiculous.

It was over.

Serenity was gone.

Sighing, he turned away and headed to his cabin.

Serenity paused on board the ship as she came face-to-face with Jake. Frowning, she looked up at the surly pirate who leaned down to whisper in her ear.

"They've no idea who I am, Miss James, and I'd deeply appreciate it if you don't educate them."

"Are you going to cut out my tongue?"

He gave a wry smile. "No."

"Then you have nothing to worry about, I think my days of writing are over."

He looked incredulous. "I don't understand."

Serenity sighed and looked back at Morgan's ship. "I no longer believe in fairy tales and happily-ever-after."

The colonial crew bustled around them as they prepared to sail.

"What about you?" she asked. "Are you heading home?"

"Aye. I can't stand another day without my wife."

What she wouldn't give to have Morgan feel that way about her. "I'm sure she misses you."

"No, you're not," he said with a twinkle in his eye. "You're probably wondering what she sees in me. If you want to know the truth, I ask myself that same question every day."

She blushed at the truth of his words. "So why did you leave your wife to begin with?"

"Morgan needed me."

"You think a lot of him, don't you?"

He laughed. "Sometimes."

"Jake?" she asked. "Why didn't you kill him when you captured him all those years ago?"

Jake sighed, and she could tell her question made him uncomfortable.

He paused so long, she was sure he wouldn't answer, and then he said, "Morgan had more guts than any man I'd ever seen. He was scarce more than a babe and yet he had the courage of a lion. How could I destroy a man like that?"

She thought about that and how strange life was. Had Jake killed Morgan that day, all the men Morgan had saved from the British would still be impressed, and she...

She would never have known love. Would never have known a man's touch.

One life touched so many.

"You know, I have a lot to apologize to you for," he said. "I should have never taken you away from your family."

His apology stunned her.

"I am truly sorry, Miss James, for any pain or

fear I caused you. I know we didn't start out on the best terms, but I hope you'll forgive me." He extended his hand to her. "Friends?"

She smiled. "Friends."

As soon as she touched his hand, the wind picked up the sails and they headed out to sea.

Serenity couldn't help going to the netting for one last look at *Triton's Revenge*.

Jake moved to stand behind her. "You know you've got a hard time ahead of you. What are you going to tell people about your absence?"

She sighed. "The truth."

He looked stunned.

"What choice do I have?" she asked. "I'm a terrible liar."

"Surely you can come up with something better. Tell people you eloped and your husband was killed, or he ran off after the nuptials."

It was a thought. But she couldn't do that. "No, Jake. My family deserves the truth."

"The truth hurts. Don't you want to spare them the pain?"

She thought about her father and his reaction to Chatty after she'd been caught alone with Stephen. He'd been cold, distant. Unforgiving.

"Tell you what," Jake said. "Why don't I pretend to be your husband. I'll pick a fight with your father and then leave without ever coming back."

She laughed at the image. "I appreciate the offer, but somehow the truth always comes out. I've lived my life dedicated to reporting the truth to people. I don't think I could live with myself if I lied to them. No, I promised myself I would have no regrets about what I did, and I shan't."

He nodded in understanding. "If you ever need a friend, you just send word to me and I'll be there for you. I'll make sure no one harms you."

"Why, Black Jack Rhys," she said with a teasing note in her voice. "You'd best be careful or I might begin to think you're actually a nice man and not a living scourge."

His smile was wide. "Ouch, lass, you've finally discovered my deepest-held secret. Now I shall most definitely have to kill you for it."

She laughed. "Never fear, it's yet another secret I shall take to the grave."

One of the boatswains came forward. "Miss James?"

She looked past Jake's shoulder to where the boatswain stood. "Yes?"

"The captain bade me show you to your room."

Serenity nodded, excused herself from Jake, and followed the boatswain below deck to a modest-sized cabin. It was clean and tidy, with a small bunk made into the wall the same way Morgan's had been.

"The captain will be by shortly to check on you."

"Thank you," she said.

He took his leave.

Alone, she sat on the bunk, and for the first time allowed the pain to wash over her. Morgan was finally gone. He would never be back.

Never.

Her heart breaking, she reached into her pocket, pulled out the crumpled note of poetry he'd written her on board his ship, and she began to cry.

Chapter 20

"Well, Captain?"

Morgan flinched at Barney's question as he sat himself down at the table in the crowded Boar's Head Tavern. The odor of unwashed bodies, roasting meat, and beer hung thick in the air as Morgan signaled a passing wench and ordered her to bring another round of drinks.

A double round of drinks.

Cookie, Barney, and Ushakii had been waiting here for him while he made yet another inquiry about Serenity.

"Nothing," he growled as the wench placed eight tankards on the rough wooden table before him. "Not a damn word. No one's seen or heard of her, or if they have, they won't tell me."

His temper boiling, Morgan grabbed the nearest tankard of ale and drained it in one gulp.

His men exchanged wide-eyed gawks, but he paid them no heed. Damn them all, anyway. And damn himself.

He was an idiot, a first-rate moron.

What kind of man let a woman like her sail out of his life?

For fifteen months, three days, and five hours now, he'd been searching for her. He'd even boarded the ship that had taken her home, but to no avail. They hadn't known anything more than anyone else.

Jake had placed her in a hired coach headed for Savannah, and no one had seen her since. No one.

She'd vanished without a single trace.

Fine, so be it! He'd had enough with this. She was gone and he was glad of it.

"Glad of it, I tell you."

"Beg pardon, Captain?" Cookie asked.

"Nothing," Morgan muttered as he seized two more tankards and drained them.

"Well, well, look what the tide washed ashore. What brings you gentlemen back to my part of the world?"

"Lay off, Jake," Morgan hissed without turning to look at the man who stood directly behind him. "I'm in no mood for humor."

"Hasn't been in a mood for humor in over fifteen months," Cookie said with a nod to Jake. "Never seen anything like it in my life."

Morgan gave him a hostile glare, but Cookie ignored it.

"We've come seeking the lass again," Barney said. "He ain't been able to find her nowhere and now he's about ready to gut the lot of us."

"You should have seen the face of the colonial captain when he boarded his ship and then took nothing from them," Ushakii piped in. "He couldn't believe Morgan had fired on his ship when all he wanted was to interrogate the crew about Miss James."

Morgan cringed as he remembered what a jack-snipe he'd made of himself that day. He'd terrified the entire colonial crew and had almost lost one of his own.

And for what?

A bloomin' chit who incensed him.

A bloomin' chit who...

He tensed as he remembered a vital fact. Jake was the last one to see her.

He reached up behind him, grabbed Jake by the collar, and pulled his face close. "You were the last person to see her. Tell me where she is, or I swear I'll have your gizzard."

Jake laughed in his face. "If you were sober, I might take that threat seriously." He wrenched Morgan's hand free. "How long have you been in port?"

"A month," Barney said. "A whole bleeding month and we've nothing to show for it. The captain won't leave until he finds her this time. Says we'll stay here till we're dried bones and the ship rots."

"Oh, Morgan," Jake said with a *tsk*. "You've got it bad for the girl, eh?"

Morgan snorted. "She can't have vanished. I know she's somewhere, and sooner or later someone here is bound to hear from her."

"Very well then, I suggest you wait it out at my place. At least I won't have to worry about the sorry lot of you getting tossed in the stocks for public drunkenness."

"I'm not going anywhere," Morgan snarled. "Not until I find her."

Jake ignored him. "Ushakii, you and Cookie grab him and be ready to hold him, because if he doesn't come willingly, I'm going to knock him unconscious."

"Go ahead and try!"

The next thing Morgan knew, the world turned dark.

"You wield a nasty blow, Captain," Cookie said to Jake as they dumped Morgan into a rented wagon.

"Aye, and it's not the first time I've had to use it on Lord and Mighty Hard-Head." Jake looked at his unconscious friend and shook his head. "What the hell happened to him anyway? He looks like he just crawled out of a pigsty."

And he did.

Never had Jake seen Morgan look so disgusting. His unkempt hair hung lankly about his shoulders. Morgan had a thick beard on a face that had never known more than an afternoon's stubble, and his clothes looked and smelled as though they hadn't been changed in a long, long while.

"He's been a raving loon," Barney said, stepping up to take the driver's seat of the wagon. "We stayed for a day at Santa Maria and then the captain decided it was time we went to find the lass."

"Then that storm hit," Cookie interrupted. "Knocked us off course so that we had a time finding the Colonials."

"And by the time we did," Barney finished, "you and Serenity had already gone ashore."

Barney shook his head. "I haven't seen him so grief-stricken and angry since Penelope died."

Jake swallowed at his words. He remembered that time in Morgan's life only too well.

Poor Morgan. His pride had always gotten the better of him, and this time...

"I think I know something that might help him out." Jake retrieved his horse from the nearby hitching post, then returned to the wagon. "Follow me."

He mounted his horse and led them the ten miles to his plantation home just outside of Savannah.

No sooner had they entered the stable than

Lorelei came rushing out, holding baby Nicholas in her arms. Jake smiled at his wife. Her red hair was swept up around her head in an intricate braid and the color was high in her cheeks.

She was every bit as beautiful as she'd been the first day he'd met her.

"What do you think you're doing?" she asked, enunciating each word in such a way as to convey her pique.

"'Tis my good deed for the year." He dismounted and handed his horse over to one of the stable boys.

She cuddled the cooing baby up to her shoulder and narrowed her gaze on him. "You can't bring him here, you promised."

"I promised I wouldn't say anything, I never said I wouldn't bring him."

"Jacob," she said in warning.

"Lorelei," he responded with a laugh. "Trust me."

She rolled her eyes as she patted the baby on the back. "I don't even want to think about what happened the last time you said that to me."

Jake gave her a quick kiss on her cheek. "Go on with you now, wench. I've some nasty things to do to make him presentable."

"I'm not your wench, *knave*, and I would beg you to reconsider, but I know firsthand how very obstinate you are." And with those words spoken, she turned about and took Nicholas back to the house.

Jake motioned for Ushakii and Cookie to drag Morgan out of the wagon and up toward the house. "We'll need to bathe and sober him," he said half to himself and half to them.

"That'll be a task," Cookie said. "I've not seen him sober since she left."

"Me, neither," Barney agreed.

Well, that didn't matter, because Jake knew a surefire way to sober Morgan.

The man was in for the shock of his life.

Morgan sputtered and cursed at the thick, smelly concoction Cookie was forcing down his throat. "I'll kill the lot of you," he snarled.

But as before, his threats went unheeded.

"Quit your blustering," Jake said. "You ought to be grateful to us. You've no idea what a chore it was cleaning you up. I ordered your clothes burned, by the way. I swear I've seen rags in better shape."

Morgan glared at him. He'd strangle the man, but at some point the four of them had tied him to a chair and he wasn't able to do more than curse them all.

And that was the one thing he was doing admirably well. "You better pray I never get free from this."

Jake just smiled at him. "C'mon, men. I think we've earned a break from the good captain. Why don't we go below and get a good stiff drink."

They left the room, with Jake trailing behind.

"Don't you leave me here, Jack," Morgan shouted.

Jake stopped and turned to face him. "The name's Jake," he said, then pulled the door closed behind him.

Morgan rattled the chair with his fury and effort to break free. The Lord better take a liking to them, because when he got out they would suffer for this betrayal.

Suddenly he heard footsteps coming down the hallway outside.

"It'd better be one of you come back to free me," he muttered between clenched teeth.

The door handle rattled an instant before the whitewashed door swung open.

"Lorelei, I was..." Serenity's voice trailed off as she looked up from the watch pin she'd been checking and met his gaze.

Morgan froze, too stunned to even breathe.

Could it be?

Her own face mirrored shock. "What are you doing here?" she gasped.

He held his hands up so that she could see the ropes that held him in place. "I'm sitting in a most uncomfortable chair," he said, and for the first time in a year, he felt the corners of his mouth lift up into a smile.

Bless Jake's soul.

But curse his twisted sense of humor.

Serenity arched one brow. "I suppose you think I'm going to free you."

His smile grew wider. "I would be obliged."

"And I would be a fool to do such a thing. Good day, Captain Drake."

To his astonishment, she left the room.

"Wait!" he roared.

But she was gone.

A few seconds later, the door opened again and Jake rushed in. "All right, Morgan, both our hides are in jeopardy."

Jake slashed the ropes holding him to his chair. "She's headed for the study downstairs. If you have any decency in you at all, you'll make her see reason or we'll both be drunken fools looking for a new place to live."

"Why didn't you tell me she was here?"

"Because I promised her and Lorelei I would never, under any circumstances, tell you she came here."

He hardened his stare. "You're supposed to be *my* friend, Jake."

"If I wasn't your friend, I wouldn't have put my neck in the noose by bringing you here today. Now get down there and smooth this over."

Morgan wasted no more time sprinting downstairs and into the study where Jake had told him Serenity would be waiting.

As soon as he opened the door, Serenity spun around to face him. Her eyes narrowed. "Oh, I swear I hate you, Jacob Dudley," she said under her breath. "All I want is Lorelei and he keeps sending me to *you*."

Morgan frowned at her hostility. "Why are you so angry?" he asked, moving to stand in front of her. "I've come back for you and this is how you greet me?"

Her face was a mockery of anger and astonishment. "You've come back for me? Oh, how delightful. Shall I put on my best gown or should I just fall down on my knees in gratitude that you *finally* remembered I exist?"

Morgan couldn't help it, he laughed. "You never could react the way you were supposed to to anything." He took her face in his hands. "God, how I've missed you."

She stepped back from him. "This isn't a game, Morgan. And I find nothing amusing about the fact that—"

"But I've been looking for you. Didn't anyone tell you?"

She turned her head to the side and eyed him skeptically. "Aye, you took your own, slow time getting here. Then you went to my father's shop, asked him and Douglas if I'd made it safely home. When they told you they didn't know where I was, you immediately left and set sail. Forgive me if that amount of care for my well-being doesn't impress me."

Morgan was aghast. "Lord, woman, I've done nothing but look for you since the day you boarded that ship. There was a storm, do you remember it?"

"Aye."

Hallelujah, mayhap there was hope for her forgiveness after all. "It knocked us off course which delayed me in getting here the first time. When I left your father's shop, I went to find that Colonial ship, to ask them what had happened to you. When they told me nothing, I came back here as soon as I could and I've been here ever since. Didn't anyone tell you *that*?"

"I—"

"And just what are you doing here anyway?"

She put her hands on her hips. "I started to go home, Morgan, but on the way back, Jake convinced me to stay here for a while. After my sister's public disgrace and disappearance, my father agreed that I should stay away from Savannah."

"But why didn't they tell me where you were?"

"I didn't want them to."

"Then why are you mad at me for not getting here sooner?"

"Because you weren't supposed to give up so easily. You were supposed—"

"Serenity, I—" Lorelei broke off her words as she entered the study and saw them standing just inches apart. Stopping in place, she stiffened her posture and eyed him coldly. "Good afternoon, Captain Drake."

Morgan was taken aback by Lorelei's hostility as she adjusted the small baby in her arms. He'd always considered her a friend, and they'd never once in all these years had a disagreement.

"Hello, Lorelei."

Smiling, he walked over to her and brushed his hand across the baby's black hair. "Is it a boy or girl?"

"A boy. Nicholas is his name," she said, her tone still icy.

"Where did he get all this dark hair from?"

"He takes after his father."

"Lorelei," Morgan said with a note of warning. "Jake's blond."

"Who said *I* was his mother?" Her gaze slid past him and focused on Serenity.

His heart stopped as he realized who the mother was, and his brain quickly calculated the baby's approximate age and how long it'd been since he last saw Serenity.

Serenity stepped forward and took the baby from Lorelei's arms. "I hope he wasn't a bother."

"No," she assured her. "He's been wonderful, but I think he may be hungry."

True to the prediction, the baby let out a loud wail.

Lorelei looked at Morgan and arched an imperious brow. "Goodness, Serenity, I think the shock of baby Nicholas killed Morgan."

Serenity shrugged. "Well, you know what I say about men and labor and children."

"He's mine?" Morgan gasped, still too stunned to say anything more intelligent.

Serenity just glared at him.

This was more than Morgan could deal with.

He'd expected to find Serenity...

To find her...

Well, he didn't really know what he'd expected to find her doing, but it definitely hadn't been holding *his* child!

Suddenly the air seemed too thick, his stock too tight. He needed to breathe. Needed time to think about this.

Unsure and quite frankly terrified, he turned on his heel and left.

Serenity exchanged puzzled looks with Lorelei, a moment before her rage took hold.

"He left?" she said between gritted teeth as she adjusted Nicholas in her arms.

Lorelei shook her head. "Why is it the only thing you can count on with men is that they will always be somewhere else when you need them?"

Serenity's sight darkened even more. "Well, he's not walking away until I've said my piece."

She handed Nicholas back to Lorelei. "Would you please watch him a moment longer?"

"My pleasure. You let that man have it!"

Serenity fully intended to.

Morgan walked on, his mind whirling. Why hadn't Serenity told him? Sent word to him?

You let her face all of it alone!

Guilt sliced through him.

"Morgan Drake."

He paused at the angry tone he knew so well. Turning around, he saw Serenity headed straight for him with the look on her face that always preceded a lecture.

And deep inside he admitted he loved that look. Had missed it greatly.

"How dare you walk away." She stopped directly in front of him. "I don't care if you leave me. I'm a grown woman and that's fine. But how dare you turn your back on your own son. You could have at least held him. Asked about him."

"I didn't know what to say," he said, his own anger rising at her accusations. "I was expecting you, not you and . . . and a baby!"

He softened his tone and reached out to touch her cheek. "Why didn't you tell me?"

"You and I had an understanding."

Morgan ground his teeth at her obstinacy. "But you went through all this on your own. If you had only told me..."

"I didn't want you here because you felt obligated, Morgan. I knew if I told you about Nicholas, then your sense of honor would force you to marry me. I told you on Santa Maria that I would never force you to give up your life."

Morgan pressed his lips together as emotions washed over him. He didn't deserve her. He knew that. She was so strong and brave.

He'd left her to face a nightmare and now he'd returned like some self-righteous Sir Lancelot trying to make things right.

If he'd possessed half her courage, he would never have allowed her to board that colonial ship in the first place.

He would have seen her grow round with his child.

Been there as she struggled to give Nicholas his life.

"Please don't send me away, Serenity," he whispered. "I came back because I need you. I want us...you, me, and Nicholas...to have a life together. To build a house...and...and farm like Jake, or maybe buy a business."

He took her hand into his. "I no longer care where I live. I just want to be with you, Serenity. With you and with Nicholas forever." He tightened his grip, afraid she would yet send him away. "Please say yes."

Serenity took a deep breath and looked up at the sky as if imploring heaven for help. When she gazed back at him, her eyes showed a mixture of deep vexation and mirth. "Of course I'll say yes, you surly pirate. How could I not?"

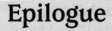

Epilogue

"Mother!"

Serenity paused her hand as she heard Nicholas storm into her study.

"Would you please make Michael return my ship to me?"

"I don't have his stupid ship," Michael said, sticking his adorable eight-year-old head in the door. "Barney and Elizabeth have it down at the pond."

"Well, why didn't you tell me that?" Nicholas demanded.

"Because you didn't ask me. You accused me of having it."

"Boys!" Serenity snapped. "I love you, but I'm trying to get some work done."

"Sorry," they said in unison.

"You should have told me," Nicholas grumbled, shoving Michael out the door.

"You should have asked."

Smiling, Serenity shook her head. She loved all

three of her children, but they were certainly a handful.

Just as she caught up with her thoughts, another knock sounded on her door.

Exasperated, she looked up again. "Yes?"

This time Morgan stuck his head in the door.

Even after ten years of marriage, he looked wonderful. "What do *you* want?" she asked with a teasing note in her voice.

He came into the room with his hands behind his back. "I have a surprise for you."

"A surprise?"

"Aye."

He placed a copy of a book on her desk. Looking down, she gasped. "My story!"

His smile grew wider. "When I was in New York last summer, I met a publisher."

"You gave him my stories? Why didn't you tell me?"

"Because I wanted to see the look of surprise on your face. And it's priceless, truly, truly priceless."

She laughed at the words that had become their own private joke between them over the years.

"And what can I say?" he asked with a shrug. "I like the idea of being immortalized."

Laughing, she traced the raised gold letters on the book. *The Adventures of the Sea Wolf.*

"You even used my name," she said with a lump in her throat as she saw "S. S. James" on it.

He laughed, then looked down at the desk where she was working. "What are you working on now?"

"Don't ask."

He rolled his eyes. "Not more of that social reform rubbish."

"Rubbish? Why, sir, I'll have you know that one day—"

He silenced her words with a kiss. "There's only one place I want my woman," he whispered against her lips. "And that's the bedroom. Care to try for a fourth child, Mrs. Drake?"

She bit her lip. "It's terribly early in the day, Captain."

"You didn't seem to mind yesterday."

And before she could protest, he lifted her in his arms and carried her up the stairs.